Nothing is Quite Forgotten in Brooklyn

D1113459

Also by Alice Mattison

NOVELS

The Wedding of the Two-Headed Woman
The Book Borrower
Hilda and Pearl
Field of Stars

SHORT STORY COLLECTIONS

In Case We're Separated
Men Giving Money, Women Yelling
The Flight of Andy Burns
Great Wits

POETRY COLLECTION

Animals

NOTHING IS QUITE FORGOTTEN IN BROOKLYN

A Novel

Alice Mattison

HARPER ◉ PERENNIAL

NEW YORK • LONDON • TORONTO • SYDNEY • NEW DELHI • AUCKLAND

HARPER ● PERENNIAL

Excerpts from this novel appeared in *The New Yorker* as a short story titled "Brooklyn Circle."

P.S.™ is a trademark of HarperCollins Publishers.

HarperCollins books may be purchased for educational, business, or sales promotional use. For information please write: Special Markets Department, HarperCollins Publishers, 10 East 53rd Street, New York, NY 10022.

FIRST EDITION

Designed by Claudia Martinez

Library of Congress Cataloging-in-Publication Data is available upon request.

ISBN 978-0-06-143055-8

08 09 10 11 12 ov/rrd 10 9 8 7 6 5 4 3 2 1

For Lloyd Schwartz

As these elegant silver cars make their way along a curved path above the streets of Brooklyn, they will bring not darkness but periodic infusions of light; and meanwhile, shards and splinters of light will pierce the tracery of their soaring supports, gladdening the beholder's eye.

—Marcus Ogilvy, 1924

Chapter 1

Even when Constance Tepper was a girl, the skeptical, blunt telephone voice of her mother's friend Marlene Silverman made her happy—uneasy but happy. Marlene knew something about life that Con's mother would never know, but which Constance seemed to have been born suspecting, looking around in her crib for an eye to catch. Their conversations were about other people's foolishness. "I *know!*" Con would say, pressing herself into her mother's heavy red drapes, her back to the room, eyeing the jagged, crisscrossed Brooklyn sky, which darkened as they spoke. It almost seemed that Marlene had called to speak to Con, not to her mother.

"Did you watch that program about the camps?" Marlene might ask. Con knew which camps Marlene meant.

"No," she'd have to say. They watched Sid Caesar. They watched Lucille Ball. Then Constance would begin to feel jealous, and soon—as if jealousy caused what happened next—Marlene would say, "Well, let me talk to Gert." Con's mother was a little dull, and it puzzled Con that Marlene preferred Gert anyway. Con's father died suddenly when she was twelve, and after that—maybe even before that—Marlene called to be of use: Gert was not a particularly sad or helpless widow, but she worried, and she didn't understand money. Marlene knew what called for worry and what didn't. And Marlene understood money.

Maybe there's always someone whose company is a delight and who can hurt by withholding it. Con grew up, didn't see Marlene for long periods, found new sources of love and pain. She married and moved to Philadelphia; she had a daughter. Marlene's interest and approval still counted. This story takes place at two times in Con's life, fourteen and a half years apart. I want to tell it this way—shifting back and forth in time—for reasons that will become obvious, but also because what interests me most about Con is not exactly that she could remember and learn—who can do that?—but that when she discovered, in middle age, that more than fourteen years earlier she'd failed to pay attention, she tried to find out what she needed to know, even though she didn't want to.

Morning sun—speckled during its passage through a dirty windowpane—laid a parallelogram of brighter color across the stripes of a tablecloth belonging to Gertrude Tepper, who was not home. The parallelogram was observed by her daughter Con, age forty-five, who was spending a week in her mother's

Brooklyn apartment (while Gert visited her old friend Marlene Silverman in Rochester) to look after the cat, a big orange beast—similar in color to one of the stripes on the tablecloth—now heavily asleep, circled by his tail, on the table, which held scatterings of his hairs. The orange stripe—*pinkish* orange; apricot? mango?—was the color of unhurried time, Con decided. She liked a dark red stripe, too. Con believed—drinking her mother's coffee and eating a bagel—that she had time, time to gaze at the striped tablecloth, trying to remember how long she'd known it. Something almost caught Con's eye, something off to the side on the floor. Without knowing what it was, she preferred not to look at it. Surely it didn't matter.

The parallelogram of sun came to a point on the oak floor. A faded blue rug, fluffy with orange fur, covered the space between table and sofa. Past the table in the other direction was an open kitchen and a back door with an elaborate bolt; it led to a dark staircase. Gert never went down the stairs but she had an agreement with the super: she left her garbage outside that door, and he ascended the three flights and picked it up. In return, Gert tipped him lavishly and often, or thought she did.

Her mother and Marlene had figured out together, Con suspected, that she could stay with the cat, though she'd have to leave both her work and her child—a tall and confident sixteen-year-old daughter. "Joanna's an adult," Marlene would have said. "And Connie told me her job is flexible." The work was flexible, but within limits. In truth, Con was glad to be where she was, in her mother's sunny, dusty apartment without her mother. Con would have preferred to live in New York, maybe alone. Her daughter could be her difficult self at home.

Con's husband, Jerry Elias, was on one of his trips. "Oh, fuck you," Con had said when he announced this one. She'd said it in the past with more energy. Jerry left several times a year, for two or three weeks at a time. He always had. It was not part of his job (he owned a lamp store in downtown Philadelphia) nor was it vacation. He studied historical topics that made him curious. She'd agreed to it when they married, as he sometimes reminded her, and it was hard to explain to her friends why the trips angered her now. Jerry did nothing with the notes he took, which were on yellow three-by-five cards everywhere in their Philadelphia apartment, disarmingly legible and so full of excitement that Con was sure he took these trips in just the way and for the reasons he said he did.

Con's bagel was gone, but a little coffee remained. She pushed her chair back. Later, she'd go for a run. Now as her eye played with the blur of cat into tablecloth and room into room, she allowed her gaze, at last, to shift to the kitchen floor. On the gray tiles was an object that did not belong: a yellow three-by-five index card, one of Jerry's cards. In her purse was just such a card, on which she had written the name and phone number of the director of a house for former women prisoners; she couldn't completely forget work this week. She didn't know how the card could have found its way to the kitchen floor. Con was barefoot, still in her pajamas. She wanted to hold on to her pleasure in the lazy morning; she delayed standing up. She merely had to remember why she might have carried her purse, which was too full, into the kitchen. If she had opened it there, the card could have fallen out.

Con had arrived the previous evening, hours after her

mother had left. The apartment smelled so characteristically of itself—of boiled meat, onions, dust, and cat—that it was hard to imagine it without Gert. Letting herself in, Con couldn't help calling, "Mama?" There was silence, except that she heard water running. The orange cat came toward her. A newspaper was spread on the table, with a mug next to it. A pair of tan lace-up shoes stood near the sofa and another tan lace-up shoe was on a bookcase. Con carried her things into the bedroom, followed by the yowling cat, whose name was Sandy. On the bed was her mother's pink bathrobe, and on the night table were a toothbrush, toothpaste, and a bottle of pills: her mother's cholesterol medication. The cold water in the bathroom basin was on.

Con (who had known Gert was forgetful, but not this forgetful) had poured herself a juice glass of cream sherry from a bottle on the kitchen counter, and drank it sitting on her mother's Danish Modern brown sofa, kicking off her shoes. As she drank, she had an idea about the case she was working on, a second idea; she'd had one on the train, too. She went into the bedroom, took her notebook from her bag, and wrote down the new idea under her earlier note, then replaced the notebook in the bag, which she put on the dresser. There had been no reason to carry the purse into the kitchen. Before sleep—in her mother's bed, which smelled like Johnson's baby powder—she'd read a few pages of *The Satanic Verses* by Salman Rushdie.

Now she looked behind her. The sticky glass still stood on the lamp table, and her own black shoes lay on their sides near her mother's upright tan ones. A crocheted afghan in orange, pink, and dark green was bunched on the sofa. At last

Con stood. As she had known it would, the card read "Mabel Turner," with a telephone number: the director of the house for former prisoners. She hastily buttoned an undone button on her pajama top, as if someone could see her. Con was five feet one inch tall, with short red hair—something like the cat's— and freckles. She considered that freckles made anyone look like a child, but her voice—her voice was strong, loud, and a little husky, with a Brooklyn accent she didn't try to overcome. She stepped forward, as big as she could be—but feeling stupid and clumsy in her pajamas—and tried the back door. She knew now it would be unlocked, and it was. In a rush, with a cry, she locked it, pushing against it; for a second she thought someone pushed back.

Then she scrambled into the bedroom, where, indeed, her purse was gone from the dresser, gone from anywhere else in the small apartment she might have put it, though she searched again and again, so determined to see it, so used to seeing it, that it seemed she could re-create it—black nylon, shaped like a briefcase but smaller, overstuffed, with "Le Sac" embroidered over and over on the trim. Someone had come into the apartment, and had entered the room in which she slept. She returned to the living room, seized Sandy the cat, and held him to her chest, but he flowed from her arms until his center of gravity shifted and he landed loudly on the floor. Then he leaped to the table and licked his orange fur.

Con looked everywhere in the apartment for an intruder, even where nobody could fit—in the broom closet, the oven. She had fastened the chain on her mother's front door the night before, and it was still in place. She dressed, but couldn't leave:

her train ticket home was in the stolen bag. So were her wallet, the magazine section of yesterday's Sunday *New York Times*— April 16, 1989—a bottle of aspirin, the notebook, a checkbook, photographs of Jerry and Joanna and Con's sister, Barbara. Also lipstick (which she wore only at work), a comb and brush, a light blue plastic case containing two tampons, and her keys— including the key to this apartment. Her address book. In her wallet were forty dollars in cash, her credit card, her driver's license, her Blue Cross card, and her library card.

She phoned the police. A detective would come to the apartment, said the dispatcher. Con should wait. "I can't go out. I can't lock the door!" said Con, but the woman had disconnected.

Fourteen and a half years later, on a Sunday morning in November, 2003, Con was not thinking about the moment when she pushed against her mother's back door and imagined she felt a responsive push back. She was not thinking about that April day at all (and when she happened to think of it, she remembered few of the details) but these days when she closed a door, a trace of the memory of that moment still made her push a little harder than was necessary or even desirable. She was not aware that she pushed too hard, but after a while doors she frequently opened and closed loosened on their hinges. This morning she intended to clean her apartment, starting with the job she liked least, the bathroom. But first she planned to tighten the loose hinges on the bathroom door. She'd tried doing it several times, but the holes were now too loose for the screws, which went round and round without catching. Con hadn't been able to imagine solving this problem, but eventually had found a home repair Web site that instructed her to fill the holes with golf tees and screw the screws into the tees. This absurd plan appealed to her so strongly that she hadn't minded buying a whole package of golf tees, even though nobody she knew played golf.

She climbed on a chair to remove the upper screws from their hinge. She then sat on the floor to remove the lower ones, loosened the door, and leaned it against the wall. She dipped tees in glue and inserted them into the holes, taking some delight in this activity, which suggested sex. The glue had to dry overnight. Then she'd saw off the part that stuck out. Now she would clean.

Con (in 1989) imagined taking her mother's largest knife from the kitchen drawer and stabbing the burglar, sliding the blade into T-shirt fabric and a fleshy male back. Surely the burglar was a man. To continue this fantasy, it was necessary to imagine a less indifferent cat, who howled and butted his head into her shoulder, so that Con awakened in time to confront the intruder. But he would have been between her and the kitchen before she could have known he was there. And he might have carried a knife, or a gun. For some reason Con didn't imagine the burglar shooting her, but shooting her mother. He shot her mother, her mother lay gasping and bleeding, and Con, having somehow equipped herself with the stainless-steel carving knife, hurtled toward his big back to stab him.

as a receptionist in a veterinary practice, a medical white coat over tailored pantsuits with shoulder pads. She refused to wear synthetics, and Gert said she spent half her salary on dry cleaning. In her white coat Marlene probably looked like a crusading woman scientist in a movie, and indeed, Gert claimed the veterinarians were afraid of her. Fierce dogs lay down and thumped their tails when Marlene gave them a look.

Con knew Marlene's phone number by heart. "Marlene," she began.

"Connie!" Marlene's voice was deep, except for the Brooklyn sarcastic lilt. She smoked. She had always smoked. "It's all right—she's here. *But*"—the voice rose in pitch, then descended—"you and I have to talk." She must have turned toward Gert. "It's Connie."

Con could hear her mother in the background. "Let me talk to her. The trip was *fine*."

"I haven't even said hello," said Marlene to Gert. Con's mother would be halfway between the breakfast table and the phone, importuning in a nightgown with no bathrobe. Of course the trip had gone badly. Gert would take the wrong train, lose her belongings on it—what she hadn't left at home or in the taxi to Penn Station—and get off at the wrong stop.

Con struggled to adopt her usual tone with Marlene; they'd gossiped and connived all her life. "So. That much is accomplished," Con said. "Mother makes it to Rochester. However—"

"One moment," said Marlene, who knew when other people were impatient, but might not care. Con was pacing as far as the phone cord would let her, then returning to lean on the kitchen counter so as to draw invisible lines, one after another—more and more firmly—on the countertop. "An incident last night," Marlene continued. "Of course I can't go into detail."

"My purse was stolen," said Con loudly.

"When?" said Marlene. "My God. Look, I know it's not a good time to bring this up—but I think Dr. Herbert should have a look at her. She's saying things—"

"Last night. My purse was stolen from my mother's apartment," said Con.

"Oh, my God!" said Marlene again. "A break-in? Armed?"

"He didn't break in. He walked in. My mother left the back door unlocked."

"Connie, you see what I'm saying about your mother? It's unbearable."

"Yes—" Con began, but Marlene interrupted. "He didn't hurt you?"

"I didn't see him. I was sleeping."

"Thank God you're all right," said Marlene (who had often proclaimed, "Since Hitler I don't believe in God. Who needs him?"). She continued, "My own experience—well, I was all right too. A black man snatched my purse, and black men chased him. Yet people talk as if no black man would do that for a white woman."

"I know."

"Of course you know, of all people." Marlene meant that Jerry was part black. "Oh, Connie, here I am going on. Are you sure it's gone? Is anything else gone?" Nothing looked disturbed—and then Con remembered something. The night before, she'd put her purse down next to a little wooden box her mother had owned since Con was a baby. Her father had brought it home from the war, and on top was a copper plate on which a faintly colored map of France was embossed; in the corner, a girl in wooden shoes pointed at the map, and as a child Con had wondered why if the girl wore wooden shoes she didn't point at a map of Holland. Standing in the kitchen, she couldn't say for sure that the box was gone, but she was pretty sure the dresser top had been dramatically bare. The thought sent a new coil of anxiety through her body.

"Your money?" Marlene said. "Your credit cards?"

"Everything. I don't have a dime." Again she heard her mother's voice. "Let me talk to her!"

"In a moment," said Marlene, then to Con, "She unlocked it when she put out the garbage." Everyone knew about Gert's household arrangements, which were the main topic of her conversation. "It could have been days ago. She could have been killed. Gert, darling, when did you put out the garbage?"

Again came her mother's voice. "The garbage? What are you talking about?"

"Is Jerry coming?" Marlene persisted.

"Jerry's on a trip."

"Oh, for heaven's sake."

"Marlene, please let me talk to my mother now." But Gert had gone to the bathroom. "Well, I suppose nature called," said Marlene. "We'll call you back." Con rushed to the bedroom. The box was gone. It was about two inches high, not very wide, with a little keyhole in front. When Con was a child, her mother had let her lock and unlock it, play with the contents and put them back. The key was kept in a drawstring bag Barbara had made in Girl Scouts. In the box Gert kept necklaces her children had made or bought her, a few old pins and bracelets. While Con stood helplessly in the middle of the bedroom, the phone rang. Only a few minutes had passed, but Gert had used the time to become afraid. "Did you reach Joanna?" she began. "Is Joanna all right?"

"Why shouldn't *Joanna* be all right?" said Con.

"The thief could go to your house," said her mother.

"I'm sure she's all right," said Con, though as she protested she became a little frightened. The burglar had her address and keys, and a train ticket to Philadelphia, an hour and a half away. "He probably kept the money and threw away the rest," she said, sternly calming herself. But she had to get off the phone. "Mama," she said then, "Mama, you left the back door unlocked."

"No, it wasn't me," said her mother. "Maybe you opened the door."

"Of course I didn't."

"Maybe the super came in. To fix something."

"You know that didn't happen."

"Go home," said her mother. "The cat's too fat anyway."

"I can't go home. I don't have any money, and I have to change your locks."

"Go home."

They hung up. Con stood with her hand on the bedroom phone, now trying vainly to see the old battered jewelry box elsewhere, moved from its former position on the dresser.

The burglar had not just grabbed. He had paused, taken two things, and decided how to hold them both as he moved quietly away. The pause made her feel his presence in the room—his recent presence—as she hadn't before. As a young woman Con had been too capable-looking to start up men's fantasies, and she'd rarely been whistled at or propositioned. Once, at a party, a drunken classmate had said he'd like to nibble her earlobe, and Con was intrigued, but the man didn't touch her; later, he apologized. Now she understood that she might have awakened to find a man leaning over her, a man with a weapon, a man twice her size and weight, and she felt a variety of fear she hadn't felt before. She was ashamed to note she was picturing a black man. She had to gain dominion over her thoughts.

The doorbell rang. The police officers had arrived—a black man and a white woman, both bulky with equipment. They took down all possible information, and were baffled only briefly about why Con was not her mother and where her mother was. They asked several times if she'd seen or heard anything. They dusted the doorknobs and her mother's dresser for fingerprints. Con at first didn't mention the box, because the jewelry hadn't been valuable, and then she did mention it. They nodded. "Anything else? Camera?"

"No," said Con, though she didn't know for sure.

They urged her to change the locks, and when she explained about her keys, her identification, and the house in Philadelphia, they thought it would do no harm to change those locks as well. "What about your car?" the woman officer said.

"My husband has it. He's away. They'll never find the car."

"They lose interest in a day or two," said the man. "If the car was on the block . . ." They closed their notebooks.

"Could you lend me a couple of dollars?" Con said then,

though she didn't know what she'd do with only two dollars. "I don't have a penny. I'll mail it to the police station."

The woman said, "There's a number for crime victims—" but the man stopped looking like a cop and looked embarrassed for Con. He took two dollar bills from his wallet and handed them to her. Con was embarrassed too, but she took the money, and didn't inquire too carefully how to return it.

The officers were slow to leave, at last shifting their solid bodies through Gert's apartment door. As Con held the door for them, fear for her daughter made her arm stiffen. It was all she could do not to slam the door into the backside of the policewoman. She had asked them if she should change her locks in Philadelphia, not whether she should worry about Joanna's safety. And they had been mildly in favor of changing the locks. She replaced the chain and dialed her home number. Joanna was not home or did not answer. She was at school or asleep. Con left a message— just "Call me at Grandma's, please!"—then regretted it. Joanna certainly wouldn't call back. Con called Directory Assistance and asked for the number of the school. Eventually she reached the attendance office. Joanna Elias was absent. Well, she was probably asleep. Con would not let herself think about Joanna.

The detectives, she felt, had not quite believed her, with her complicated story about her mother. She could not account satisfactorily for herself, but although they had sensed it, they had not cared. New York cops were used to tricksters and the confused; if she was pathetic or despicable, she was still entitled to be heard on the subject of her puny losses. She went to put the two dollars into her wallet, but she had no wallet. She put them into her pocket.

Con spent a foolish half hour studying ads in the phone book for locksmiths, trying to guess which one would trust her for the money. She had no experience in being penniless— or, unable to put her hands on the money that was hers and Jerry's. She had no identification. She stopped studying ads and began searching the apartment, pulling drawers from the night table, looking for money. Her mother's apartment was only superficially disorderly—there had been one dirty mug, not six—but it contained innumerable dressers, old scarred desks, and battered end tables with drawers. Each drawer was dark with jumbled objects or dense with paper. Con searched them all, though she thought Gert would know enough not to keep money around the house. Con called her home number again, then resumed looking. She found three or four afghans and an unfinished sweater that her mother had been knitting for her years ago. She had half an idea that if she found a piece of identification of her mother's she could perhaps convince someone she was Gert, though why that would get the locks changed and herself on a train to Philadelphia she didn't know. Then she began to feel that she almost *was* Gert, that she was turning into Gert, as if her mother had left the pills, the bath-robe, even the running water, so Con could give up her own life and smoothly take over her mother's. Something was holding her mind, slowing it and making her afraid. She looked in the mirror. She looked like herself, but maybe it was something in the air here, in the cat dander or flying orange fur, that gave her mother a stubborn passivity underneath the exterior of a sturdy old woman who could take the train to Rochester. (Why had Marlene invited Gert? Marlene's mind was supple and quick.

17

How did she endure Gert?) Like Con, Gert had short reddish hair—now dyed. Her face was thicker than Con's, but similarly shaped. Con couldn't go out for a run, but she ran the short length of the apartment several times because she couldn't imagine her mother running.

Her mind swirled with fears she couldn't quite separate and name; this must be the feel of her mother's mind. She found a piece of paper and a pencil and made a list, something either she or her mother might have done. *Call a locksmith*, she wrote. *Find the super.* She dialed the superintendent's number and got a machine. She left a message. Then she unlocked the door, stepped onto the landing—nobody was there—and rang the three doorbells on the floor. Nobody answered. Inside, she replaced the chain, but even with it in place, the door could be opened a couple of inches.

The locksmith was not going to change the locks for free, that was undeniable. She wondered if there really was a phone number for crime victims, and doubted that whatever service it reached would pay to have the locks changed. When a locksmith did call back, she explained what had happened. But he wouldn't even take a check, he said, not that she had a checkbook. "I'm sorry," he said, and did sound sorry.

Con couldn't think of anyone in New York City from whom she might borrow money. She now couldn't make any call at all. She stood with her hand on the phone and took her hand away again. She stared at the newspaper her mother had left on the table, which offered a week-old story about airport security. New procedures were going to require that passengers be asked if they'd had help packing their suitcases. She ate lunch—her mother was well stocked with soup and canned tuna—and touched the wall phone in the kitchen again, then went into the bedroom, where she put her hand on the receiver of the bedside phone, then took it away, got into bed, and slept. She fell asleep thinking of her mother on these sheets.

When the phone woke her, she was momentarily disoriented, then reminded herself it was afternoon, still Monday. The machine on the kitchen counter picked up and from the bedroom she heard her mother's announcement, reciting the phone number. Gert recited it twice. Meanwhile Con realized that the caller might be Joanna, and reached for the phone near the bed. "Hello?" she said as the announcement continued.

Marlene's voice said, "Can you turn that thing off?" but the announcement had ended. "I'm going to wire you money," Marlene said then.

"Don't bother," Con said. "But how would you do that?"

"Western Union."

"But I'd have to go to the Western Union office. I can't leave."

"You can't get somebody to stay there for a few minutes?" Marlene said skeptically. Then, "Did you reach Joanna? Your mother keeps asking. She's taking a nap, so you can tell me the truth."

Con hesitated. "I can't reach her but I'm sure she's fine."

"She's not at home?"

"Or not answering."

"Should I call her?"

"Definitely not."

"I wouldn't make things worse, Connie," said Marlene. "You

know I'm no dope. I'm right about your mother. The things she's been saying! I'm not even going to tell you. Of course it's not true."

"What's not true?" said Con. Now and then something reminded her of the past—certainly a complicated past and maybe even a mysterious past—that Gert and Marlene had shared for years before Con was even born. She envied them that time, as if she somehow knew that they'd spent all of it telling secrets they planned to keep from her.

"Look, she should be tested," Marlene said.

"You think she's got Alzheimer's?" said Con. "What did she say?"

"Last night," said Marlene, "she woke up and thought she was in the train. She kept asking me what stop it was."

That didn't seem so bad. "Marlene, I should hang up."

"My doctor is wonderful. I'm making an appointment. I'm trying to spare you heartache, Connie, heartache."

"I'll call you back."

"But she'll be up. I think I hear her."

"Okay, so long then," said Con, and hung up before Marlene could speak again. She liked this attention from Marlene. The question of the Western Union office had been unresolved. Con looked in the Yellow Pages but didn't recognize any addresses of Western Union offices in Brooklyn. Anyway, she'd have to leave the door unlocked—it couldn't be locked without a key—and would be afraid to return. The phone machine was flashing. It had recorded their call; Con listened to the first few words and erased it. She expected more from Marlene—rescue—but that had never quite happened. As an adolescent, when Marlene still lived in Brooklyn, Con enjoyed the fantasy that Marlene might someday invite her to come and visit all by herself—maybe for weeks at a time—but when she was finally invited for an overnight visit, Con had become lost in the tangle of subway lines. There was no good way to travel across Brooklyn to Marlene's apartment, and eventually she gave up and made her way home. "Connie, I'm ashamed of you," Marlene had said.

Now Con dialed her home number again. School would be out, so Joanna might be more willing to pick up the phone. But these days she never spent her afternoons at home, where Con was often working. When Joanna was younger, Con would stop work when she turned up. They'd eat and talk, or she'd drive Joanna somewhere while Joanna talked confidingly from the backseat. Later they'd return reluctantly to work, Joanna to her homework, Con to the case she'd been working on, with their papers intermingling on the kitchen table.

Con had a law degree, but after working in a big firm before her daughter was born, she hadn't wanted to return to that life—to hours away from home, to pantyhose and skirts. She worked part-time, taking on cases for a women's legal project and doing some of the work at home, barefoot. At present she was trying to keep the house for women ex-prisoners from being closed down. It had existed without trouble for two years in a neighborhood just outside Philadelphia, but now neighbors claimed the women were prostitutes, soliciting on the street. Joanna scoffed. She proposed that they drive to the street in the evening and see what happened. Con thought the women probably *were* soliciting on the street, but should be allowed to stay in the house anyway.

She tried the super again, left another message. She wondered if he was the burglar. Her mother would regard that supposition as unfair, and maybe she'd be right. How long could he keep his job if the tenants grew suspicious? But Con liked the thought that the super was the burglar: then he would stay where he was, rolling trash cans. He would be too busy to travel to Philadelphia, using her train ticket, to rape her daughter.

Con never returned the police officer's money. Fourteen years later, in November, 2003, she no longer remembered the two dollars. She tried not to think about that week in 1989, and as she'd grown older, she'd become more adept at not thinking about painful subjects. This is not a story about memory. Now she herself lived in Brooklyn, in a quite different apartment, not squarish and sunny but oddly shaped, dark, with rooms that were a little hard to find, off corridors, and were full of not-quite-finished objects—bookcases made of unpainted boards, tables stripped but never refinished. Con and Jerry had had some of them for decades, and Con had acquired others, leaving them also not quite finished. The apartment had a gray metal desk in a study that might have been a living room, separated from the living room (which should have been a dining room) by a homemade partition. She had no dining room and the kitchen was small, but she had a spare bedroom, and she was glad the study was the most noticeable room. What mattered was work, even if work was often unsatisfying.

On this November Sunday, Con was not at her desk. When she'd struggled with the hinges on the bathroom door as much as possible, she started cleaning, as planned. She didn't mind scrubbing the basin and toilet, but disliked cleaning the bathtub—bending, reaching. If Jerry had been present he'd have done it. He undressed and climbed into the tub, cleaning quite thoroughly, and then he mopped the floor, having slopped water over it. Con and Jerry no longer lived together—they had been divorced for some years, and during a period of three years Con had met, married, and divorced someone else, a psychologist named Fred—but when Jerry was in New York he stayed in her extra bedroom. Con had moved to Brooklyn after her divorce from Fred. A few years later, she heard the crash of the first plane into the World Trade Center while walking to the subway. When she left Philadelphia, Jerry's lamp store was still open, but in the final stages of failure; on the downtown block where it had stood for decades, it was the last independent store.

For some reason Jerry often cleaned the bathroom when he visited, though she'd never asked him to, and Con might glimpse him padding with wet feet back to his room, his clothes in a bundle under his arm. She wouldn't have walked naked through the apartment, but Jerry was nonchalant, or maybe he displayed himself to provoke her.

This morning Con felt like taking a walk, but if she walked before cleaning, she wouldn't clean. When she'd finished the bathroom except for the bathtub, she found herself in her study, checking the *New York Times* Web site. It was more than seven months after the start of the war in Iraq, and the United States was considering recruiting units of the old Iraqi army to speed the creation of a new one. Though the government had claimed casualties would be few in this war, twenty-two Americans had died in the last two weeks, and a long story discussed the effects of their deaths on those at home. Con checked her e-mail to further put off scouring the tub. She had no new messages, but she answered a couple of old ones. When she sent the second one, she saw that a new one had come in, and recognized Marlene's address.

Marlene's messages didn't begin with the recipient's name or end with her own. "I must see the leaves in Central Park," she wrote this time. "I just decided to go to New York next weekend. If you don't have room I'll stay in a hotel." The leaves were pretty much gone, but Con knew Marlene wouldn't care. She didn't mean the part about the hotel, either; she assumed she'd stay with Con. She'd like to go to a show, she said, and proposed that Con buy the tickets. She said she'd pay her back, but Con knew she might never do it.

Con didn't clearly remember that April week in 1989, but she did remember being thrilled, over many decades, by Marlene and Marlene's attention. It was still a thrill, but Con was busy—more than busy. These days—or weeks, or years—she was not in a good mood. The apartment was messy and likely to stay that way, and Jerry had asked if he could come later in the week. A consultant to small family businesses now that the store was gone, he came to New York to see clients, taking the train.

"Of course you'll stay here," Con nevertheless replied to Marlene.

Still postponing the tub, she wrote a message to Jerry. He'd cross the living room in the Philadelphia house from the remaining easy chair, around which newspapers, local and New York, would be distributed. He'd lean down past the long bones of his legs and haul his laptop from the floor, where it lived. Jerry was an impossibly tall and thin man who had grown up learning not to break the lamps in his family's store by stand-ing up in slow stages, checking in all directions, and he still did, though his living room had little furniture in it. A table on which the laptop might have rested was here in Brooklyn, but when Con had last stopped by the Philadelphia house, Jerry hadn't replaced it. She didn't know whether he checked his e-mail sitting on the floor, or unplugged the laptop and carried it to the chair.

Jerry, now with gray in his curls, still did what he did with-out much explanation or inquiry. He was a persuasive man. The businesses he advised had been in families for a long time and were struggling as his had struggled. He liked to tell his cli-ents that he'd kept the lamp store going well beyond its natural lifespan by putting all the lamps on a series of extension cords and plugging the last one into an outlet at city hall. Con wasn't sure what that was a metaphor for—what he'd wangled from the city of Philadelphia—but he seemed to manage equally well advising others in the City of New York or other cities.

"Hi," she wrote. "Marlene just issued a royal edict: I'm to set aside a bed, she's on her way—next weekend. I can't remember when you're coming. But you'll be gone by then, won't you?"

At last, Con cleaned the bathtub. When she returned to her computer, she had a new message. However he managed it without a table, Jerry checked e-mail often.

"I have an appointment with a real estate agent for Wednesday morning, so I'll come to you on Thursday. I'll be there about a week."

Con wrote back: "A week? Did I agree to this? Why? And don't tell me you're finally putting the house up for sale!" Jerry had long ago bought her out of the house they'd owned together, but he had far more room than he needed.

Con went back to the *Times* Web site, and when she returned, Jerry had written, "Yes, I'm selling the house. A week because this is one of my trips." He meant his expeditions to historical sites. He continued to take them. They continued to irritate Con, but didn't infuriate her now that she wasn't married to him. "I did ask permission," the message continued, "but I guess you didn't realize what you were getting into, so you forgot. It's a good trip—I'll tell you about it. Did you ever hear of Marcus Ogilvy?"

"No," Con said out loud. How odd. After all these decades, one of Jerry's trips was *toward* Con, not away from her. "No," she typed. "I never heard of Marcus Ogilvy."

Before dark that April Monday, Con spent many minutes staring out the two windows in her mother's living room, from which she could see sidewalk and an apartment house opposite. Cars passed. A delivery truck double-parked. She read the newspaper story about airports, though the story was continued from page 1 and she didn't have page 1. A whole new way of checking in airline passengers was about to start, including, according to the *Times*, "a process known as profiling": a response to the bomb on Pan Am Flight 103. "Details of the profile, used to select some passengers for further examination, are secret, but may include behavior, nationality, and other factors." Con didn't think her mother would have taken an interest in this story. She had happened to buy a paper, and happened to leave it—for a week—on the table, open to page 9.

The airlines' plan seemed silly to Con, not to mention unconstitutional. Joanna did not phone. Con found no money, though she searched without shame, even reaching her hand into her mother's nylon underwear, feeling for coins. She stopped staring at the newspaper and checked the pockets of everything in the closet—her mother's familiar shirts and jackets, all festooned with cat hair and recalling Gert's squarish shape. The pockets bellied slightly because Gert put things into them or kept her hands in them. Con found seventy-eight cents in change. She tried her house again, hanging up before the answering machine finished its message. She could call Marlene's house again, but she didn't want to. When Gert and Marlene were together—even bickering and complaining—they both were less interested in Con than when she was alone with either.

Gert and Marlene had met in the thirties. Gert was already engaged to Abe, but they couldn't afford to get married, so she still lived at home with her parents. A receptionist for a company that made bathing suits, Gert had to summon the assistant to one of the bosses—Marlene—when a buyer asked to see a bathing suit on a model. Marlene was young and considered glamorous, and she didn't object to going into the ladies', taking off everything but her girdle (keeping it on made the suit look better), putting on the suit, and entering the reception area flouncing her shoulders, a hand on one hip. When she told her daughters the story, years later, Gert would demonstrate, slapping her own hip.

Gert said that though she admired Marlene's looks and vivacity, they didn't become friends for several months because Gert was shy and Marlene barely noticed her. But one day, one of the buyers was rude to Marlene. (Con thought her mother meant that he'd said she didn't look good in the bathing suit; much later she realized he must have propositioned Marlene.) Marlene was afraid to leave the office—it was winter, so it was dark outside at the end of the working day—and she asked Gert to walk her to the subway. Naturally, Marlene was dressed again when they left the office, but such a point had been made of her dazzling appearance that as a child hearing the story, Con pictured her stepping out into the cold in a bathing suit. The two young women walked to the subway station. Gert thought she spied the man in question, edging into the shadows near the building. They talked loudly about Gert's boyfriend, so the man might think Abe would show up at any moment and defend Marlene.

At the subway station, they conferred again. Marlene was still afraid. They lived in different neighborhoods in Brooklyn, and their neighborhoods were reached by different trains. So kindhearted Gert went with Marlene on the Jamaica el, instead of taking the IRT—but as everybody knew, once you got to Brooklyn there was no way to get from the northeastern part (where Marlene lived) to the southwestern part (where Gert lived) without going most of the way back: the lines in Brooklyn fan out instead of connecting. At Marlene's stop, Gert went home with her. Marlene, astonishingly, had her own tiny apartment, and of all things they ate bacon and eggs for supper. Then Gert spent the night on the couch in a borrowed nightgown. After that, they were friends.

Marlene told Con her own version of this story three times, several years apart, apparently forgetting she'd told it before. The first time, she said she'd only pretended to be afraid of a man: she simply wanted to make friends with Gert. Nobody had lurked in the shadows. The second time, she said she was dating her boss, and had quarreled with him. She had an appointment to meet him, but if she kept walking, talking loudly to Gert about another man (Abe), then the boss—waiting in the shadows— would become jealous. The third time she said again that she'd only pretended to be afraid: she had been trying for months to think of a way to make friends with Gert. She considered Gert refined, because she came from a nice family. Marlene's relatives were in Toledo, Ohio. Her parents were dead. She wanted to become part of a family—Gert's family—but she was afraid Gert disapproved of her for modeling bathing suits (and occasionally dating the buyers). "And I don't mean just having a drink, if you follow me," she'd said to Con.

The various stories raised more questions than they answered. Con didn't believe Marlene would go to so much trouble to make her boss jealous, but it was even harder to believe she'd schemed to make friends with Con's ordinary mother. But Gert's story raised the same question—why did she want to be friends with flighty Marlene? And the trains—did the problem with the trains make sense? Was traveling in Brooklyn *so* difficult that Gert would have spent the night at Marlene's when she didn't even know her? The past was lit only partially, and in the dappled light of the little she knew, what Con wanted most to see was hidden. She could picture Gert at an old-fashioned switchboard, and Marlene coming out of the bathroom in that sleek black tank suit, with her hips swaying. But she couldn't see the expressions on either girl's face. Now Gert needed Marlene, but Marlene didn't need Gert, and wasn't in the habit of making sacrifices. Con couldn't imagine why Marlene—who made no secret of her frequent irritation with Gert—stayed friends with her.

She was supposed to call her office, and since she remembered the number, she finally did, trying to distract herself from the question of Joanna's whereabouts. The secretary was glad to hear from her. Something was up but she didn't know exactly what, and the head of the office was on another line. Con gave her mother's number. Now she was waiting for so many phone calls that she felt justified sitting near the phone, waiting, just running her finger down the orange stripe on the tablecloth. She couldn't think how long her mother had owned this tablecloth, but she knew from the way she felt, looking at it, that it did not go back to her childhood, to the time when she was so small that her mother seemed infallibly interesting and trustworthy.

It didn't have the sad, dense purity of objects that had been around longer than she could remember, from the times, during the war, when Gert had repeatedly packed up her baby—and then two babies—and moved. There were such objects: the stolen jewelry box with its map of France; a small oil painting Marlene had done, of an orange sand dune and blue sea and sky; a big square glass ashtray, dark red, with beveled sides and smooth cuts at each corner, where a cigarette might rest. It had one broken corner. The striped cloth was much newer than these things. It came from a time after Con had discovered that her mother, though frantic with good will, could not—maybe because she was frantic—guess what her children felt.

Con ran again. Ten steps from one end of the apartment to the other, ten back. The phone rang at last: the director of the office, a lawyer named Sarah. Mabel Turner had called. Con didn't mention her present predicament. "I'll call her," she said. That number had escaped the burglar.

"It's probably not the decision, this soon," Sarah said. "But if it is, and it's a no, we've got to move fast." There had been a zoning hearing.

Con suspected that Sarah considered her foolish, not quite capable of seeing for herself what mattered. She hung up and tried unsuccessfully to reach Mabel. She wondered whether, when they were in prison, women had the use of a phone. She tried Joanna again and left a second message. "I don't care if you stayed home from school. Please call me. Something happened."

A week ago she and Joanna had argued about Jerry's trips. "It's easier for me to understand him," Joanna had said. "I'm African American, like him." Jerry did not usually describe himself as African American. He refused to discuss race or specify what his was. His father had been a Jew, his mother a light-skinned black woman from the neighborhood who worked in the lamp store and married the boss's son; Jerry looked ethnically ambiguous. Joanna was only half as African American as Jerry, but her skin was as dark as his, with a rosy tinge, and she sometimes said, "I'd have been a slave." At other times she remembered she was mostly Jewish and said, "Hitler would have killed me." Joanna had a restless, strikingly mature laugh. Would she laugh at a man with a gun? And what would he do then?

If Joanna was perfectly all right, anything Con might do to find her would be the needless effort of a neurotic. If Joanna was not all right, a sensible mother would call anybody, whatever anyone might think. But without her address book, it was difficult. The people in Philadelphia whose phone numbers she remembered were somehow—like people she thought of in New York—the wrong people. At last she called the lamp store—she knew that number—and reached the manager, Howard, a loyal and humble man with scraps of gray hair around a wide, bald crown. When Joanna was a baby, Con would sometimes walk to the store with the stroller. Howard would pretend to pinch off Joanna's nose, then solemnly show her the tip of his thumb between his fingers. "I got your nose," he'd say. Now he listened intently. "Shall I call the police?" he said when she paused.

"No. But if you could go to the house . . ."

"I'll find her," said Howard.

In her mother's house, she was only a daughter. She had never lived in this apartment, in Park Slope. Gert had moved in when Con was in college, and on vacations she slept on a sheet tucked around the sofa cushions. Mornings, she'd gaze out the window at the polygon of sky between the tops of nearby buildings. Her mother would be drinking coffee at the table, her back to her daughter, wearing a pink bathrobe, an ancestor of the present pink robe.

She and her mother, during those vacations, were alone;

Con's sister, Barbara, had her own place in the city. Gert was still working then—she had eventually become a school secretary—and she told funny stories about the pupils and teachers. Earlier and later her stories never arrived anywhere, but in those years they had punch lines. Gert was competent though slow, puzzled by those who were less conscientious than she was. Some teachers never did paperwork on time, no matter how many times she mentioned it.

Gert had been a single parent through the war, with her husband in the army. Then she'd been a married woman for what must have seemed, in retrospect, like a minute—eleven years. And then Con's father had a heart attack and died, and Gert returned to the single life, which probably felt a little more natural, though harder and sadder, as she brought up her girls.

The doorbell rang. It was dark outside. The day was gone. At the door was the building superintendent, a tense, quick-talking Puerto Rican man. He was sorry about the break-in. "I tell her, make sure you lock that door! Does she listen?"

Con was sure he had never said such a thing. She was annoyed with him for condescending to her mother, though she knew she did the same thing herself. She demanded to know how she could get her locks changed and he shook his head sympathetically. "Aren't you supposed to *do* something?" she asked. The super was vague. He said he'd bring new locks, but he didn't know when. He went away.

The phone rang. "I went to your house," said Howard's voice.

"Howard, what is it?"

"It's locked up. No lights. The newspaper's outside. The mail."

"Did you ring the tenants' bell?"

"Nobody home there either. Their mail was taken in."

"I'm calling the police."

"I already did," said Howard. "They want her friends' names. I have a number for you to call. Have you got a pencil?"

"She could be in there—"

"At first they wouldn't even listen—teenagers are always taking off. You got a pencil?" he said again.

Gert kept pens and pencils in a bowl; after several tries Con found a pen that worked. She hung up quickly. "If only Jerry was with you" was the last thing Howard said, but she didn't want Jerry. She wanted to touch Joanna's taut, lithe shoulders so badly her fingers hurt. Howard had spoken quickly. She'd never heard him speak quickly. In a moment she found herself talking to a police officer for the second time that day. He wrote down all the names she could think of. "The parents never know the real friend," he said, "but sometimes the friends that the parents think of can tell you the name of the real friend."

"I understand," said Con miserably.

"You don't have numbers for these kids?" She explained where she was and what had happened. There was a pause she didn't like. "If you can get here that might be better," he said. "You could notice something."

"Do you think the burglar—"

"I'll get back to you," said the officer. She hung up. She could pour some cat food into a bowl and leave the house, taking her suitcase and leaving the door unlocked. She had enough money for a subway token, and she could go to Penn Station. Conceivably she could sneak onto Jersey Transit. But what if she was caught? And if she got home, how would she get in? Now, anyway, she didn't want to leave this phone. Joanna had this number. To her slight embarrassment, Con was hungry. There was more canned soup. There was bread. There was vanilla ice milk.

The police officer had said there was no reason to break down the house door and find out what or who was inside, or not yet. Con did not call him back. She sat near the kitchen phone all evening, turning on the television and turning it off again, unable to concentrate on the Speaker of the House or the *Exxon Valdez*, the ship that had run aground in Alaska, causing a huge oil spill. She wanted to call Howard, who seemed wise and fatherly, but he might not continue to be wise.

Con brought a blanket and slept on the carpeted floor near the table that night, just where she'd so luxuriously studied the striped tablecloth in the morning. She could not have said why she was sleeping on the floor; a phone was next to the bed. By then she was rigid, unable to think what to do, unable to do anything. She woke often, slept, then woke again. At six, she lay looking at the brightening sky above the building tops, unable to remember a painful dream. At some point she'd moved to the sofa.

She had slept in her clothes. She lay unmoving for a long time. Her pants were twisted uncomfortably against her crotch, but if she stayed where she was, maybe she could keep clear of fright; maybe fear filled some but not all the air in the room. She reminded herself that the only trouble she was sure she had was the missing bag. It wasn't logical to think that Joanna was in trouble simply because Con couldn't find her. Tentatively, Con moved her legs, stood up, and shifted her clothes. Then she sat down again.

For an hour, she sat with her legs drawn up under her. Sometimes she played with the dark red glass ashtray on the end table next to her. She remembered fitting her fingers in the cuts for cigarettes when she was a child, and now she ran her index finger on the ashtray's broken edge, then on its whole, smooth slopes. At the edge of memory was the knowledge of how it had broken, but when she tried to focus on the event, she couldn't. She had been little, her father had been present, and the memory had a wolf in it, but that part must have been a dream. Something had frightened her—that was all she knew. At last she stood and loped back and forth in the living room, in a sloppy way, not fast enough to call it running. She went to the bathroom; on the floor near the toilet her mother had left a copy of *Prevention* magazine, open to a story about the benefits of oat bran. She returned to the living room. When the phone finally rang, the call was from Mabel Turner, apologetic for not calling the day before. They'd received legal papers. She'd given them to her boyfriend, who worked in a law office.

"But I'm your lawyer," said Con.

"That's why I'm calling."

"I have to see the papers."

"He'll bring them back. I didn't know when I could reach you."

"Well, call me when you get them. I need to get off the phone," said Con. "I'm expecting a call from my daughter."

"I hear you," said Mabel, and Con thought she might mean something uncomfortably close to what Con was feeling: that

Con would like to hear from her daughter, but had no convincing reason to expect a call. The women Mabel worked with—and for all she knew, Mabel herself—probably knew about daughters who didn't call: errant daughters, missing daughters, hurt daughters. Con determined to fix her life, at least for the moment. If she fixed her life, nothing bad would have happened to Joanna. She brushed her teeth, showered, put on clean clothes. She straightened her mother's apartment a little, replacing what she'd disarranged the day before. She ate cereal with raisins and drank coffee. As she ate she remembered a phone conversation with her mother, just a few days before this trip. "Not that my old friend Marlene is always nice—you shouldn't think that," Gert had said, in the middle of a conversation about something else. "She thinks I'm stupid."

"No, she doesn't," Con had said. "She wouldn't have invited you if she thought you were stupid."

"I invited myself," said Gert. "I just hope I'm not so stupid I make her mad."

Con in her Brooklyn apartment in 2003 finished cleaning the bathroom and went for a walk. She liked to walk fast because it felt more like running, which, lately, made her knees hurt. In her crowded neighborhood, even fast walking wasn't always possible. Pedestrians pushed strollers and talked on cell phones, and there were constant small disasters of breakage, spillage, and the discharge of bodily fluids. Today the weather was cloudy and surprisingly warm for November, and Con opened her jacket. She carried money in one pocket and a cell phone in the other, but though she kept the phone on, she hoped it wouldn't ring. At the corner she turned toward Prospect Park, falling into step behind families with children; it was almost like a summer Sunday. A woman ran with a stroller next to a little girl who pedaled a wobbling bicycle, pink streamers floating back from the handlebars. They stopped when the bike wobbled. As Con walked on, her cell phone rang.

The call was from Joanna. Even when Joanna had been missing—back in 1989—when Con could calm down she understood that her daughter was probably not dead, and indeed, though Joanna's disappearance would make Con change her life, Joanna was not only alive but, in 2003, had been staying with her mother until a few days earlier. She lived in Durham, North Carolina, with a boyfriend named Tim, and just now she'd interrupted a three-month stay in New York to go back there for a week or so. "What are you doing?" Joanna said.

"I'm on my way to the park." The woman and children passed Con. At the corner they all waited to cross Grand Army Plaza.

"I've got a problem," Joanna said.

"About Tim?" Without an excuse—she'd never met him— Con didn't like Tim.

"No, nothing's wrong with Tim," said Joanna. "Barney called."

Joanna had flunked out of one college and interrupted attendance at another to spend time in rehab because of a drinking problem. Eventually she'd graduated with a degree in art, and had become a sculptor, making her living waiting on tables. She'd quit her restaurant job and come to New York when she'd been awarded a three-month internship with a well-known sculptor in TriBeCa. Staying in Con's spare bed-room, she filled the apartment with her work and kept Con up late talking about sculpture and the famous sculptor, whose name was Barnaby Willis. Barnaby Willis worked in steel, and Joanna was learning techniques she had never picked up in school. "I could work like this too, maybe," she'd said, a couple of weeks earlier.

"I thought you didn't want to," Con had said.

"I think I do want to." What Barnaby Willis did was expensive and even dangerous—welding, manipulating metal—but bold and ambitious, and Con liked hearing Joanna sound ambitious. "Sculptors have to learn so much," Joanna said. "Things people in hard hats know."

Another day she said, "I once did a piece in aluminum. Aluminum sucks. But steel—you can bend steel, twist it. Steel has ductility." Joanna's present sculptures were large but not rigid shapes—something like sea creatures, something like plants, made of industrial gray-green twine that she secured from a factory. Sometimes she knotted it until it took on a shape, sometimes she actually crocheted or knitted. Con loved to look at them; she could scarcely believe that her years of worrying about Joanna might be over. Sometimes she didn't believe it, and worried.

"How did you learn to do that?" Con had said one night, watching as Joanna crocheted an irregular gray shape with an enormous needle. "It looks like something you'd have to have surgically removed."

"That's the idea," said Joanna. "Grandma knitted and crocheted. Don't you remember, all over her house?"

Con didn't remember.

"She made sweaters and blankets," said Joanna. "Wonderful ugly colors."

"Did she teach you?"

"I guess so." She paused and continued, "I wouldn't mind working in wool. A ten-foot monster made of green alpaca. It would cost ten thousand dollars to make, but maybe I'd sell it and make a hundred thousand. An investment. Want to invest?" Joanna was tall and sturdy, with roughly cut black curls. She looked up from crocheting and her eyes snapped. When she wasn't angry with Con, she teased her.

"I've invested plenty in you already," said Con, pleased.

"Somebody has to. You can't make sculpture out of nothing. Well, I guess you can. Maybe I'll collect garbage and make garbage sculpture."

"Not while you're living in *my* house," said Con with mock ferocity. She liked conversations like that. "Aren't you upset?" she had asked when Barnaby was called out of town and Joanna said she thought she'd go back to North Carolina until he returned. "This is your time with him."

"Oh, mostly I just clean up after him," Joanna had said, sounding quite different from the way she'd talked about Barnaby Willis before. "And watch my ass to make sure he keeps his hands off it. Two weeks away will be fine, and I've got to talk to Tim." She sounded slightly drunk that night; Con kept changing her mind about whether to be concerned.

Now, on the phone, she tried to concentrate. "What about Barney? What does he want?" It had taken her a moment to remember that Barney was the sculptor. For the first couple of weeks, Joanna had used his full name each time, with a slight laugh that told Con she was excited by her good fortune. He'd become Barnaby only recently, and in the last days before Joanna went to North Carolina, he'd become "Barney, who can't be bothered to pick up his own laundry."

"He's back in New York. He wants me there."

"Is that bad?" Con said. She entered the park. The leaves were definitely gone, or were shrunken, shattered and dull brown. A woman in an Islamic head scarf, on her way out, organized treats for three small children.

"Of course it's bad," Joanna said impatiently. "But do I have to go? I'm asking you as a lawyer. Just because of the internship, do I have to?"

"You'd rather stay with Tim?"

Whatever her feelings about Tim, Con hoped that Joanna would stay in the south another week. Joanna had never liked Marlene, and it would be better if they were not in the apartment together. It would also be good if Jerry were gone before Joanna showed up. The three of them had not lived together for many years, and the situation would require thought.

"It has nothing to do with Tim," Joanna said. "I'm not sure I want to work with Barney anymore."

This was not good news; Joanna had a long history of incompletion. But something about the tone, this time, was different. "Jo, you're not sleeping with Barney, are you?"

There was a pause. "Not so far," said Joanna.

"Then what is it?"

Joanna sighed. The park was not crowded after all, and the cobblestone path was peaceful, framed by late fall's dull, subtle colors. Here and there a tree was still yellow. Con took her usual turn, so as to pass the lake. "It's not like that," Joanna was saying.

"Well, I guess I don't know how it is, then," said Con. "Listen, the connection isn't good. Call me in a few minutes, okay?"

"I thought you were an expert on sexual harassment in the workplace," Joanna said.

"Nobody's an expert in that subject," said Con. "I can hardly hear you," she said then, and hung up.

But she didn't turn the phone off and in a moment it rang again. "The truth is, Barney raped me," said Joanna. "I really don't want to come back."

Con was almost at the lake. A flock of furious black birds—a flurry of black spots—made noise in the tops of trees. *"What?"* she said.

"Well, maybe it wasn't rape. It wasn't rape."

"Was it or wasn't it?"

"Surely you of all people know that's a complicated question, Ms. Attorney!" Joanna hung up.

In her mother's apartment, younger Con—more worried Con—stared at the phone and it rang again. This time it was Mabel Turner's boyfriend. "She said you were mad at me."

"I'm mad at her, not you," said Con. "If she expects me to represent her, she has to show me what comes, not give it to somebody else."

"Yeah, I apologize. I talked her into it. I thought the lawyers in my office could give it a quick look. I didn't look at the papers—I just gave them to my boss."

"Could I talk to him?" said Con.

"I don't think that's such a good idea. He does a lot of real estate law. He doesn't think much of that house. Prisoners. He keeps telling me it's probably illegal."

"It's not illegal."

Before she'd ever heard of the house, the irate neighbors had gotten a building inspector to order it closed down for a zoning violation; there was a law against more than a few unrelated people living together. Somehow Mabel or her boyfriend had learned enough to request a hearing. Nervous at last, Mabel came to see Con only after the hearing was over, and Sarah had immediately taken an interest in the case. She'd been hoping for one like it. Everyone in her office assured Con that the results of the hearing wouldn't be announced for several weeks more, so Con had felt able to come to New York. She'd planned just to give Mabel a call that week, to encourage her.

Now Con was pleased with herself for being able to sound something like a lawyer on the phone despite her state of mind. As she hung up, she found herself wondering if the women really were turning tricks outside the house, and suddenly recalled Joanna's insistence that they weren't. Joanna had wanted to go and see. Might she have gone, now that Con wasn't around to stop her? She could have reached the house on a SEPTA train. What if the women were soliciting, and Joanna had run into their pimp? Con didn't let herself continue that line of thinking.

The next phone call was from Barbara. Con's sister had lived in London for ten years. Con wouldn't have thought to call her sister when she was in trouble, but when she heard Barbara's cranky but cheerful voice, "Mom? Wait a minute, Connie?" she sank to the floor where she was—in the kitchen—and leaned back against the cabinets, almost in tears. "Barb, Joanna's gone, nobody can find her," she began.

"*Joanna's* gone? I thought you were going to tell me something's wrong with Mom."

"Why?"

"Because you're answering her phone."

"She's with Marlene."

"Oh, I forgot. She told me. She told me several times." When Barbara was in New York, they stayed up half the night talking and when Con got herself to London they rode around on buses and on the tube, both talking at once. Con followed her sister at such times, at ease, wondering why life ordinarily felt so much more difficult, but when she was alone again she was relieved. Nothing quite worked out for Barbara beyond today—she couldn't keep a job or a man for long—but somehow she always had enough money for today, and today was interesting or even brilliant. She would have been a tourist anywhere, and it made sense that she'd settled in a city she'd never know in any other way. But Barbara could listen and give advice, and sometimes she made Con's life seem more interesting just by its proximity to hers. What was happening to Con just now did not feel interesting but sickening—gray and ugly and, somehow, all her own fault.

Once again she told the whole story. "She's run away," Barbara said.

"Why would she run away?"

"All kids her age want to run away. Didn't you? It was my

primary fantasy. As soon as you left, she packed a bag and took off."

"I'm afraid she's in the house and she's dead," said Con—making herself say it.

"No, no. She ran away. God what a stinker."

Run away was better than dead.

"Can you reach Jerry?" said Barbara. Everyone assumed she needed Jerry.

"No. I had to cancel the credit card. I thought he'd call when it didn't work."

"You have to talk to Jerry. Maybe she said something to him." This was possible. "More cops," said Barbara. "Is Fort Ticonderoga a town or is it just a fort? Are there cops?"

"But all they could do would be look for the car," said Con. "I suppose I could call the fort."

"Call the fort."

Con was able to get a number for Fort Ticonderoga. A message said the fort wasn't open until summer. There was a museum. It sounded like history for children, not the kind of history Jerry liked, in which scraps of reality might be lying around. This history had been tamed, the blood scrubbed away. She called her mother, feeling obscurely that if she could just explain to Gert what had happened, Gert, despite everything, would know where Joanna was. Marlene answered the phone. "I was just about to call you," she said. "Did you at least change the locks?"

Con had forgotten the locks. "No," she said, "but that's not what I'm thinking about."

"Don't you know anybody who could lend you some money? Go to the neighbors." Marlene was getting impatient.

"Yes, I should do that. Marlene, may I speak to my mother, please?"

"I've got an appointment for her tomorrow. They're squeezing her in."

"That's good," Con said. A doctor's examination could do no harm. Marlene's beloved Dr. Herbert had been her friend and advisor for years; Con had sometimes wondered if she slept with him.

Again, Con could hear her mother's voice, demanding to talk to her. This time Gert succeeded. "Connie," she began, "can you explain something?"

"Hi, Mama, how are you?" said Con.

"I'm fine, but Marlene says I have to go to the doctor. Why should I go to the doctor?"

"A checkup is always smart," Con said lamely.

"But I'm not sick."

Now that she had Gert on the line, Con couldn't imagine how to confess to her mother that she didn't know where Joanna was. "Well, just in case," she said. Then, "Marlene's worried about your memory."

"Oh, my memory. I can't think straight. That's not what you go to a doctor for. Just this morning, I couldn't remember—you know Barb's friend? I couldn't remember that name no matter what I did. I was lying in bed trying to come up with it."

Con supplied the name of Barbara's closest New York friend, but that wasn't the friend Gert meant. She mentioned a girlhood best friend.

"A man," said Gert.

"You mean Donald?" Donald was the name of Barbara's former husband.

"Donald!"

And then Gert didn't remember that Con's purse had been stolen. It came out gradually. Con said, "Well, I'm still trying to deal with everything here." She was determined to tell her mother that Joanna was missing, but somehow to do it in a way that would not alarm her.

"The cat is trouble," said her mother.

"No, of course not," said Con. She had forgotten the cat. She hadn't seen him all day. "I mean changing the locks. But also—"

"Why should you change the locks?" said her mother.

Eventually Con told the whole story over again. She waited for her mother to decide, as she had the day before, that the person they must worry about was Joanna, but today Gert's mind didn't go in that direction. "Why would somebody do that? He took your purse?"

"Marlene knows all about it. Marlene will explain." And Con got off the phone. She sat down on her mother's brown sofa and put her hands to her face. Marlene was right. Marlene would call back, she knew, and sure enough, she did. "Okay, kid, see what I mean?"

Con wanted to talk about Joanna. "Don't you care . . ." she began. She said it with more force than she usually used with Marlene, then felt she might cry, and paused to breathe.

"If you knew how much I care!" Marlene said, with a self-conscious sob that embarrassed Con. The woman couldn't stand opposition. How could Con have loved such a person all her life? "She's breaking my heart," Marlene was saying. It was Gert who was breaking Marlene's heart, not Joanna. "Whatever she says, promise me you won't believe her. Last night she thought—well, I didn't want to say the main thing, but you won't mind—you'll just laugh, you're no baby. She thinks I had an affair with your father. What might be worse, she doesn't mind. Twice this morning she wanted to know if Abe gave me money when he was my husband."

"What?" But Con liked "you're no baby." She'd always feared that Marlene considered her a baby.

"Isn't that ridiculous?"

It was not ridiculous, it was simply too large to be looked at right now. "Marlene, please, I need to talk about Joanna." She explained what Howard had told her.

"Oh, Connie," said Marlene. "Oh, baby. Everything at once. What shall we do?"

"I don't know." She wept. "Marlene, I don't know." Weeping was luxurious.

"Tell me again where Jerry is," said Marlene. "He may know where she is."

"That's what Barbara said," said Con. "He's at Fort Ticonderoga."

"That silly tourist trap?"

"Yes."

"I'll call you back."

Waiting for more phone calls, Con searched the apartment again. She could not have said what she was looking for. In Gert's bedroom were several chests of drawers: in one, Con's mother kept her big bras, her nylon panties with cotton crotches. On top—next to the wooden box—Con had set her purse the night she arrived. Two other chests, which had belonged to Con and Barbara as children, were side by side against the wall. Now Con pulled out a drawer from one of those and sat on the bed with it. She believed that if she could pay such close attention to what she found that she forgot Joanna, the girl herself would phone.

The drawer contained shoe boxes, their lids held on with yellow tape. The first ones she looked into were full of photographs. In one box, she and her sister were little girls. There were few baby pictures, but many of two children in sunsuits. Sometimes a graceful arm—Gert's—stretched between the children or pushed hair out of someone's eyes.

In another box, her father, in uniform, squinted into the sun. He'd been younger than fifty when he died. He looked very Jewish for a soldier; Con always thought that about pictures from the war. In another drawer were old clothes, smelling of mothballs. Con found two dollars in a pocket and transferred them to her own pocket.

Then she found a stack of letters from her father, written during the war. A rubber band holding them together came apart when she touched it. Once he wrote that Bob Hope performed for the men. Another time, a friend had received a "Dear John" letter. "I sat with the guy playing checkers for hours," said her father.

"There's nothing wrong with the baby," he said in another letter. "She will be as smart as Barbara." In another letter he wrote, "You don't have to say anything to your friend Marlene. She is the way she is and she'll never be any different."

Gert would never miss these letters. Con put them into her suitcase, then considered that she was stealing her mother's love letters, and replaced them in the drawer. She picked up another bundle. More letters, in a different handwriting.

On top lay what looked like the second page of a letter, hastily written.

How should we have known about the fire? The
doll carriage was in the alley between the buildings,
its inside was charred and sodden. Brenda was asleep
against Bernard's shoulder. She drooled in her sleep
and his lapel had a round damp patch. He handed her
to me and she woke up and tried to hit me. Her mother
dresses her in little dresses and she had wet herself. Her
legs were bare and wet. It was freezing out.

Con had no idea who Brenda and Bernard were. The next page was in the same handwriting, but apparently from a different letter.

There's no reason for you to give me that kind of
advice. I'm doing fine. So is he. Let me know if you want
me to send the coat. I know it is hot in Florida but it
isn't hot every minute. Your loving friend, Marlene.

Gert had moved to Florida with Barbara when Con's father had first been stationed there. Then he was sent overseas. These letters were from the war years, of course. Marlene had been single, living in New York.

Con turned the pages of the letters. Most were in the wrong order. Some were stained, as if Gert had left them on the kitchen table for weeks, living around them. She read a piece of another one.

All this is a little silly, anyway, this volunteering. The mayor is trying to get us to feel as if we're part of the war effort. I feel that anyway, just living. I don't need this kind of thing but now I'm glad I'm doing it, because of Bernard. Also, maybe I can become a photographer or a radio operator.

This time Con was less scrupulous. She shuffled the letters together. The original rubber band had lost its elasticity. She went into the kitchen for a plastic bag large enough to hold them, and for a moment caught herself thinking that there wouldn't be any plastic bags because it was only 1944. On her way back, she was stopped by the ringing of the phone.

"Hello?"

"I got you the numbers of five motels near Fort Ti," said Marlene.

"That's a good idea." Her own voice sounded unfamiliar. *Who was Brenda?* she wanted to say. *How did the fire start?* She wrote down names and numbers on a used envelope. Then she hung up and without much hope dialed the first motel. Jerry was not staying there, but when she looked again at the name of the second one—Mountain View—she knew it was right. "I don't think he's in his room," said the proprietor. "But maybe his daughter is."

"His daughter?"

"She went out with him yesterday," he said, "but today I think she hung around."

"Try the room," said Con. She heard ringing.

"Hello?" said Joanna's sleepy voice.

Chapter 2

Con reached the lake in Prospect Park. She approved of this time of year, of its colors—richer browns than the exhausted tones of late winter—and of the annual surprise of open sky when the leaves had fallen and light outlined tree branches. She liked to be cold; she liked wind flattening her hair, but today was foolishly warm for November, which suggested global warming and thus made her grouchy and guilty, though she knew that one warm day in November was not necessarily the result of global warming. In cold weather, she walked fast and felt young, though she wasn't.

Con told people she was the oldest of the Brooklyn newcomers, most of whom were Joanna's age: artists, teachers, and writers in their twenties and thirties. She needed to say she had lived in Brooklyn as a child, but she was unlike people her own age who had lived in New York all along. She cried more easily. She had missed the toughening events: the muggings of the seventies; the eighties' frenzy for real estate while homeless people lined the walls in Grand Central Station; Mayor Koch, much of Mayor Giuliani. But she'd been in New York for September 11, 2001. From the windows of her apartment, in the cold months she could see a scrap of the Manhattan skyline, which she now didn't like looking at because the World Trade Center—which she'd never liked looking at—was gone.

Con was no expert on sexual harassment in the workplace, whether such experts existed or not. At present she was a lawyer for a project that fought job discrimination against women. Just now, like almost everyone else in the office, Con spent her time on a big case against an insurance company. If the company's employees were beaten up at home, they didn't get time off to go to court, and seemed less likely to be promoted. Victims of domestic violence often became victims of sexual harassment in the workplace as well, and Con was studying that issue too. Both Joanna and Marlene had long taken an interest in Con's work, but both seemed disappointed that she wasn't more straightforwardly aggressive. "What did you do *yesterday*?" Marlene might ask. On a typical day, Con spent time in the law library and attended two meetings. Marlene wanted her to swoop down on discriminatory offices, or at least on courthouses, but Constance was not a litigator. She was trying to find the perfect client.

She sometimes wondered what her life would have been like if she and Jerry had lived in Brooklyn all along, if the store had always been on Flatbush Avenue, or if some member of the Elias family had moved it there. Would she still be married to

Jerry? Would the store be gone now—like the actual store—or would it be stalwartly selling lamps to schoolteachers from the Midwest, upwardly mobile Caribbean families, and stubborn Chasidim?

On her way home, the cell phone rang again. "Forget I said he raped me."

"All right, Jo."

"Now, can I get out of this? I mean, given the terms of my internship. Do I have to come back?"

Con said, "If it's sexual harassment, there's lots you can do, starting with reporting him to the people who gave you the money."

"They'd laugh. It happens every year. Each intern thinks she's different."

"Well, still—"

"Look, that's not what I want. Forget what I said about rape. I just don't want to go back to New York."

"Because of Tim?" Tim was a photographer who earned his living taking portrait photographs of children. He'd be out at the moment—Sunday was his busiest day.

"No, not because of Tim. That's a long story, too."

"When you say each one thinks she's different," Con said— she had reached her building and was feeling for the right key—"do you mean each one thinks he'll leave her alone?"

"Or that he'll mean something by it. Or both. You've been a woman. Or maybe you haven't."

"Watch it, Jo."

"Sorry, I'm edgy. You're not going to help me think this through, I can tell."

Con was getting into the elevator. "But what do you *want*?" she said. The phone died. Often Joanna went too far. Once, she'd destroyed a wooden sculpture she'd made, just before a critique in art school. "I thought I was improving it," she had said to Con. "When I started with the knife, I thought I was improving it."

Con didn't want Joanna home right now—but even more, she didn't want her to resign the internship, whatever had happened. If Joanna did come home, however, she'd have to be polite to Marlene. For a start, she'd need to vacuum around her sculptures, which tended to shed. If Joanna didn't come, Con would have to vacuum, sometime before Friday. But today was only Sunday. She tried to decide whether she was morally bound to mention Marlene's visit, if it meant Joanna would give up her internship to avoid seeing Con's old friend. She could never figure out just why Joanna disliked Marlene.

The motel near Fort Ticonderoga was more than two hundred miles from Brooklyn, but when Joanna's voice reached Con's ear she grabbed air with her free hand as if to seize her child.

"What's wrong, Mom? Are you crying?"

"I didn't know where you were."

"Sure you did," said Joanna, sounding uncertain.

"Did you run away? How did you get there?" Con said.

"Bus. Dad gave me money. He told you," Joanna said.

Con felt physically ill, as if the room had just lurched. "What do you mean?"

"I had money. He gave me enough for lunch, and emergencies."

"Before he left?"

"Of course before he left. Look, he told me last week you said this was okay."

"He told you I said it was okay?" said Con stupidly.

"You didn't know," Joanna said, her voice flat.

"No." Jerry had deceived her, and the news shoved itself into Con's body with as much force as if the deception had been sexual, maybe more force. He had conspired with their child to deceive her.

"I sort of knew you didn't know," Joanna was saying. "That's why I didn't say anything, just in case. Stop crying, Mom. I'm fine." Then her voice became quiet. "I'm sorry."

"But why didn't you call me?" Con said. "Why didn't you tell me, once you were there?" She wasn't angry with Joanna. She pictured Jerry, somehow overhearing this conversation and shrugging, his shoulder moving in an easy way as he dismissed any notion that Con might have been consulted, as he dismissed *her*. She saw his shoulder, his neck, the way his thin arm would slightly rearrange itself as the one-shoulder shrug moved down through his fingers, as he shook out of his fingers the very idea of telling her. The imagined arm and shoulder made her know what she felt. She was in the kitchen, and as she talked to Joanna, the objects belonging to her mother, there on the counter—the bottle of sherry, a dying plant, the cat food and water dishes, some bowls and canisters—looked more and more fragile, sadder and sadder, as if they were the last quiet frame of a tragic movie. Joanna didn't answer.

Con took the receiver to the table and sat down with it. "Where is he?"

"Driving around. Figuring out old roads. Tomorrow we'll be in a boat, if he can find some local to rent us one."

He had never given Con a thought. He was figuring out roads, he was not even making sure that she didn't discover what he'd done. Once he'd made the plan with Joanna, Con had not been in his mind at all. It was as if the marriage had ended so long ago that she was no longer still opposite him at the imaginary table we all carry in our minds—she was not a loved presence and not even a presence. She said, "When is he coming back to the motel?"

"I don't know."

"I need to talk to him," said Con. She hadn't told Joanna anything. "Tell him my purse was stolen."

"Stolen?"

"Yes. Look, I better hang up and call the police. The police in Philadelphia are looking for you."

"I hope they don't talk to the school!" Joanna said.

"Maybe you should have thought of that." Con said good-bye. She was too relieved to be more than slightly angry with Joanna, even though Joanna was old enough to have known what was wrong with her escapade, whether Jerry knew or not.

She phoned the police and called off the search. She phoned Howard and got his machine. She was glad she didn't have to talk to him. He admired Jerry. He'd make an excuse for Jerry.

For years, she'd felt angry with Jerry much of the time, but her anger was based on love. Lately she'd felt weary—not surprised enough to be angry—and sometimes she realized that a week or more had passed when she hadn't thought about Jerry, except in practical ways, at all. At some point she'd excused him from her own mental table, whether he was present in life or not. Maybe it wasn't fair to be shocked that he seemed to have dismissed her as well, but Con was shocked.

Jerry was indefensible, but Joanna was safe, and Con was hungry. She had never eaten lunch, and it was now well into the afternoon. She wanted fresh vegetables, but her mother had only frozen peas and frozen broccoli. She found some rice and an onion, and cooked what she had with plenty of salt and pepper. She ate mounds of rice. By the time she was done, it was five o'clock. Five o'clock on Tuesday afternoon. Con put her dish in the sink and took the packet of Marlene's old letters from her suitcase, where she'd put it underneath her clothes. She wanted distraction. She wanted the rest of the story about Brenda and the fire. Some letters were still in envelopes, but some were just loose sheets. Others were folded together, sometimes with pages from a different letter. Marlene wrote a large, sloppy script, always on onionskin—presumably to save postage—but with big margins, so not many words were on any one page. Some letters weren't dated at all, others were dated "Friday." She seemed to write often on Fridays. Some envelopes had legible postmarks, some didn't. The letters seemed to have been sent from New York in 1943 and 1944.

Con looked over the letters but was too tired to read them. She took a long shower. When she came out there was a message from Jerry: "You're hard to reach, I'll try tomorrow." She didn't call him back. She turned on the television and watched a little of *thirtysomething*, then went to bed, read Salman Rushdie for a few minutes, got hungry again, and ate toast with jam, belatedly weeping with gratitude because Joanna was safe. Then she wept with rage at Jerry. Then she slept.

On Wednesday morning, still in bed, she reached for the letters again.

"I went to Saks this morning looking for a present, but that's silly. I can't buy him anything there and anyway what would he do with it" a long, crumpled page began.

Another page that seemed disconnected from everything else said only:

When you think about it you'll see I'm right. There is nothing wrong with it, only with what was before. I'll write again in a couple of days if I can. I have to do a lot of things. Your loving sister-friend, Marlene.

There was a P.S.: "Kiss baby. If she's good." Con might have been the baby. She had been born in January, 1944. Was she to be kissed *only* if she was good? Marlene had left a space at the bottom of the page. In pencil, in her mother's handwriting, was a list:

Evap
Fruit Cocktail
Bread.

Another disconnected last page said:

You're not going to believe this, there was an article in the paper saying if we bring the contents of wastebas-

kets to donate for the war effort we should leave out the
cigarette butts. I'll tell you, Gert, they are going to have
to win the war without the contents of my wastebasket,
with or without cigarette butts. Wish me luck.

Luck with what? Not with donating the contents of waste-
baskets, apparently.

As well as she could, Con arranged the letters in order and
tried to link up parts of letters. It took a long time, time when
she felt pleasantly suspended from problems she should have
been solving. Then she put aside the fragments and began
reading at the beginning.

Dear Gert,

Well, you can imagine that I was glad to get your address after all this time. I thought you'd probably left the
baby in a foundling home, if they still have such things,
and taken off with an attractive sailor like—what was
his name? The room sounds small. I know, you'll cope.
How far are you from the beach?

I know Eleanor is your sweetheart [it took Con a
moment to think of Eleanor Roosevelt] but it says in the
paper she agrees with La Guardia that women air raid
wardens should not wear slacks. I'd like to know how
she'd feel walking in the cold, night after night, with the
wind going up her legs. I might wear slacks under my
dress, that will show her.

I've had my own adventures, nothing like what you're

up to. To make a long story short I met a Catholic man
at a bar. I went there with Sherman but he was tired so
I said I'd take the subway home alone, and then I went
back and got into a conversation with the man, Mike. He
had a cross around his neck believe it or not. He asked me
to marry him. Turned out he promised his mother when
he went to New York he wouldn't kiss any girl he wasn't
engaged to, so he gets engaged to all his dates. Very funny.

We had a few laughs but that was all. I saw him
again when I went back with Sherman, but we both
pretended we didn't know each other. Or maybe I pretended and he forgot.

What do you think of calling the baby Babs? Someone in my office has a sister Babs. You'll tell me Jewish
Barbaras aren't called Babs but since when was Barbara
a Jewish name? Then you'll say you named her after
your Aunt Basha and I guess you did. I know you don't
hear from your aunt these days, but that could mean any
number of things, not just Hitler.

Got to go, if I don't get some sleep I'll start laughing at the jokers in my office and you know where that
would get me.

Your friend,
Marlene

Dear Gert,

I didn't get an answer to last week's letter but I'll write
and tell you the news from here. First of all I looked up

where you are on the map, and I guess Starke isn't too near the beach. Do you get to see Abe? Maybe they'll end up using him at the base and he won't have to go overseas. There must be a need for people like him with moderate-sized brains in their heads instead of noodles. As you know I have never considered Abe a genius (not since the alphabet incident) but he is no dope either.

We won't tell the army about the alphabet incident.

Anyhow, I'm still wearing out my shoes and my feet walking the streets of Brooklyn at night. Imagine how we would have felt in peacetime, just a few years ago, if somebody said it was her job to walk up and down the street and make sure you couldn't see any light through the window curtains. I have gotten to know a very nice fellow, also a warden. He wasn't drafted because of something he doesn't like to talk about. I think he had an operation. He showed me pictures of his daughter. I can't guess how old—maybe four, maybe seven. As you know I don't know anything about kids.

Better go. Write soon.

Love from your friend,

Marlene

P.S. I miss you. Maybe there will be a letter tomorrow.

In Gert's apartment, the doorbell rang.

When cell phones were invented Con was not interested, and when she finally bought one she often left it turned off. Alone at home on Sunday afternoon (in November, 2003), she left it on. She didn't like to use it except away from home—she hated the thought that two phones could ring simultaneously—but Joanna rarely called on the apartment phone, as if she preferred to talk to her mother when Con was distracted, elsewhere. She checked her e-mail again, then opened a memo she'd been writing. She read what she'd written—she'd been studying interviews with potential clients—and changed a few words. It felt good to do this work. Then she made herself a cup of coffee and cleaned the kitchen. When she checked her e-mail again, she had messages from Jerry, Marlene, and her friend Peggy. She read Peggy's first. "Are we still on for dinner this week?" it said. "Which night? In the last weeks I have performed the impossible in all areas—work, family, love. Eating fewer carbs too but everybody's doing that." Con and Peggy had dinner every couple of weeks. Two years ago, Con had been at dinner with Peggy when she'd received a cell phone call from England telling her that Barbara had died. She and Peggy had stayed together all night that night in Peggy's apartment, never sleeping.

Jerry had forwarded a message he'd received from Joanna: "Dad—Tell me I'm not crazy. I want a boyfriend who respects me. I'm working up my nerve to break up with Tim." That didn't fit with what Joanna had said to Con, and Con didn't know why Jerry had forwarded it. Was he bragging that Joanna had turned to him in her perplexity, or asking Con to answer her? He'd added a message, but it didn't refer to Joanna. "Marcus Ogilvy is a footnote in the history of Brooklyn who makes the inside of my head light up, though the story doesn't have a happy ending. I'll tell you when I come."

Marlene wrote, "The City Opera is doing Turandot Saturday night. I can't remember Turandot. I wish it was Tosca or Aida. I like doomed passion."

Joanna didn't call again.

Con blinked, as if the doorbell had not just interrupted the reading of Marlene's old letters, but awakened her. Would she ever know the story of "the alphabet incident"? Probably not. And what did her mother know of handsome sailors? She hadn't washed her face, brushed her teeth, or eaten breakfast. It was nine thirty Wednesday morning, and she still hadn't changed the locks, couldn't go outside, and had done nothing about the case she was supposed to work on.

At the door was a woman about Con's age or maybe a little older, dressed in indoor clothing—black loose pants and black sweater—hand on one hip. She had a long, narrow nose and long fluffy curly gray hair. Her nose made her seem like a thin person but her breasts were big. "I couldn't imagine," said the woman. "I came to see. You're somebody else, for a start. Were you *marching*, yesterday? Are you going to do that a lot?" She looked as if she could be Jewish, but her name, which she said next, sounded Italian. "Peggy Santoro. I live underneath." She wore red nail polish; she seemed like someone who'd lived all her life in Brooklyn, but the black clothes meant that she worked in Manhattan, or "New York," as Brooklynites put it.

"I was running," said Con.

"Maybe you ought to run outside?" said Peggy Santoro.

"I'm sorry," said Con.

"Are you her daughter? Shopping cart. That's my name for her."

"I guess there aren't too many of those left," said Con, disliking this woman. The shopping cart was folded in the broom closet. "Her name is Gertrude Tepper. She's my mother. She's away. She asked me to stay here. My purse was stolen."

"What do you mean, stolen?" said Peggy, who didn't seem to care whether she was disliked or not.

"What do you think I mean? The first night I was here, somebody came into the apartment and took my purse."

"That hasn't happened for a long time," said Peggy. "It has happened here, but not for a long time."

"Well, it happened to me."

"So I understand."

Peggy Santoro sounded less cranky so Con said, "Have you lived here long?"

"Five years."

Gert had been in the building for twenty-five years.

"Your mom's one of the old-timers," Peggy was saying. She took a step farther in. "She probably knew my aunt. I took over my aunt's apartment when she moved to Florida. Nobody in my family gives up an apartment."

"Come in," said Con, since Peggy wasn't going away, and since she was finally talking to someone.

Peggy came in and sat down, smoothing her pants under her hips. "Especially because I'm not married," she continued. "They don't think I could find an apartment on my own. For me to move, somebody has to move out of a better apartment or die, and somebody else in the family has to be ready to move into my place." She had long fingers and a ring with a rectangular stone, the color of butterscotch, in the middle of her right hand.

"My mother hasn't mentioned you," said Con.

"We nod. Sometimes we talk. Your mother is a little uncertain, you know?"

"Suspicious?"

"Not quite suspicious." She shook her hair off her shoulders as a glamorous woman might have during the forties.

"I was running," Con said again. "I can't go outside because I don't have keys to lock the door—the burglar took my keys. I need to change the locks but I don't have any money."

"They'll bill you."

"But I asked them—"

"Well, you don't *ask* them. You tell them you need your locks changed. When they're done, you say, 'Please bill me.' What are they going to do? Change them back?"

Con looked at her, walked over to the table—the phone book was on the striped tablecloth—and looked up locksmiths once more. She stepped into the kitchen, called the first one, and arranged to have the locks changed.

"I'll keep you company while you wait," said Peggy. She wiggled her hips as if to carve a comfortable place on the sofa cushion. "I'm going crazy anyway. I took a day off from work to catch up on everything at home, and all I'm doing is waiting for my boyfriend to call. I fooled myself. I thought I truly wanted to deal with laundry, shopping, cleaning. Then I heard myself tell him I was going to do it."

Con excused herself, leaving Peggy in the living room. She

washed her face and brushed her teeth. She dressed in a fresh navy blue turtleneck. When she returned, this confident guest was standing at the table, leaning on one hand and reading the newspaper story about airport security. "I saw this last week," she said. "It's another world."

"I thought it was kind of funny," Con said.

"It's not funny," said Peggy. "I see you're married," she said then, returning to the sofa. "I've never been married." She pointed to her bare left ring finger. Con had been wondering how old Peggy was, and Peggy said, "I'm fifty," as if she'd heard Con's thoughts. Then added, "He's married. Of course."

"I'm forty-five," said Con.

"That's so cultural," Peggy said.

"What is?"

"When I said 'married—of course.' As if you'd already know that the boyfriend of somebody like me would be married. Did you see the story about China the other day? Ever since I read that, I keep thinking about cultures."

Con had read a story about China in the magazine section on Sunday, but had not seen the paper since.

"Deng Xiaoping, apparently, is not as popular as he used to be," Peggy said, standing up straight and sounding particularly alert. "The story explained that 'Xiaoping' can mean 'small bottle' in Chinese. So it seems when he was popular, people would put *small bottles* in noticeable places to show their support. And now they *smash* small bottles. I can't stop thinking about that. Imagine if people grew bushes if they supported Bush, and rooted them out if they changed their minds."

Con liked what Peggy was saying but she wasn't quite listening. She had never thought of her mother as suspicious, but when Peggy used the word—or when she used it herself—it had made her understand that Con was the same, without quite knowing it was possible to be otherwise. Con found herself marveling at Peggy as if she'd never been allowed out of her mother's house, as if Peggy was the first person she'd ever met. Gert was not suspicious but wary. Con was wary too: she expected that things were likelier to go wrong than right. She saw now that her mother had taught her to be that way. "My mother's friend," she said, "thinks my mother is losing her marbles."

"Is this the friend she's visiting?" Peggy said. Then she said, "That locksmith won't be here for a while. Want to go out for a few minutes, and I'll keep an eye on the place? You could buy a paper."

"You're not the burglar?" said Con. "Yes, that friend."

"I'm not the burglar," said Peggy. "I want to stay here because it will make my phone ring."

"That doesn't work if you have an answering machine," said Con.

"Of course it works. The laws of the universe have not been altered by answering machines," Peggy said. She turned on the television, and Con didn't stop to put on her running shoes and sweat pants but picked up her coat. "What does she do for this friend?" Peggy said then.

"Do for her? Not much," Con said. "The friend does a lot for her. They've been friends forever. Why?"

"We meet on the stairs. Last week," Peggy said, "she said she was taking a trip, so I said something polite and she said, 'It's trouble to go, but she needs me.'"

"She did?" said Con. "That makes no sense at all." She went downstairs and walked around her mother's long block as fast as she could. It was amazing to be outside. Surely she'd been locked up for weeks; everything looked fresh and interesting. Her mother lived in an apartment building near a corner, but brownstones filled most of the rest of the block, their high stoops and tiring stairs less grand than formerly, but not too cracked and crumbly. One or two were being restored. Two old women talked on the sidewalk outside, and Con tried to decide which one needed the other. When she climbed the three flights back to Gert's apartment, the television was off and the kettle was starting to boil. Con was slightly put out that Peggy had made herself quite so comfortable, but also pleased. She made a pot of her mother's coffee. Peggy made tea for herself from Gert's supply of Lipton. She talked about her work—she worked in admissions at NYU. "April is not the best time to take a day off," she said, "but I was exhausted. At least at NYU I meet guys."

She put a second tea bag into the mug. "Before that—briefly—I was a dog groomer," she said. "I never met men, only dogs. The wives brought them in." She searched in Gert's cupboards for sugar. "Before that I went to graduate school in romance languages. Not for very long."

Con remembered that she had used up the milk. She disliked black coffee.

"What's wrong?" Peggy said.

"No milk." She decided to put ice milk in her coffee. Opening the freezer with her back to Peggy, she said, "I am so angry with my husband I am going to leave him."

"They'll do that to you," said Peggy.

The doorbell rang and they brought their cups into the living room. The locks were changed. A trifling event, except that now—halfway through Wednesday—Con finally had keys to Gert's apartment, though Gert didn't, as if Con were its true occupant. After watching the man for a while—perhaps making sure he'd do—Peggy gulped her tea and departed. When Con said, "Please bill me," the locksmith took down her name and address in Philadelphia. If her mother wanted to reimburse her, fine. Probably she wouldn't think of it, and Con wouldn't mention it either. When she realized that she would rather pay for the new locks than explain once more what had happened—and that this line of thinking was habitual—she understood that her mother had been finding it hard to think for a while.

But no sooner did she understand this than instead of wanting to go outside, now that she could, she wanted to call her mother. She was hungry. She had $4.78. She had been too shy to ask Peggy—such a new friend—to lend her some money. Despite hunger, she went to the phone. "Mama, I got the locks changed," she would say. "I met your downstairs neighbor. I'm leaving Jerry."

"*Why* leave Jerry?" her mother would say. Her mother cherished Jerry. Maybe Con would omit that part. She called Marlene's number, but nobody was home. They had probably gone to the doctor. She didn't leave a message. She'd go shopping. She went out and walked in the spring sunshine; she found a grocery store and made her way up and down cramped aisles. $4.78 wasn't much money. Finally she decided she wanted spaghetti with meat sauce. Con bought a package of chopped meat and a can of tomato sauce. She bought some apples and a quart of milk. Gert had spaghetti. On the way home, she stopped for coffee and a muffin, and felt rich, though she'd now used up all her money. On her table in the luncheonette was a copy of that morning's *New York Times,* opened to a story about Babylon. She couldn't have said what country Babylon was in, or even whether it existed in modern times. It did; it was in Iraq, and the Iraqi dictator, whose name was Saddam Hussein, was having the palace of King Nebuchadnezzar restored. Sudanese laborers were doing the work, since the Iraqi men were all fighting in the war with Iran. The paper said, "Iraqis enjoy Nebuchadnezzar's emerging palace, flooding to Babylon on their Friday holiday by rickety bus and car. 'It's prettier than where we live,' said Sadia, a teen-age technical-college student who was visiting with classmates." Con flipped the paper back to the first page so as to see the headlines. The Speaker of the House was defending himself against charges that he'd failed to declare much of his income. Thousands of people in China had marched to Communist Party headquarters, chanting about democracy. As soon as Con got back to the apartment, opening the door with the sharp-edged new key (there was no message from Jerry), she tried Marlene's number again, and this time her mother answered the phone.

Con felt a rush of pleasure. "Mom, it's Connie!"

"I know that," said Gert. "Did you try to call before? We were at the doctor."

"I did." Long before answering machines were invented, Con's mother had always known if Con tried to call. "Then I remembered you had an appointment. How was it?"

"All right," said Gert. "An old man. He thinks I should take those pills my real doctor gave me."

"Yes, you saw Dr. Herbert—you know, the famous Dr. Herbert." Marlene had talked about Dr. Herbert for years. He was her friend if not her lover, and neither Con nor Gert had ever been sure whether Herbert was his first name or his last. But her mother seemed to have forgotten all that.

"If I take them, I go to the bathroom every minute," Gert said.

"For blood pressure. Don't you take those?"

"No, I'm up six times a night. It's crazy to take them."

"But maybe you should. Listen, Mama—how's it going, this visit?"

"The visit to the doctor?"

"No," Con said. "I mean visiting Marlene—are you comfortable there?"

"The bed gives me a backache," Gert said. Then, "Did you get the locks changed?"

"Yes, yes I did!" said Con, inordinately pleased. "I could have done it right away. I called someone and when he was done, I asked him to bill me. It wasn't a problem. And you know who made me do it? A neighbor of yours." Con slowly told the story of Peggy's arrival and opinion, gesturing vigorously in the empty room. "And she was so smart—she just said I should tell them to bill me later."

"She paid?" said Gert.

"No, I told them to send me a bill."

"That was nice of her to pay."

"No, I told them to send me a bill. But anyway, do you know who I mean? She has curly hair. She lives downstairs."

"The woman with the shoes?"

Con was stumped. "High heels?"

But now came the usual skirmish, and then Marlene had the phone. "So you finally got the locks changed?" She sounded amused.

"It was simple. What did the doctor say?"

"Let me change to the portable phone." There was a pause. "Sweetie, I hate to say this. We talked while she had a chest X-ray. He wasn't hopeful. He was surprised she lives alone. He couldn't say what's coming but he looked awful. I can't keep her—we wouldn't get along. I try, but I see how it would be."

"Nobody thinks you should take her!" said Con. She too had decided her mother could no longer live alone, but now she resisted. "We could put a good lock on that back door— something that locked automatically. Or if we pay the super, maybe he'd come up for the garbage."

"When we were young," said Marlene, "we said that when we were old we'd live together. But I don't want to."

"Of course not."

"I don't think you should take her either," said Marlene. "Sooner or later Jerry will get impatient."

"I forgot something I have to tell my mother," said Con.

"She's taking a nap. The doctor wore her out. Listen, there's something else. He emphasized that someone has to take responsibility. You know—her money. I think I should have her power of attorney, Connie. You shouldn't be burdened with that."

"Her power of attorney?" Con said, startled.

"Yes, you know, paying the bills, signing the checks—"

"Yes, I know. I'll do it."

"I did it for my aunt," said Marlene. "It's work. Let me deal with this. I may even be able to deal with it while she's here."

"I'm not sure this is necessary," said Con. She didn't want to deal with her mother's money, but of course if someone had to do it, it should be Con, not Marlene.

"Think about it," said Marlene. "I'll call you back."

Monday, November 3, 2003, was as warm as it had been on Sunday. Con checked the *Times* Web site before work. Sixteen Americans had been killed when missiles in Iraq brought down a helicopter. A gay man had been chosen as Episcopal bishop of New Hampshire. She left home a little early, then emerged from the subway a stop before she had to, to get some air.

At the office, a letter had arrived from the London law firm that was slowly handling Barbara's estate. Con was still shocked that Barbara had died, though her death had not been truly sudden: she had not been run over by a bus, Con sometimes found herself saying to friends. But it was as if she'd been run over by a bus, by one of those big red London buses they'd loved. Barbara had died of a brain tumor over the course of five months. She'd left her meager estate to Joanna, a fact that made Con weep. She'd flown to London several times while Barbara was sick, but avoided going now. Each time it made her think she should have gone more often when her sister was well. Now the impersonal letters about money caused hours of regret and grief. Con put aside the one that had just come, and returned to the interviews she'd been examining.

Clients who lived nearby came to the office, where they were interviewed by a young paralegal named Aaron, who Con privately feared was incompetent. He was sweet and maybe too conscientious, and prepared long lists of questions that he asked in order, no matter what the answers. Sometimes, reading his transcripts, Con wanted to know only the answer to the question he hadn't asked. What made the woman think she *should* have been promoted? How many people in her position *had* been promoted? Aaron would have needed to sound less sympathetic to find the best clients.

Con's office was on the sixth floor of a prewar building near Union Square, with dusty streaked windows. Sometimes she pressed her forehead to the glass, looking at the tops of heads of people below, watching them move in the aggregate, as if they were loosely tied together with invisible cords. Considered as a group, the clients—like the people on the street—seemed to have experiences and problems in common, but when she considered each one in turn, that woman was hardly ever a good example. She didn't seem like someone Con would have promoted either. Or she seemed to be lying. Con had been thrilled to get this job—looked at from above, it too made sense—but minute by minute it frustrated her.

Often Con ate lunch at her desk but on this warm November Monday she wanted to be outdoors. She walked with her jacket open. As she passed the Strand Bookstore on her way downtown, her cell phone rang. It was Joanna at last—their first conversation since the phone calls in the park a day earlier. "Well, I may be moving," her daughter began, "but I'm not going back to New York."

"What was that e-mail you sent Dad?" said Con.

"He told you about it? He didn't answer."

"He forwarded it. I should have answered. Did you have a fight with Tim?"

"When I said Barney wanted me back, Tim accused me of wanting to leave early so I could sleep with my new lover, the famous sculptor."

"Isn't that something I accused you of?" said Con. She crossed the street.

"I hope not," said Joanna.

"I'm at the restaurant," said Con. "I should hang up."

"But still," Joanna continued, "I think maybe I should stay here, or go somewhere else, internship or no internship."

Con was sure that was a mistake. Even if Marlene was coming, even if Barney was whatever he was, the internship mattered. "Think about it," she said. "Ask Barney to give you another week. You've been so excited about working with him. Maybe you just have to make clear— Well, I hate to see you give it up."

"What difference will a week make?" said Joanna.

"You'll have time to think," Con said. She was standing outside the noodle shop and people kept jostling her. "And it might be better if you didn't come here this week. Marlene's coming for the weekend. And Dad. It will be crowded. Next week we can talk more, and maybe we can figure out together what you need to say to—"

"Marlene's coming?" Joanna interrupted.

"Yes."

Joanna was silent. Con said, "I know you don't like Marlene."

"I don't know if I like her or not," Joanna said. "One of these days, there are some questions I want to ask Marlene."

"What questions?"

"I'll tell you sometime. But if I did come, could you pay the difference in the plane fare?" said Joanna. "It's going to cost a hundred dollars to change the flight. If I decide to come."

Con was now chilly, warm day or not. "Sure, I guess so," she said, baffled, and got off the phone.

Marlene's wartime letters were at the cleared end of the table. Late Wednesday afternoon, Con picked them up again. She liked reading about Marlene's love life. Sex life. Con wondered whether her mother would have been shocked. Maybe not.

Dear Gert,

Your letter came two days ago and I've been waiting for a spare minute to answer it. Are you sure about your period and so on and so forth? Well, there's only one explanation I suppose. I don't know what you're going to do in one room, sharing a bathroom, with two kids.

Bernard came home with me the other night. I told him I had a picture I wanted to hang and I didn't know how. I had mentioned it the day before, so he brought a hammer and came home with me and did it. Then we sat and talked and had a beer and a cigarette and the next thing it was late. We laughed, but when I saw him again he looked embarrassed.

He likes me because I'm an artist. He said he never
knew a Jewish woman who was an artist before, he
thought all of us just cooked. I said he better not try
my cooking. But I don't have time to paint what with
working all day and walking the streets at night. Call me
Marlene the streetwalker. It's getting cold these nights.
I'm not scared. They tell us what to do if there's an
attack but I figure it's not my time. Too much is happening. I've got Bernard, I've got Frank. Frank doesn't like
Bernard but that's not my business.

What do you know, they figured out a way for us to pretend we're in Europe, as if we needed such a thing. They're
having a mock air raid in Brooklyn: fireworks, very realistic,
people running around and taking care of the make-believe
wounded, coffee and doughnuts. I want to be wounded but
I'll probably end up making coffee, my luck.

He's not Jewish, not that I want to marry him, he's
already married.

Is it hot there?

Your friend,
Marlene

Dear Gert,

It's two a.m. and I have to get up for work tomorrow but
I can't sleep. Maybe I'll feel better if I write you a note. I
think I spoiled things with Bernard. We had a real fight.
My big mouth, I said something about Brenda and I should
have known better, he thinks she's perfect, but she's a pest

and we do what she wants because it's the only way to see each other except if he sneaks home with me at night. He takes her to the zoo or something and his "friend from work" (me) comes along and then we have to make up stuff about our supposed office. She's just old enough to figure it all out and tell the wife—if the kid was smart. But I don't think she's smart enough, and I said so.

Now don't go and tell me how you'd feel if Abe did something like this, you don't know a thing about Bernard's wife, she's probably nothing like you.

Anyway probably it's all over now. I should have apologized right away but instead I said something back and it's too late now. I don't know what I could have said, the kid really isn't too bright. She brings her reader sometimes and he tries to get her to read simple sentences, but she won't or can't.

What do you mean the baby won't listen to you? She is a child and you are her mother. You are a fool if you can't make her listen. I don't think I would like to have children but if I did they would listen or else. But what do I know? Now they want girls to volunteer to look after children in the slums but I would rather be an air raid warden.

Don't worry, the new baby will be all right, that doctor doesn't know what he's talking about. Too many soldiers' wives and he's not getting any sleep so he can't remember what they taught him in medical school.

I better try and sleep.

Your sister,
Marlene

Dear Gert,

I keep explaining but you don't seem to get it. They're
not going to use real bombs but there are going to be
real fires. Well, smoke. I think I'll get to be one of the
wounded. I might get to ride in an ambulance. I don't
know if they'll use the sirens. I had another fight with
Bernard. He wanted me to take care of Brenda but
she wet her pants again the last time we had her and I
wouldn't know what to do if that happened. You know
I'm not good at that kind of thing. Bernard has an idea
he started to tell me about and I'm afraid now he won't
tell. I don't know what it has to do with exactly but I can
guess, don't want to say in a letter, you never know.

Your friend,

Marlene

Con stopped reading the letters and went looking for something to eat. She didn't feel like meat sauce after all. She found
a couple of potatoes. They were starting to sprout so it made
sense to cook them. When she took a carton of eggs from the
refrigerator she saw that Gert had written on it, "Connie, use
up—I don't remember when I bought." Her mother, it seemed,
had touched her shoulder. Con made herself an omelet with
potatoes and an onion. The onions were sprouting too.

As she ate she remembered another time when she'd been
alone in this apartment, during her last year in college. Gert
had to spend a night in the hospital after minor surgery, and
Con—who had just had her heart broken by a man she'd slept

with once—had come home from school for a couple of days to help. Alone in the apartment at night, she'd thought not about her mother but her lover, and as she brought her mother home in a taxi the next day, Con had told Gert the story, leaving out sex. Ordinarily she didn't tell stories like that to her mother, but Gert hadn't tried to make Con feel worse. She'd said, "Somebody once did that to me. After a long time it's almost a nice pain—like sad love songs."

Now Con was alone again in the same place. She'd gotten over that man—he was not even a comfortable pain. She hadn't made much progress, she considered, in acquiring the sad stories women loved telling and reading. At ten p.m. the phone rang and it had to be Jerry. She could tell from the ring, that "Who, me?" ring.

"I tried to call you," Jerry began. "The first day she was here. But your line was constantly busy. And I tried a couple of times today."

He had never wanted Con on his trips, not even when they were young and in love, before Joanna was born. Once, she'd wept. "I'll bring books," she'd said. "I'll eat alone and make up my own things to do." She was ashamed to have been so craven. Her old hurts were either gone altogether or still painful; she had no comfortable ones. At the time, Jerry had said, "I have to do it this way." They had been in bed, and he'd turned over and curled his long body into its oval nighttime shape.

Now—finally on the phone with him—she was more curious than enraged, as if he were a stranger. The sound of his voice, which was light and quick, and had always pleased her, made her sad. She said, "Jerry, what made you do this?"

"You mean, letting Joanna come?" he said lightly. "She's been wanting to for years. And she found out something I wanted to know."

"What, she got a tourist brochure from Fort Ticonderoga?" Rage came into her voice after all.

"I don't care about the fort," said Jerry. "It's not even open until summer. I'm interested in where Allen was coming from and how he got across the lake. And she found something at the library. I didn't even remember telling her what I was thinking about."

Con was sitting at the table in the living room, stretching the cord to talk on the kitchen phone. Over and over, she ran her free index finger down the edge of the orange stripe on the tablecloth. "But you took her out of school. And you didn't tell me. How could you not tell me?"

"You'd have said no."

"You were never going to tell me? Didn't you think I'd phone her?"

"Sure, but she's always hard to reach. I didn't think you'd think anything. She was going to call you and not say where she was."

"Jerry, you told her to *lie*?" Her hand flattened on the table.

"Well, it was a game," he said. "Like a play. Surely you can see that this was good for her. Joanna's a kid with so much anger, so much inborn rebellion, that she could just turn against everything good." He paused. "Con, I know you're not going to listen. You're not going to agree—and that's why I didn't tell you in the first place. But I'm trying to save this girl for something worthwhile. School does nothing for her. She could turn against it and go on drugs or get pregnant. She could be twenty-one with four babies."

She said, "But Jerry, Jerry, wait a second. I'm asking you something simpler. *What did you think would happen?* What did you think I'd think? Do you know the police in Philadelphia were looking for her?"

"The police! Why the hell did you call the police? Half the time you don't know where she is. You were hysterical."

"Howard called the police," she said. "I phoned Howard when Joanna wasn't there and wasn't in school. I was afraid—did she tell you my bag was stolen?"

Joanna had not quite understood or had not thought to say. Jerry didn't know about the burglary, Con's stolen purse. It was hard to understand that Jerry had no idea about something so important. This is what it would be like when they were separated. It seemed a waste of time to tell him. They could start the separation more efficiently if he never knew. But the credit card.

"Haven't you tried to use the credit card?"

"I brought a bunch of cash," he said. "What about it?"

She told the story succinctly. He said, "But this burglar wasn't going to go to Philadelphia and kill Joanna. Surely you didn't think *that*."

"Nobody I talked to would dismiss the idea."

"This was a little overdone," said Jerry.

"But what you did would have been terrible even if nothing had happened."

"No. It was great. It *is* great. She's excited."

"She spent the whole day in the motel."

"You don't appreciate Joanna," he said. "You have no idea what a great kid she can be."

Con didn't answer. Now she was pacing from the kitchen to the living room and back, stretching the cord. Peggy had asked, "Were you marching?" Now she was marching. She had to march a long way to get where she had to be.

The cat butted his head against Con's leg. It was the first time she'd seen him in a long time; she'd forgotten him again. He jumped onto the table, then yowled at her. Con was silent, noticing the cat and watching herself get ready to speak. When she heard her own voice again, it sounded tentative, youthful, but that wasn't because she was uncertain about what she wanted to say; she was only uncertain about how to say it. "Jerry, there's something we need to talk about," she said, and in answer—it was the one moment in the conversation when he reminded her of the young husband who amused and delighted her—he said, tentatively too, sounding finally a little scared, "What?"

"This is not just because I'm upset at what you did," she said. He was silent. Sandy paced on the table and socked her forearm with his orange head. With the phone tucked against her shoulder, Con washed his dish, took the can of cat food from the refrigerator, and forked some food into the dish, then added dry pellets from the box on the counter. She thought to herself in words, as if she said it to an interviewer, *While my marriage was breaking up, I fed a cat.*

As she put the bowl on the counter, she heard herself make a sound—not a sob, not a sigh, something more primitive—a soft, low-pitched wail such as someone might emit before a battle in which people who were dear and well would scream and die. It was a sound for the last moment before the battle, when everyone was still all right and no skin was broken.

"I can't live with you," she said.

"I've been thinking—" said Jerry.

"What?"

"I know you've been thinking this way."

Yet she hadn't known she'd been thinking this way. It wasn't until she found Joanna that she had known what she'd been wanting to do. Somehow he had known before she did. He continued, "I know you want this. I don't. I want us to stay the way we are. I thought maybe we should figure out what you could do that would be like these trips. These trips are why I can live with you—not just you, with anybody. I couldn't live with anybody if I couldn't do this."

Con hadn't thought about whether she could live with anybody. She couldn't live with Jerry, with his smooth surface that couldn't be blemished or even grasped, with his solipsistic happiness.

"You never let me come on the trips. You let Joanna."

"She's a child."

"So what?" she said.

"There are things you can share with a child and still keep to yourself."

Again, he sounded firm and confident. This was all he had to offer: the suggestion that Con take trips—or something—of her own. From here on, it would be up to her to end this marriage. Jerry would simply watch.

"Of course I've thought of it, too," he said now, surprising her.

"Of what?"

"Of breaking up. Of living apart. There are plenty of reasons. But I don't want to. Well, I guess if I had wanted to I'd have said so. But if this is something that will help your life—well, you'll have to do it, Con. I mean, if it's like my trips are for me. If it's the only way you can breathe."

Could he give it up so easily?

Maybe it was the way she could breathe.

"I think I'll talk to someone I know who does separations and divorces," she said.

"A lawyer friend."

"A lawyer friend."

"We won't fight," he said.

"We'll talk."

"Maybe it doesn't have to happen," he said. "Con, I'm sorry your bag got stolen. I'm sorry I picked the wrong time to have an adventure with Joanna."

He'd never apologized before. She was slightly awestruck. They hung up and she went to bed and lay rigidly under her mother's blanket, looking down at her still, separated body, nearly an unmarried woman. She was in the middle of leaving her husband, and in the middle (past the middle) of a week looking after her mother's cat. She hadn't told Jerry her mother might be losing her mind, or that Marlene wanted power of attorney.

Lying in bed, she realized her period had started, a week early. This happened lately, and she had a box of Tampax in her suitcase, but it was almost empty. Peggy would lend her tampons, she thought, slightly consoled. Or money.

In the morning she got up and went about her business, not

exactly grieving, almost convalescent: each act—showering, dressing—was noticeable, even startling. She watched the news on television. There was always something about the *Exxon Valdez*. They kept trying to figure out what had caused the ship to run aground. In China, ten thousand people had now taken over the central square in Beijing, demanding increased democracy. And an enormous asteroid had passed within half a million miles of the Earth. Barbara called.

"Are you at work?" Con tried to figure out what time it would be in London.

"I don't have that job anymore. But it's all right. Have you heard from Joanna?"

Con was appalled at herself. She hadn't let her sister know Joanna was all right. She told the story. "I'm leaving Jerry."

"Just over this?"

"No, of course not." It was hard to explain. "It's because this was so clearly Jerry. It's his defining act, taking Joanna and not telling me."

"What's *my* defining act?" said Barbara. "Does everyone have a defining act?"

"I don't know but Jerry does."

"Quitting that job," said Barbara, "was my defining act. Anybody wants to know anything about me, they could see a two-minute clip of me walking out of that office."

"Well, I guess so." Con couldn't recall when they'd begun discussing Barbara's personality instead of Con's marriage.

"I really called to ask you about Mom," said Barbara. "I talked to her yesterday. What's this stuff about a doctor? Was this your idea?"

"Of course not."

"It seemed like your kind of thing."

"My defining act?"

"Maybe. Worrying."

"Mom sounded strange on the phone the other day," said Con. "She didn't remember what I'd told her. She'd forgotten about the burglary. Marlene's worried. She wants power of attorney."

"Marlene's overreacting," said Barbara. "Be careful of Marlene."

"Oh, I'm used to her," Con said. "She's bossy, but you have to admit she's helpful. I don't let her bother me."

"You didn't tell her she could have Mom's power of attorney, did you?" Barbara said. She spoke differently—maybe more slowly—as if Con were a child or someone who might not understand.

"No, of course not," said Con. "I'm a lawyer. But she'd probably handle it all right if she did it."

"Maybe," said Barbara, "but don't."

"What?"

In London, Barbara sighed. "You idealize Marlene," she said, "but Connie, you *have* to see . . . well, Marlene's risky."

Con found a reason to hang up. Too much was going on; she had no time for Barbara's theories.

On Monday evening Con left the office with a sheaf of papers stuffed into her tote bag to read at home, because she'd had no time for them during the day. A meeting that should have lasted an hour had been twice that long, slowed by quarrels between one lawyer so abstract she dismissed practical difficulties and another so practical that the first lawyer drove her wild. Con had said little. She'd intended to stop on the way home for groceries—would she actually have all three visitors at once?—but she left the office late, having accomplished little, and went straight home. The warm November weather was starting to annoy her. At home she e-mailed Peggy, suggesting dinner on Wednesday. The bathroom door was still leaning on the wall. Con looked at it with some nervousness, then went for her tools. Finishing the project was easier than she had expected.

In the evening she read fitfully, feeling herself slide into gloom, trying to remember any single case she'd worked on in her entire career about which she was sure she was right. She was good at what she did—reading and thinking, then persuading others to see things as she did—but at times what she could do felt like no skill at all; anyone could do it. Fixing the bathroom door had pleased, then depressed her. Why couldn't her real work have such clear results? The cases she worked on lingered and lingered. Nothing was obvious. Newspaper stories made justice and injustice more distinct than they were in Con's mind, though she'd been a lawyer for so long. From the first paragraph of a newspaper story she could tell which side she was on. Working on a case, Con was never as sure as she had to sound.

She kept the cell phone on in case Joanna called but it was silent. Finally, to cheer herself, she made a list of tasks for the rest of the week. That night she slept poorly, unable to make the parts of her mind—the parts of her life—make sense to one another. Instead of thinking about work, she thought of Joanna, of Barbara, even of Jerry. She thought about the war in Iraq, slept, then awoke recalling mistakes she'd made in jobs over the decades. She'd worked most of her life on the problems of those without money and power, and those people seemed to have less money and power now than when Con and others like her had begun. And she'd failed them more than once.

But it was morning, and she stepped through her apartment, which got sun only in the afternoon, when she wasn't usually home. Con associated sun with weekends. She assembled what she needed, watering a few dark plants with thick leaves, plants that didn't need much sun. Joanna's hairy sculptures looked ungainly but compelling in the morning dimness. Con liked this apartment, though it was elongated and dark. Marching back and forth, gathering notes, checking e-mail, preparing breakfast, she seemed to make the rudiments of a trail.

She checked the *Times* site: Iraqis in Fallujah hated Americans even more than in the other cities. She postponed reading the story. Once she'd trekked through the apartment and was ready to emerge into the light—her body clothed, down to those annoying but pleasantly smooth tubes of nylon on her legs, her stomach soothed by granola and banana and yogurt, her bowels emptied—she could perhaps do a measure of work worth doing. And so, although she was inadequate and the world was full of sorrow, she got herself to the door of the building, along the speckled gray sidewalk, and down the gray steps into the subway. From there on, other people made some contribution. Nobody expected Con to drive the train.

At work that day Con walked in on one of Aaron's interviews. She'd seen the client go into his cubicle, and could hear their low voices. She herself was reading cases, searching for lines of reasoning that one court or another had adopted. She stood and stretched at the window, and then walked down the hall toward the voices. The client was a young, muscular woman who looked older close up, her face strained. Aaron—a possibly gay black man of indeterminate age and impenetrable reserve—looked baffled, his forehead creased. He often whispered.

Con introduced herself and asked if she could listen in, saying she wanted to get a better sense of the clients. Aaron looked annoyed but said he didn't mind. "So this was the second time you worked in that office, or the first?" he said, staring at his questions.

"I don't remember—he never liked it when I worked."

"And that was why you quit, the first time?"

"There were so many reasons to quit," said the woman.

"So when was that?" said Aaron.

"Wait a second," said Con. "Did you quit because your husband hit you?"

"It's hard to say," said the woman, turning to look at her.

It was intolerable to have to question people about subjects so intimate. Let Aaron do it. Probably he did it better. But she couldn't stop herself from saying, "If you didn't quit, he'd have hit you?"

"Well, he hit me anyway," said the woman, with a little laugh. "But yeah."

Later that day came an e-mail from Joanna. "I just told Tim we're finished. I'm going to a motel. Love, Jo."

Con didn't know whether this was good news or bad, or whether it meant Jo would come home or not. "Are you all right?" she replied. "Now what?" She went back to the *New York Times* site and read the story about Fallujah. Sunni Muslims who lived there still favored Saddam Hussein and resented the American presence. When American soldiers threw candy at children, the children didn't pick it up because they thought it was poisoned. When American soldiers hung their feet out of the back of helicopters, Iraqis were insulted, because in their country it is disrespectful to show the bottoms of one's shoes. Reading the story, Con put her feet down. They'd been curled around each other, so anyone passing might have seen the bottoms of her shoes.

She worked until evening. On the way home, she bought a free-range chicken. She didn't hear from Joanna again, but there was an e-mail from Marlene: "There's an El Greco show at the Metropolitan Museum. And did you buy the opera tickets?" Jerry wrote that he was coming Thursday evening. That meant he'd be in New York for a day before Marlene arrived. But who was Marcus Ogilvy?

Con still didn't have any money and her marriage was over, but she forced herself to spend some of Thursday working. She had to learn what was on the missing papers. She talked to Mabel, who still didn't have them, but admitted it was true that two of the women had been soliciting in the neighborhood. "I told them not to," she said. "Nobody looking for a whore is going there."

"Were they trying to get you closed down?" If Con had her lost notebook, she felt obscurely, she'd know what to do. There was a short paragraph in blue ink, written on the train, and a longer one, in black, that she'd written in her mother's apartment. When she'd visited the house, one resident had said, "If I weren't here I'd be in jail. Or dead." The women did not bake cookies and sew quilts—nothing that wholesome was going on—but they had ordinary conversations about shopping and laundry. Con had been happy there, despite the irritating TV in the background and the smell of cigarettes.

"Some people have a hard time with rules," Mabel said now. "Did your daughter ever call?"

"I found her. Thank you," said Con.

"She was missing?"

"She was with her father. She was fine."

Twice Thursday morning her mother called. Now Gert kept fretting about the burglary. She couldn't be persuaded that Peggy hadn't paid for the new locks. Marlene had gone to work. "She told me a million things not to do," said Gert. "Why would I leave the stove on? She made coffee and put it in a jar but I can't open it."

"You'll be home soon," said Con.

"Saturday. Will you be gone?"

"No, of course not. I'll make dinner. I'll sleep on the sofa and go home Sunday."

"I miss you," said Gert.

"I miss you, too," said Con, and found that it was so. She pictured her mother slightly dazed in Marlene's house. Then she said, "I think Jerry and I may separate for a while."

"You're separated now," said her mother. "You're in my house."

"That's right." It was all Con could say on the subject.

"My husband and I were separated during the war," said Gert, as if she'd forgotten to whom she was talking.

"Yes, Daddy was in the army."

Something terrible was happening to Gert. Marlene was right.

"I was thinking about Papa," Gert continued, "because I was looking out the window here and all the time I see birds. My friend lives in an apartment, but there's grass outside."

"I know. A condo."

"A condo. I keep seeing the kind of birds my father had. During the Depression, my father kept birds."

"Pigeons?" said Con. She thought she'd heard that her grandfather had kept homing pigeons. Con's father and Gert's father had become the same person.

"Pigeons. It was on the tip of my tongue. Four pigeons. He would take them to Coney Island and let them go and they would fly home. He loved to watch them come down to their house. One day during the Depression my mother said to him, 'We have nothing to eat. Tomorrow we eat the birds.' The next day my father sold them."

"That's sad," said Con, but she was hungry and impatient to get back to work. Marlene was right, but what could she do now? She got off the phone, ate toast standing up, and made some more phone calls. She wasn't sure, after all, if an appeal would make sense, if the zoning commission decided against Mabel Turner's house. Finally she called Sarah, who said, "Of course. We'll argue that these woman have a disability. Aren't they addicts?"

"I think that would be hard with ex-prisoners," said Con. "The judge is used to thinking of prisoners as bad, not sick."

"Then we'll have to change the judge's thinking."

Con phoned Mabel to find out if the women were in treatment. "Do you have AA meetings at the house?" said Con.

"Some of the girls go to the meeting at the church."

"There's a church? Would the minister vouch for the house?" How could she make a judge understand that these women were fixing their lives?

"We threw out the ones who were turning tricks on the block," said Mabel.

"You did?"

"Sure. This is a decent place."

"So they're gone?"

"They're leaving soon."

Con lost her temper. "I can't defend you if you don't throw them out. What am I supposed to do for you?"

"Oh, you'll figure out something," said Mabel.

Late morning on Thursday, Con finally got money. Like changing the locks, it became easy. She called Howard and asked him to wire some. He too knew about Western Union and she found an office not far away. It was a breezy day, and she gulped air as she walked there, as if she were in the country. Brooklyn had trees, and their leaves, sticky looking and light green, had just unfolded. At Western Union she was handed money. She folded the bills into her front jeans pocket, and felt rich, with a comfortable awareness of money when she swung her leg. She stopped at the grocery store, treating herself to cheddar cheese and Häagen-Dazs chocolate ice cream, and bought a chicken to roast for her mother. As she walked back to the apartment, Con found herself trying to feel sure that if she left Jerry, she didn't have to move in with Gert. When her mother returned, maybe Peggy would take an interest in her. Some people made pets of frail old ladies. Con told herself a quick story in which Gert continued living in her apartment, quite fine because Peggy dropped in once a day and looked around, trying the back door. Once a month, Con would visit them both. And then a new thought occurred to her. When she was apart from Jerry, men might want to have coffee with her—even go to bed with her. As she turned her key in the lock, she remembered that she should have bought tampons.

She was hungry again. Mabel had left two phone messages. She made herself a cheese sandwich and called her back, trying to chew quietly as they spoke.

"I got it back," Mabel said, and read the paper aloud. It was the decision of the zoning commission after all. They'd lost. "It says it's an illegal rooming house," said Mabel. "It's not a rooming house at all. I don't run some rooming house!"

"That's just the term they use," Con said. She hung up and called Sarah, who wanted details Con didn't know. "Can't you get back?" Sarah said. "We need to see those papers. How much time do we have to appeal?"

Con didn't know. She hadn't wanted to tell Sarah about the stolen bag and her mother's confusion, but summed up her week as briefly as she could.

"That's disgusting," said Sarah. "Anyway, we'll make some

kind of claim. These cases are working out, but it'll be harder than if they'd come to us before the hearing."

"I wish our clients were a little more picturesque," Con said.

"We'll deal with what we've got."

"The whole thing started with some of the women soliciting on the block," said Con. "Mabel said she'd throw them out, but they were still there the last time I talked to her."

"The whole thing started when the neighbors saw a black face," said Sarah. "Depend on it."

"It's so quiet there," Con said. "Everything they do will stand out. Wouldn't they be better off somewhere else? Or wouldn't we be better off using a different house to bring this kind of suit?"

"This is the client we have, Constance," said Sarah. "If those women get thrown out of that house, they'll all bust parole. They'll be back in prison in a week or two or three. Look, I don't want to argue the merits of the case. File an appeal. If we lose that, maybe we can go to federal court."

Later, Con was sorry she'd sounded so negative. She was tired and didn't feel like talking, but the phone rang, and it was her mother calling. "Did you get money? Did you eat?" said Gert.

"I'm fine. I've got a bit of a crisis at work."

"You have to go to your office?"

"No, it'll wait."

"You mean you're going home now, to your house?"

"No, I'm working from here."

"Who will feed Sandy?"

"I'll feed Sandy."

"You'll feed him before you leave?"

"I'm *not leaving*," Con said emphatically. She began to talk as to a four-year-old. "When you come on Saturday, I'll meet you at the station, and we'll take a taxi here. I'm going to roast a chicken, and we'll have a good dinner. Then, on Sunday, I'll go home."

"That's right," said her mother, and put Marlene on. "She doesn't understand," said Marlene. "She thinks you're leaving."

"Is this happening a lot?"

"I told you," said Marlene. "It's breaking my heart. We'll talk about power of attorney later. You're busy now."

"Sometimes she makes perfect sense," said Con.

"Listen, let's be realistic."

Con said, "Maybe there's medication."

"The doctor didn't seem to think it would help," said Marlene.

The doorbell was ringing. Marlene tried to keep Con on the phone but she thought it might be Peggy, and Con wanted to see this new, interesting person. "I'm just making sure you're home," Peggy said when Con opened the door. "I'm bringing lasagna up."

Con winced at "home." She declined politely. "I went shopping." Really, she should use up the chopped meat.

"No, this is my mother's lasagna. I was there last night and she made me take a big pan home."

"I'm sure it's wonderful."

"What it is, is authentic. This is real Italian lasagna made by the downstairs lady's mother. You don't say no." Peggy raised her arm to lean on the doorjamb. Her arm was long and slender.

"I'm sorry," said Con. "I bought food. I should use it up."

"Your mother will eat the food you bought."

"I'm sorry." If she were alone, she could read more of Marlene's letters.

"Homemade lasagna will go to waste," said Peggy. "There are criminal penalties for that kind of thing."

"All right," said Con. She could freeze the meat. Her mother would eat it eventually, if she didn't burn the house down, cooking. "When?"

"An hour?"

"An hour." Peggy turned and Con said, "And could you lend me a few Tampax?"

"Sure," said Peggy. She went down the stairs. It would be all right. They could talk about families. Con was wistful to think of having a mother who fed her daughter lasagna—who still looked after her daughter.

Though she'd have to be at the office a little early the next morning for a staff meeting, Con stayed up late Tuesday night. When the phone rang at 3 a.m. she struggled out of the blankets and hitched herself across the bed to answer. Then she realized it was her cell phone, next to the bed on the other side. Joanna's voice was tense. "Mom, this is my phone call. I'm in jail. I was arrested."

"You were *what*?" said Con, though she had heard her daughter and was already struggling to stand, feeling for pen and paper.

"I was stupid," said Joanna, "but also I was absolutely right.

I went to a bar because I was so upset about Tim. The TV had something about Iraq, and I said something. This guy started arguing—" There was a pause. "Okay, okay. They're telling me to hurry it up. Nobody in this state believes in freedom of speech. I got into an argument about Iraq and I was arrested."

"Have you called Tim?"

"No, I'm not dealing with him. I called you."

"What do I have to do?" said Con.

"Bail, I guess. It's all right. They're putting me in a cell with women."

"I'll get you out, but I just wish you hadn't—"

Now Joanna was really crying. "Mom, get me out. Just get me out." Someone from the jail came on the line and explained to Con what to do. Nothing could be done until morning. She hung up, stunned. She sat up in bed for ten minutes, poised to run, as if she could rush to North Carolina in her pajamas. But then, even though Joanna was in jail, Con slept. The alarm was already set to go off early. She woke before it, dressed quickly, had a bowl of granola, and left the house. On the way to the subway she began making calls on her cell phone, trying to reach a bail bondsman. When she called the police station to say bail would be coming, Joanna had been released. Con tried Joanna's cell phone. "Hello?" came her voice.

"Where are you?"

"I'm eating at a diner."

"What happened?"

"I have to go to court. There's going to be a fine. Will you pay it?"

"Of course, but what the hell happened?" If Joanna had to

go to court, there could be a delay. Maybe Con should fly down there.

"I was mad at Tim so I checked into a motel, and there was a bar. I had a few beers."

"Were you drunk?"

"No."

"Did the owner ask you to leave? They said the charge was refusing to obey a police officer."

"Why should I do what that cop told me to do? Trust me for once, okay? I wasn't drunk. I was just a little high. You know how you get high from crying a lot. You're sort of broken up in pieces from crying, and as soon as you drink anything, the pieces float off in different directions. But in fact I'd had one and a half beers when all this happened."

"What happened?"

"They had a TV on and I said 'Shit' when there was something about more deaths in Iraq, and the man next to me said, 'At least they died for a reason.' And I turned toward him and said in—not a loud voice, but a very clear voice, 'They died so our government can control Iraqi oil.'"

Con was proud. She wondered if she'd have had the courage to say anything.

"So he turned nasty, and I kept arguing—and the next thing I know, the bartender is calling the cops. I kept talking about the First Amendment but I swear they never heard of it. They just called the cops."

"They do have a right to ask you to leave," said Con. "It was private property."

"That's crazy," Joanna said. "What about the First Amendment? Mom, they never heard of the First Amendment. Literally never heard of it. I kept asking them and they didn't answer. Finally I realized the answer was no, they never heard of it."

"Was the jail horrible?" Con said. She would explain later. The cops couldn't legally ask her to stop speaking, but they could ask her to leave.

"It wasn't so bad. The other women were prostitutes, and they were used to it. They keep toothpaste in their handbags. They lent me toothpaste, but I had to use my finger instead of a brush."

"Baby," said Con.

"You have to call the ACLU. You have to do something."

Con took a breath. "It would be hard to prove that what they did was illegal," Con said. "If the bartender asked you to leave, and the cops asked you to leave, and you didn't, the arrest was legal."

"The cops didn't ask me to leave, they just told me to shut up."

"They did?" said Con. "That could make a difference. Were there witnesses?"

"No, nobody was on my side. But we have to do something."

Con sighed. "What will you do now?" she said.

"I can't come home, because I have to go to court, and I can't go back to the apartment, because Tim and I are very very broken up. But as soon as I pay the fine I'm taking the first flight to New York. You should have kept me there and bought me alpaca. You're going to be paying for a lot of stuff."

"Okay," said Con. "But Marlene—"

"That's all right."

She should say something more. She took a breath. "Honey, I'm glad you spoke up but I don't think there's much we can do about it."

"Of course there is," said Joanna. "All I did was give my opinion."

Her cell phone died. Con couldn't help liking the quiet, walking the last half block to the office. At least Joanna was free. When she looked again, the phone was working. She and Peggy were supposed to have dinner that night, but Con decided she shouldn't go. She should stay home and make phone calls and do whatever Joanna needed to straighten out everything. She called Peggy as she approached her building. "I need to change our dinner date. Joanna was arrested."

"Oh, for heaven's sake!" said Peggy.

"It's outrageous," said Con, and told the story.

"You have to do something. Call the local paper."

"I know. But can you have dinner tomorrow, or next week?"

"No, I can't change. She's in jail right now?"

"No, but I think I should make myself available."

"You can still have dinner with me. Keep your cell phone on and if she needs you, she'll call."

"I can't."

Peggy sighed. "How about Friday?"

"I can't," said Con again. "Marlene's coming. And the place is a mess, and Jerry is coming for a week. It's already Wednesday and hordes will descend by Friday. I shouldn't have made a date with you in any case."

"Marlene! I have to see Marlene!" said Peggy. She had met Marlene once or twice. "Is she going to rebuke rude people in the street and explain nutrition to waiters? Whatever it is, count me in."

"All right," said Con. "Saturday, I guess. But I really need to change our dinner date."

"You don't. You really don't."

"I'm not just being an overprotective mother," said Con.

"Yes, you are."

"Well, let's see what happens," said Con. Sometimes Peggy could not believe in a feeling she didn't have. It was the only thing wrong with her.

Con arrived an hour before the staff meeting, and tried to get some work done. The meeting was distracting, but after it was over she found herself agitated again. She was angry that her daughter had gotten herself into complicated trouble. She turned on her computer and went to the *Times* site. Bush was having trouble talking about the casualties of the war, and his strategy was not to talk about them at all. In Iraq, a total of 375 Americans had died through Tuesday. On Tuesday, November 4, 2003, the dead were Daniel A. Bader, 28; Steven D. Conover, 21; Maurice J. Johnson, 21; Brian H. Fenisten, 28; Joel Perez, 25; and Bruce A. Smith, 41. Smith was the only man to die who was older than Joanna.

She wrote to Jerry, explaining what had happened, then turned to her work. She'd received some citations from a lawyer who was working on a similar employment case, and reading them had been part of the task she'd set herself for the week. She had to read slowly and think hard. When something turned out useful, she knew, it wouldn't be for reasons she had expected. If it were obvious, everybody would be talking about it already.

She returned to the day's messages. Now one had come in from Jerry. "Do you think it had to do with race?" he wrote. Sometimes Con had to remind herself that Joanna might be identifiable as a black woman. Her skin was slightly darker than Con's, and her dark hair had what could be considered—what presumably was, except that plenty of Con's Jewish relatives had similar hair—an African American frizz.

"How far are we going with this?" she wrote back to Jerry, but she knew the question didn't quite make sense. So far they had gone no distance at all. They had not talked to a reporter, or consulted a local lawyer, or phoned the ACLU or some other organization—the NAACP? She didn't want to go any distance, even if the bartender and the cops *had* told Joanna to shut up. She wanted Joanna to stop drinking. She wanted Joanna to set her mind on her art, and on turning her art into making some kind of living, and on finding a man she didn't despise. In a moment Con had invented a hypothetical storyline in which Joanna gave up two years of her life to a vain pursuit for justice in North Carolina.

Peggy's lasagna smelled good. She came up the stairs with the hot pan between two potholders, and a handful of tampons in her pocket. She offered to lend Con money. "I don't know why I didn't think of that before."

"I'm newly rich," said Con, "but my mother is out of her mind and I'm divorcing my husband."

"You're not having a good week," said Peggy. She preceded Con to the kitchen cabinets and set the table while Con made a salad with dressing from her mother's refrigerator. Peggy listened to both stories, then began telling stories about men she'd loved. It had all gone badly but Peggy did not seem to hold that against herself or the men. They ate. "I'm freezing," said Peggy. She was wearing a thin blouse.

Con went for one of her mother's afghans. Fourteen years later, she wouldn't remember her mother's knitted and crocheted objects when Joanna mentioned them, but in 1989 she knew they were there. She didn't like them. Crocheted afghans were too lacy to provide warmth. Knitting was more promising but Gert knitted so loosely that clothes were invariably too big and blankets shapeless.

Peggy wrapped one of Gert's afghans—mustard, orange, and green—around her shoulders, and looking at it, Con rather liked it after all. It looked lively, draping over the striped table-cloth, which was more stained than it had been on Monday morning, but still pretty. They drank wine. In the middle of the salad preparations, Peggy had run downstairs again and returned with half a bottle of chianti.

Eating and drinking, Con was surprised to hear herself talk in considerable detail about Jerry and her decision to leave him. Somehow it connected to Peggy's stories, and she told one in response about her present boyfriend. "I'm the kind of woman with a married boyfriend," Peggy said, and Con remembered that she'd said something like that before. "Half the married men who are accused of having little nitwit girlfriends have lovers who look just like me. The rest really do have little nitwit girlfriends, except for a few who have young brilliant girlfriends." Peggy was used to being unhappy. Yet she feared it, and feared it for other people, and it turned out that was the connection between her own situation and Con's. "It will be hard for you," she said. It was a simple observation but somehow they'd talked through many subjects, arriving at it, arriving at what seemed like agreement between older friends than they were: the shared sense that it was hard being unhappy but intolerable not to keep taking chances on happiness.

"I'm not doing this just because he didn't tell me what Joanna was going to do."

"I know. And it's not because you're jealous that he took her on a trip and not you." Con was not certain that was completely true, but let it pass. Peggy continued, "First husbands are unbearable. I never got married because I'd have to start with my first."

Con laughed, and Peggy said, "No, I mean it. First husbands just drive you crazy. Second husbands are better—all my friends with second husbands are always compromising and making rules for their marriages. They say, 'We had a long talk and from now on I'll visit his parents only once a year' or 'We're scheduling sex.' All that negotiating is exhausting." She reached for a crisp edge of noodle from the remaining lasagna—which was not great, but good—and bit off a piece of it. "What I want is a third husband," she said. "My friends who have third husbands—it's all cherishing and forgiving, day and night."

Con laughed at her again but she was still thinking about herself and Jerry. "When we're apart, I'll be able to take deep breaths," she said.

Peggy said, "All I want in life is to take big breaths. One guy or another—somebody's always making my diaphragm clench. Even at my age." She stood to leave.

"My mother's friend—" Con said. "Her friend wants power of attorney."

"Really? You'd trust her that far?"

"Oh, I can *trust* her," Con said. "I've known her all my life. But I should do it, if anybody does."

"She brought it up?" said Peggy.

"Well, the doctor said something."

"It's a big job," Peggy said. "If she's willing, and you're sure she's—you know."

"Marlene has a criminal mind," Con said, laughing. "But she's not a criminal."

"Oh, well then," Peggy said.

Chapter 3

After Peggy left with the empty lasagna pan, Con wrapped herself in the afghan and read more of Marlene's letters from the war years. She had to find out just what Marlene got away with—whether she always got away with everything.

Dear Gert,

Frank accused Bernard of taking money but of course that's not what happened. It was a lousy ten dollars. But that does it, I'm finished with Frank. Mostly this is a good group of people and there aren't many girls so I am popular. We have a few laughs.

Even you would be having a good time. We end up talking most nights. Sometimes Bernard comes home with me. When we have the simulated air raid, he's hoping to be picked for the

head of our group, but I tell him we might not even be in
the same group. La Guardia is all worked up about it or
so he says when he makes speeches. We're going to be in
New York for the next one. It's supposed to be more like
the real thing than the first one, in Brooklyn. I might
be a casualty. It will be fun. Not that it tells us a thing
about what it would be like if the Nazis really showed
up. Nobody thinks it's for real except the mayor. But for
Bernard and me it's time together.

You can't imagine how dark New York is. Don't worry
about the money. If you can't send it I understand, I'll
borrow it from somebody else. I do have friends besides
you! I thought it might not be too hard for you because
things are better, or so it seemed. Don't get a sunburn
down in Florida.

Your loving sister,
Marlene

Dear Gert,

Bernard had a fight with Frank. I don't see what he's
supposed to do. He can't leave Brenda home by herself.
I can't take her. I love her but I am not gifted with children, so you'd better not ask me to babysit your girls.

I know I told you that was the last time and I wouldn't
need any more money but just one more time should do
it. I won't tell Abe, of course. Don't worry about that. Why
would I tell him? I can see he wouldn't like it if you've
been making up something about doctor bills when you're

really sending it to me. Twenty-five would be great but I suppose that's too much to expect. How about fifteen?

Frank really has it in for us. I should never have had anything to do with him. It was only that one time and only because we got drunk but now he treats Bernard like hell and I'm afraid he could go to people I don't want to mention and make some kind of deal. This would not be fair because as you know the whole thing was his idea in the first place, but you never know with guys like that. He and Bernard have that Irish temper. Frank supposedly doesn't know about me and Bernard but I guess he does.

I am sorry about your back and the baby being sick. I wish you could rely on Abe but at least he is still stateside. When is the new baby due, I forget?

Love from your sister,

Marlene

Another letter was missing the first page.

I think as you are my close friend—sister, really—you could trust me about this. I wouldn't do anything with your money you wouldn't like. This is quiet and not a big deal. Frank deserves trouble, he's a lousy supervisor, always yelling at the women and saying we're going to be responsible when the Nazis bomb the block and we all get killed. Well, what do you know, he might get killed along with us. I know you don't have extra money with Abe in the service and the baby and being pregnant, but this is not a lot and you know you'll get back more than I'm asking for. It's a good plan and with all of us together we know the right people to talk to. Rationing doesn't make sense anyway. If somebody didn't do this, where would we be? But they have to buy the stuff—they won't trust us.

Dear Gert,

Well, I didn't mention Bernard for a while because you said you didn't want to hear about him but it's getting difficult. He can't stop worrying and nothing is fun. I guess he promised the guy in charge that we'd give a certain percentage of the money to the men who are providing the meat, and on the basis of that we got more than we can deal with, and now what? I'm sure it will work out but if you can send another twenty, even ten, it would be good.

I told you they had me making coffee at the mock air raid, didn't I? It wasn't good coffee. I made sure of that, so maybe next time they'll give me something better to do. But I didn't spill it on anybody.

Nothing much to say today, just hoping you can put together a little something. I still hope we'll get some benefit from all this and that will be nice. I'll send it to you the minute I have it. You'll be able to buy something pretty for the baby and the new baby.

Oh, I almost forgot to tell you, I met the big boss of this thing we're doing, the mighty Lou. You never see Lou, but everything that has to do with you know what—well, you keep hearing Lou wants it this way, Lou wants it that way. You would not think little Marlene would meet this guy, who for his own reasons would rather not be seen too much. But, I was with Bernard one night last week. We decided to knock off a little early and get together, and then he kept me waiting on a street corner, freezing to death. This was the start of when he began worrying, but I didn't know then what was on his mind. I was mad and he kept saying, "Hey, honey, hey, honey." Finally we went into a bar to warm up and talk things over, and as we're going in, he says, "Oh my god."

I go, "What? What's going on?" and he motions me to keep quiet, and introduces me to a guy at the bar, only he doesn't say his last name, only "Lou." The guy says hello—this is a tall guy dressed in brown with a hat and a glass in front of him on the bar, and he's playing with both of them. He turns back and sort of talks to us over his shoulder about the weather, which is terrible, and he's playing so fast with his hat and his drink I think he's trying to do a magic trick. He's one of those people who can't sit still, apparently. He's talking mostly to Bernard, of course, but then I say, "What are you going to do with that drink?" just meaning is he going to spill it, and he ends up buying us a couple of drinks. And somehow I find out how the side of his leg feels, sitting on the bar stool. Of course at this point I have no idea who he is. The name didn't ring a bell.

So when we leave, Bernard goes "Oh my god" again, and I go, "What? What's going on?" and he says, "That was Lou."

"I know it was Lou. You said it was Lou. Lou who?"

He says, "I'm not sure he wants you to know Lou who."

So I say, "Oh, for crying out loud." And then I catch on. "You mean Lou as in Lou this, Lou that?" The boss. If he gets in trouble, I hope nobody saw me. But I'll tell you, Gert, this was a smart guy. I like smart guys. I don't know how I could tell he's smarter than Bernard, but sitting there, that's what I was thinking. I don't spend enough time with smart.

Stop worrying about the baby. She'll be fine. Abe has nothing to think about but worrying? Tell him to watch his rear end, now that he's almost overseas. We can't do without him.

Hurry and write.

Love, your sister,

Marlene

Dear Gert,

Well, lots of luck! I didn't think you'd have the baby for another week, so I wasn't even looking for a letter. I'm glad it's another girl though you may not agree. Constance is not my favorite name but I'll live with it, and Connie is cute. At least Abe was there, but I know it's hard now when he's going any minute. I get news of this one and that one in Europe, and mostly news of no news. With this war, no news is bad news. People say, "My mother-in-law hasn't heard from her aunt in Poland" and first you say, "A stamp costs money, probably she has nothing to eat." The person doesn't answer and you say, "I know, I know." But what do we know?

Thank you for what you sent, and I understand that it couldn't be more, but if you can make it a little more in a week or so, that would be very sweet of you.

Love,
Marlene

Wednesday

Dear Gert,

Don't worry about your money, and stop asking me to send it back. You know I can't do that yet. Things are not easy here. Bernard's wife found out something. I think Brenda told her about the fire and what happened that day. I didn't think she'd do that. It will work out about the money. A lot of people are excited and willing to be part of this. The man Bernard knows is good at getting hold of butter, meat—things people want. I'm not sure if this is Lou, who I told you about, or somebody else who answers to Lou. People say rationing isn't even necessary. There are all kinds of things they want us to do, donate foil and stuff like that. Maybe in Florida too.

Still another letter had lost its first and last page.

No, it's not what you think. I didn't see him again and maybe it would be better if you don't mention him. I don't have time to write anyway. We're getting ready for the second mock air raid and this time I'm going to be a casualty. Some women have to cook because there is going to be real hot food and real doughnuts and the Red Cross and so on and so forth. But I'll be lying there. Then I'll be carried. They better not drop me. There are going to be real internes and maybe I'll meet a handsome young doctor. Mayor La Guardia came and talked to us. He mentioned people making fun of the simulated air raids. He knew he was talking to volunteers so he said we were heroines and criticized people who laugh. But some of us were the ones doing the laughing, little did he know. Not too many. Bernard and I are the only ones without stars in the eyes. It was interesting to see the mayor close up. He walked past me taking off his coat. Somebody held it for him. He didn't look as short as people say.

I don't know what colic is but I hope it went away.

Dear Gert,

You'll never guess. I spent last night at a swanky New York hotel that has a name you would definitely recognize. I stole an ashtray, so you'd believe I was there. It's huge. Maybe I'll give it to you—I better do something with it because sooner or later Bernard is going to see it and ask questions. Or somebody is going to ask questions. I'll keep it in my bottom drawer and give it to you when you come home. It's dark red, very heavy, very big, or I'd mail it. But then Abe would ask questions. By the time the war is over nobody will be thinking about anything like that, and you can tell him the beautiful dark red ashtray was a wedding present you put away. You're wondering how I happened to spend the night in a very very swanky hotel and I am going to let you guess, but it has to do with someone I have mentioned once or twice. Enough said.

In fact I'd better give it to you. I don't think I want anybody to know I know this guy, and who knows what he wrote down on the register. Well, I'm tired. That's all for tonight. I wanted to tell you about it. A very classy guy.

Your friend,
Marlene

Dear Gert,

I think I know better than you what risks I am taking. You think you're not taking risks, having two children when your husband—well, who knows what could happen? I'm sorry to suggest something like that, but you know what I mean. I don't do anything foolish, I can tell you that. I know the difference between somebody where it's going to work out and somebody where it isn't. I have a feeling this is going to last. For one thing he isn't married. Or so he says.

Stop worrying about your old friend and just take care of those little girls. I wish I could see a picture. Maybe somebody has a camera. Does Connie have red

hair? I should buy her a present, I never bought her anything. What do you need? If I were a real friend I would
knit a sweater, but I never learned.

Write soon. Don't worry about me. Don't worry, I'm not
mad.

Love,
Marlene

Dear Gert,

It was pretty exciting. It happened in Bryant Park, right
behind the 42nd Street Library. They had fake fire and
fake bombs, the Red Cross, City Patrol, ambulances.
The light was eerie. A whole lot of us supposedly got
trapped in the building across from the library. It was
smelly. Your girlfriend almost died, only pretend. But
was saved. I was on a stretcher, and they put me in an
ambulance. Then they carried me out and some young
guys—people said they were real internes—asked me
questions and felt my arms and legs. I kept trying not
to laugh. I wish Bernard was here, even if he's not as
classy as some people. I think he may go to prison, and
I just hope this isn't because I said the wrong thing,
that night at the hotel, and you-know-who got mad at
him. I was up half the night at the mock air-raid but it
was worth it.

Love,
Marlene

Again, a letter began with its second page. Or had begun in the middle of things.

Of course I understand about the money. I know what things cost and I can do simple arithmetic. All you have to do is say no, there is no need to get huffy about this. I'm sure I never expected you to send anything unless you wanted to be part of this plan that could benefit everybody, and I thought that was the understanding all along. But I'm afraid I can't return what you already sent. That wasn't the idea and you knew that. True, I thought it would all work out sooner than this, but it is just a matter of time.

I have no way of getting in touch with the person in charge I shouldn't mention, and I haven't even seen Bernard.

There's nothing wrong with the baby. I wish you'd stop using that as an excuse, for heaven's sake. Everyone has told you there is nothing wrong with the baby.

Maybe I should write to Abe. Let me know how to reach him. I will explain that you are under a lot of stress and it is natural for you to worry, but he shouldn't worry about her. I hate to think of him up nights worrying that his daughter is feeble-minded just because she can't roll over and some stupid neighbor is upsetting you about this. Just let me know how to get in touch with Abe. Don't worry, I won't say much—maybe I'll let him know a little of what has been going on, very carefully of course, so he won't think you've been extravagant. He must be worried about money. If you don't want to send

me his address I think I know how to get it from someone else, don't worry.

Love, your sister,
Marlene

Dear Gert,

Now don't be angry. I had to do something or people I can't
name would take off my head, and something bad would
happen to Bernard, and it would be my fault. I'll explain
it all when you get home if that happy day ever comes.
Anyway, thanks for sending it and no I am not going to
write to Abe. Not yet anyway. Oh, by the way I saw the big
guy again. More than just saw, if you follow me.

Love,
Marlene (your fascinating friend from Brooklyn)

Dear Gert,

The main thing is that I think Bernard is the man for me.
I don't know what would have happened if we had met
before all of this, and now that events have happened I may
never see him again. His wife knows and I don't think he'll
stand up to her, even if we get away with the rest of it. He
has never been willing to talk about divorce and all that.
Gert, you have never told me how to live even though you
don't live the same way I do, and I appreciate that, and I
know I haven't made things easier for you. Now I wish I
had lived the way you would have wanted me to.

I'm glad you heard from Abe and he is all right.

Make sure the girls let you get some rest. You can't be picking up after them every second and if the landlady complains, well, she would have a hard time getting somebody as good as you. So be nice but just go about your business. You've never learned to stand up for yourself but who am I to talk about that, you've done better than I have.

Brenda is upstate with his wife's sister, I forget where. His wife thought he wasn't a good influence and now that she's working such long hours he would have to keep her all the time and she didn't think that was a good idea, so she has been sent off somewhere. Which would make it easier for Bernard and me to be together if he would only listen, but his heart has gone out of everything. He thinks he has nothing to look forward to but trouble, but I think when the war is over, and that will be soon, everybody will forget all about this stuff, and once rationing is ended it will not matter who tried to find a way around it and who didn't. We didn't do anything wrong, when we were able to get the meat it worked out very well and I'm sure there are kids growing up in New York with strong bones and teeth because we went to all that trouble and expense. Or is it milk that gives you strong bones and teeth?

Well, I'm going on and on. Better see if I can get some hot water. I need to soak my feet.

Love,
Marlene

Of another letter, only a page survived.

> Bernard has been arrested and his wife is taking Brenda
> and going to her mother's in Ohio. I don't think he'll go
> to jail. I think you should stop complaining about your
> lousy money given this eventuality which nobody could
> have foreseen. It was in the *Brooklyn Eagle,* just a small
> item. They got it mostly wrong. The trouble is, Bernard
> and I are just small potatoes but others I may have men-
> tioned are not small potatoes.

> Gert, dear,

> Could you burn up any letters from me that you kept?
> I don't know who they're going to talk to or when, but
> I know there are things in my letters it would not be a
> good idea to spread around, for other people's sake if not
> for mine. Think of Brenda, who is just starting out in life
> and doesn't need this trouble.
>
> Thanks,
> Marlene
>
> P.S. I think I better not write for a while. I hope
> you'll be home soon anyway.

It was extortion. Marlene did not just have a criminal mind,
she was—had been—a criminal. Marlene got money from Con's
mother for a black market scheme, then threatened to tell Con's
father if Gert didn't send more money. Con put down the letters.
Marlene was not alluring and splendid, she was selfish and crafty.

It was much better not to think this thought. Con couldn't ask Gert and Marlene about these letters, and it would be best to forget they existed. She didn't put them into her suitcase, but left them on her mother's dresser. She put the afghan on top of them.

The phone rang as she turned from the pile of letters and went into the kitchen, wanting something sweet. "I was looking at that letter from the zoning," said Mabel Turner's voice. "I think there's a deadline."

Con tried to focus on this very different letter, and eventually she got Mabel to read everything aloud. She had until Monday to file an appeal. How could she do that from Brooklyn? "Call me tomorrow, okay?" she said.

As soon as she hung up the phone rang again so quickly that she expected Mabel's voice again, asking a forgotten question. But it was Marlene. "Baby, I've been thinking. I know you're busy, but I think we should talk about this now," Marlene said. Her voice sounded more confident than ever, more certain that Con understood a great deal less than Marlene did—probably a great deal less than anybody should. And yet it held, as well, the old promise of intimacy, of *possible* intimacy, as if—if Con proved worthy, and with proper tutelage she might—together they'd escape the well-meaning ordinariness that was apparently essential to anything connected with Con's mother (such as this prison of an apartment). At any minute Con and Marlene would achieve charm. They'd achieve glamour.

"Talk about what?" Con said, startled; she was scared but expectant—as if Marlene had seen her reading the letters. Marlene could explain; maybe Con had misunderstood. She eased herself back against the kitchen counter, but remained standing.

"Power of attorney," Marlene said.

Now Con felt a tendril of anger make its way through her body. She tried to control her voice. She stood up. "I'm a *lawyer*," she said.

"Well, I know *that*!" Marlene crooned.

"I'm actually practicing law right here in the middle of the night in my mother's apartment. I was just on the phone with a client." She was competent, she meant. It was not precisely Marlene who doubted Con's competence; it was probably Con herself. She didn't know exactly how to acquire her mother's power of attorney, though she could find out. She didn't want to know. She didn't want to manage—or even look at—her mother's records of money coming in, money going out; they were personal, like food going in, being digested, becoming blood or shit. But if acquiring her mother's power of attorney became necessary—and Con was not sure that it was necessary now—if it became necessary, of course she could do it. She would find out how, as she was about to find out how to file an appeal in Mabel's case.

"I'm not sure you can," said Marlene, and Con sucked in her breath. "You don't live in the same state as your mother."

"What does *that* have to do with it?" Now she was walking with the receiver once more, as in the conversation with Jerry. No wonder she was so tired. She had to get rid of Marlene.

"I think the person who holds power of attorney must reside in the same state. I've been through this quite a bit. My aunt, my cousin."

Con had never heard of this aunt or cousin before—had no memory of Marlene looking after frail relatives—and had certainly never heard of a law against out-of-state holders of power of attorney.

"And Barbara's not even in the country!" Marlene was saying triumphantly.

"You're mistaken," Con said. She'd never worked on a case involving power of attorney, but Marlene's claim was decidedly unlikely. "I'll look into it."

"Don't," said Marlene. "Let me take this on. I feel bad that I can't have your mother come and live with me, but honey—things aren't good. Something has to be done. And this is something I can do. If there's anything I don't understand, I know people to ask. This is something I'm good at."

As if her mother's voice had emanated from the stained couch cushions, Con heard Gert say, "Marlene is smart about money," as she had said it many times during Con's girlhood and later: when a decision had to be made about insurance, or Gert's pension, or investment of the death benefits and life insurance money that had come into Gert's hands when Con's father died. "I'll ask Marlene," Gert would say. "She'll know somebody." And Marlene had always known somebody.

But now, though it was late, and Con didn't want to think about her mother right now—her marriage was ending, actually ending—and though it was tempting just to say, "Okay, Marlene, thank you," Con didn't. The pile of onionskin pages, marked with Marlene's large, elegant loops and angles—expertly shaded by a nicely controlled fountain pen that had probably cost more than the young Marlene could afford (and who had bought it for her?)—was still nearby. Maybe she'd jumped to a hasty conclusion about extortion. Maybe it wasn't that. But even so.

"I just don't think it's a good idea," Con said. "Let's talk about it again in a day or two. Let me see how my mother seems when she gets home."

"You're being unreasonable, Connie," Marlene said. "We all know there are times when our dear Connie is unreasonable, and this is one of those times."

"I don't think I'm being unreasonable."

"Well, of course not! You never do, do you?"

Con sat down at the table and fingered the stripe in the color she liked so much. She would have liked to enter that orange or maybe pink stripe—would it be called coral?—as if it were a room, a quiet room. "I'm not being unreasonable. This is hasty, Marlene."

"Have you any idea what your mother may be doing with your inheritance? Have you looked over her records?"

"I'm not sure she keeps records."

"That's even worse!" said Marlene, but she sounded delighted with Gert's degree of helplessness. "People like Gert, when they get this way—they do crazy things with money and there's not much you can do about it if you didn't secure power of attorney." Marlene's voice seemed to deepen as she spoke. Maybe she was smoking while talking. Con thought she heard an intake of breath, as of someone inhaling. Smoking was dangerous, but not for Marlene. No cancer cell would dare invade those lungs. She'd stare it down. That would be that.

"No. No. I'm not going to agree that you get her power of attorney, and you'd better not take her to a lawyer in the morning and just do it!" said Con, and now she was becoming unreasonable after all. It was heady to fight like this with Marlene—

risky, but thrilling. "Because if you do, I'm not letting you get away with it," Con said. The problem was that she was starting to cry. "This is going too far, Marlene. You're not in charge of my mother, and I'm a lawyer, and there are ways to stop you."

"Stop me from what? What in the world are you accusing me of?" Marlene said in her deep, almost masculine voice. "What am I going to do to her? Who takes better care of her than I do? Who keeps track of her if it isn't for me? You have no judgment when it comes to something like that. You'll probably believe the nonsense she's going to tell you, about me, about the past, about your father."

"She's my mother!" Con found herself crying. "Leave her alone! She's my mother!"

There was silence, a much longer silence than phone calls ordinarily include, as if Con might never hear that voice again. Then Marlene spoke, and her voice had dropped in volume and in pitch. "Oh, Connie, I didn't mean to upset you. Of course she's your mother. Nobody doubts that she's your mother!"

"The answer is no," Con managed to say.

"Don't worry about it," said Marlene, and despite herself, Con was glad they weren't going to hang up in the middle of a shouting match, and was also still worried that Marlene didn't really respect her, was just changing her tactics.

"I'm going to bed," Con said. "I'll talk to you tomorrow."

"You know me," Marlene was saying. "You know Marlene. You know me." It was a kind of goodnight. The conversation, at any rate, was over.

❖

Con turned to her computer, and now she thought about nothing but employment discrimination for the rest of Wednesday morning and much of the afternoon. One woman had been fired for having repeated black eyes. "You're a face," her boss had said. She'd been a receptionist. "It would be different if you weren't a face."

Except that suddenly Con remembered Peggy. Peggy had been right. There would be other occasions to fret about Joanna. She wrote a quick e-mail message. "I can have dinner tonight."

"Wonderful," Peggy wrote back. They usually met at a quiet place near Peggy's apartment. Con would leave the office early enough to get home and take a bath. A nap would be welcome, but she didn't think she'd get one. She e-mailed a friend about Joanna's arrest, a law school classmate who worked in a firm that handled political cases. The woman was interested, but not interested enough. Her message said, "It's too bad she was drunk. If we knew for sure they told her to be quiet, that would be different."

She shouldn't have said Joanna was drunk. Con should find out whether arrests like this were common. She went to a few Web sites. Civil rights groups were busy with larger issues: prisoners were being held without charges at Guantánamo Bay; American citizens who looked as if they might be Arabs were being harassed and arrested. The cops who had arrested Joanna knew they'd done something at least ambiguous, since the charges had been dropped. Still, Joanna had spent a night in jail.

Con didn't leave work early. Aaron stuck his head into her office just as she was starting to think about turning off her computer. He wanted to talk about the woman whose interview Con had witnessed. She ended up back in his office. Everything felt more possible after the conversation—which was good—but half an hour had passed. She could be on time at the restaurant only if she went straight from the office. But she hadn't showered in the morning. She couldn't enjoy Peggy unless she was clean. She'd be late, but would apologize, and Peggy would forgive her. In Brooklyn, she walked home quickly from the subway station, jabbed at the elevator button, barely glanced at the mail, and began taking off her clothes on the way to her bedroom.

The shower soothed her. When she turned off the water she heard a voice.

She wrapped a towel around herself and opened the bathroom door. "Joanna?" she said. "What are you doing here?"

"I called the airport and there was a flight." Joanna came toward her mother, still in a jacket, keys in her hand. "I barely made it."

Behind her Con could see that the apartment door was open. "Go close the door," she said. Joanna's bag was in the middle of her study.

"I think I love Tim. I never should have broken up with him," Joanna said then. "You shouldn't have been so negative about him."

"Go close the door," said Con. She reached up, clutching her towel, to give Joanna a damp, one-armed hug.

"Oh, my life," said Joanna, suddenly in tears. "I shouldn't have broken up with him in the first place. I wouldn't have gone to the bar. None of this would have happened."

"Jail was horrible, wasn't it?" said Con quietly.

"It was horrible."

"But close the door." Joanna turned, and Con went into her bedroom and dressed. She wouldn't cancel dinner with Peggy, who would already be on her way, or in the restaurant. Before leaving, Con perched briefly, in her jacket, on the arm of her gray squashy chair, and listened to Joanna, who was already distractedly clutching her green fibrous twine ,as she spoke, walking back and forth across the dusty living room rug, pushing her wild curls back with her free hand.

"I have to leave," said Con. "I'm having dinner with Peggy."

"I'll be all right. There are eggs, I guess."

"Yes." Con lingered, though she was already late. As she left she asked, "Is there some reason you *want* to see Marlene? Is that why you came home?"

"I don't do or not do things because of Marlene," said Joanna.

When she and Marlene hung up after the argument, Con stood with her hand on the phone. She'd been unable to mention the letters. Did she have to think differently about Marlene from now on? Marlene had stolen money from her mother as the burglar had stolen money from Con—or so it seemed. Of course, this was a long time ago. As Con brushed her teeth, she thought not about the crime or the argument or even Jerry. She'd turned from the letters stunned at how time passes and life changes, how the young become the old, yet remain who they are until they lose everything. Her mother—the silent one in the correspondence—seemed much as she was now: mute, helpless before her friend's fearless competence. Con knew a little more about that friendship now, but she still didn't understand it. Marlene hadn't been friends with her mother, surely, only for Gert's pathetic contributions to the black market scheme? Did she want to show her power over Gert—to cause timid Gertrude Tepper to participate, even marginally, in wrongdoing?

All this time Con had forgotten to think about herself and Jerry, but when she went to bed, that grief overtook the others. She fell asleep feeling a kind of dread, as if that ordinary frame house full of ex-prisoners—in an old, crowded, humdrum Philadelphia suburb—were sliding into an abyss, as if ground crumbled beneath it, and everything else—all Con knew—would go with it. She was sad about arguing with Marlene and astonished by her decision to leave Jerry, but no less sure. It was necessary, but terrible. She was asleep in her mother's bed when the phone rang. It was dark. "I'm afraid of losing you," said Jerry's voice.

She didn't want to talk lying down. Her mother's bed had no headboard. No wonder Gert's head was slipping off her neck, Con found herself thinking. She wasn't awake yet. "Look," she said, thinking she was being clear. "What would make me feel better?" Then she said, "Wait a minute," and put down the receiver, reached for the afghan, then rolled it and used it to prop up the pillow. When she took the phone again she was not quite lying down. "You woke me up."

"I couldn't sleep. I thought maybe you couldn't sleep."

"What time is it?"

"Midnight. Ten after twelve."

Within a substantial silence she thought as clearly as she

could. "There's nothing in me I wouldn't reconsider," she said, "except loving Joanna and believing—"

She tried to say what lay behind her work, what it was on which she could not compromise. "Believing in the Bill of Rights," she said.

"The Bill of Rights?" he said.

"Freedom of speech. Freedom of—"

"I know what the Bill of Rights is," said Jerry. "I guess I wouldn't stop believing in it either, but I don't think about it often."

"I thought maybe you wanted to know if I'd stay married after all," she said.

"It crossed my mind," he said. "Do you mean the Bill of Rights gives you the right to leave me?"

"No, I'd have the right to leave you whether the Bill of Rights existed or not. The Bill of Rights makes it possible to resist injustice." He wouldn't try to imprison her. He could not wrap her in the cords of the lamps and keep her. The pillow was slipping. After all, maybe she could talk lying down. She pulled the blanket around herself.

"Do you think I compromise on those things? Is that the trouble?" Jerry said. She had still not been clear.

"No," she said. "I would never stop loving Joanna, and I'd never stop believing in the Bill of Rights."

"You said that."

"But anything *else*—if you had asked me—" She began to cry because she had used the past perfect tense. "If you had asked me, I would think about changing my mind."

"So you can change your mind about loving me? I don't think I can change my mind about loving you."

These last two days, she'd sometimes thought she was only pretending her marriage was over, but now she felt the kind of fear she'd experienced not when she first realized that her bag was not on the dresser, but when she continued not to see it, when certainty replaced anxiety. "I'm talking about you, Jerry," she said, and she was now sitting up, legs crossed, leaning forward with her elbows on her knees. "I'm talking about being willing to consider being different."

"How can anybody be different?"

"I can be different. I can at least consider being different."

"You mean giving up my trips?" said Jerry. "You'll stay married to me if I give up my trips?"

She hadn't put it to herself that way, and she didn't want to know what he'd say if she said yes. She didn't want to hear him say that he'd give her up rather than give up the trips. She was cold. She leaned forward and pulled the blanket around her, making a tent that covered her head. Inside, it was dark, but if she could sit in the dark she'd know what to say. The receiver's cord made an opening in the tent.

For a moment she wanted to tell Jerry about Marlene's letters—and about the argument—but she knew she wouldn't. It would all be part of the archive of separation, the eventually large body of what would not be common knowledge between them. Common property would be hard enough to sort out, but common knowledge . . . it was sad to think of the jokes they'd lose.

She said, "If I'd found out—if I'd overheard you and Joanna discussing it, and if I had asked you very seriously not to let her go, would you have changed your mind?"

"We didn't discuss it when you were in the house," he said.

"I know, but if."

"I wouldn't have invited her if I couldn't have done it privately."

"You're not private about the trips. You leave your cards everywhere."

"I'm private about some parts. I don't write everything down," he said. She was hot, now. She shook off the tent of blanket, and gleams of light came from the window and from the hall, where there was a nightlight. "Why can't you compromise?" she said. "I think I'd be all right if I could understand why you can't compromise about *anything*. That's what I'm saying," she said. "I'd reconsider everything except those two things. You reconsider nothing. It's not just the trips. You reconsider *nothing*."

"I don't?"

"I want to go to sleep."

"Maybe I don't know how to reconsider. I don't think I consider, in the first place," said Jerry.

"You sound pleased with yourself. I don't think it's anything to be particularly proud of."

He ignored what she said, but had become interested in the topic. "I don't think I make decisions," he continued. "I think they come to me ready-made. I couldn't reconsider—I'd have to know how they began, so as to begin them differently."

"Did you ever try?"

There was such a long pause that she thought he'd gone to sleep, and she considered putting down the receiver. Then he said in a low, uncertain voice, "I don't know."

She started to speak, but he kept talking. "If we separate," he said shakily, "will Joanna be all right?"

"She won't like it. But she might be less surprised than you and I," Con said.

Another long pause. "She'd be mostly with you?"

"Yes." He didn't want Joanna to live with him, she noted, though he claimed to think so highly of her. And Con did want her daughter to live with her.

"Do you mind if I talk to her about it?" he said.

"Don't," said Con quickly. "Not yet."

Again there was a long silence, while she wondered if he was talking from the room where Joanna slept, or somewhere else. Again she grew cold. This time she lay down under the blankets, but still held the receiver to her ear. She didn't know what she hoped Jerry would say.

"Maybe it's time to be apart for a while," he said at last. "It's going to be hard to figure out."

"You reconsidered?" She was joking, in a way.

"Maybe not."

"I still love you," said Con, though she had thought she didn't.

"I love you too."

"It's terribly, terribly sad," she said, as if it were a story about other people.

"The saddest of sad," he said. "Good night, dear."

She hung up and wept in the bed, but then she slept soundly. When she awoke it was light, and for a moment she didn't understand that her mother's phone was ringing again. Then she thought Jerry had called her back and had been dialing all night. All night the phone had been ringing, and yet the machine hadn't picked up. She wondered why not, and thought that possibly someone had broken into the apartment again and had taken the answering machine. Then the ringing stopped and the announcement began in the other room, and she understood that she'd slept through only two or three rings. She picked up the phone and said, "Hello."

Her mother's voice, once again, explained as if it might be surprising news that she wasn't home right then, and pronounced numbers. "Hello?" said Con. "Can you hear me? I don't know how to stop the machine."

"It's me," said Marlene. Then more loudly. "It's *me*. Your friend Marlene."

"I know," said Con. "What time is it?"

Marlene sounded stymied. The machine stopped and there was a beep. "I don't know. About nine."

"I was asleep. Look, about last night—"

"Never mind about that. Sweetheart, I have to tell you something," said Marlene, and Con understood that if Marlene sounded strange, it wasn't because of their argument.

"Is something wrong?" said Con. Then, involuntarily, "Joanna?"

"What?"

"Nothing," said Con. "What is it?"

"Connie—I don't know how to tell you," said Marlene. "Connie. Sweetheart," she said. "Gert. Your mother."

"*What?*" Con said, with the start of a scream.

"Connie, she died— she's dead. I found her dead in my house."

"No!" Con shouted, and then, "You can't say that, it's not true."

When Con stopped making sounds, Marlene was in the middle of a sentence and she continued to talk. She said, "It's for the best" but it was not for the best. It was true, however. A doctor had said so. Marlene had already called a funeral home and they were coming for the body. "It's going to be complicated, getting her wherever you want her—New York, I assume. Where is your father?"

"He's dead," Con said, and it took her a while to understand that Marlene wanted to know where her father was buried.

Finally she said, "I'll call you back," because she was afraid she might faint. Con hung up the phone and went to the bathroom. Her mother's copy of *Prevention* was still next to the toilet, still open to the article about oat bran. Then she got back into her mother's bed. She turned onto her stomach and breathed the smell of the bed—her own smell, her mother's perhaps still—and then she just lay there. She was sure the news wasn't true, but if it wasn't true, there would be no reason to say it, so it had to be true. She didn't cry and didn't sleep. Her body hurt—her shoulders, her arms, her legs—and she lay as still as she could. She thought only in short sentences. It was impossible to think anything that made sense, anything she might think in a week or even a day. She was aware of light coming through the window, and the cat, who had emerged from some hiding place during the night and was sleeping near her. Now he jumped heavily off the bed, and soon she heard him scratching in his litter box in the bathroom. He returned, and wanted to sleep on her head. She pushed him aside and he tried again, but after that he slept on the blanket pressed against the protuberance that was Con's buttocks. She wondered when she would get up, when she would want to eat, as if she were someone else watching herself. An hour passed.

She had to pee again, and finally got out of bed. Her bare feet were cold. She returned to the bed and sat on the edge. For a long time she thought about warming her feet and at last, with what seemed like all her energy, she stood up, found the socks she'd worn the day before, and put them on. Then she put a sweater on over her pajamas—she was freezing—and went into the living room. It looked like a photograph of itself. When she saw the answering machine on the kitchen counter she knew it had recorded her entire conversation with Marlene. Then she wasn't sure. She could press "announcement" and hear her mother's voice, Gert's unbearably trusting and needless repetition of the phone number. Con could not bring herself to hear her mother's announcement. But she had to know if she and Marlene had been recorded.

Con and Peggy met at an Italian restaurant not far from Peggy's place, a long walk from Con's, so she took a taxi. The waiters knew them by now and deferred to Peggy, who sometimes talked a little Italian with them. When Con was late, Peggy ordered a glass of wine and gossiped with the bartender, mostly about real estate in the neighborhood. Tonight Con was more than half an hour late. When she came in, the warmth was welcome, and small piercing lights picked up gleams in dark woodwork and tabletops. Peggy, looking more like a lifelong neighborhood woman than usual, was wearing a possibly too elaborate tight knitted sweater with silver around the V neck and a flower pattern. It made Con nostalgic.

Peggy's long thin nose had wrinkles at the top that softened her face, which would otherwise have been severe. She'd once told Con her whole career at NYU had come about because she had a scary face, so she could say no and get away with it. Con now caught her eye, slid into the seat facing the wall, and ordered a glass of Pinot Grigio when the waiter appeared at her elbow. She looked down at her own sweater. "You remind me of old Brooklyn," she said.

"Old Brooklyn?"

"Women with lots of sisters and sisters-in-law," she said. "Dressing up and getting together with family."

"We still do that," Peggy said. Then, "I was just thinking about your mother."

"You were thinking about my *mother*?" Con said.

"I was thinking about when you and I met, when she died."

"I don't think about her death," Con said. "I don't like to think about it."

"I was remembering that when she died, I brought you lasagna my mother had made."

"Because she died? I don't remember. I bet it was wonderful."

"I think the lasagna wasn't particularly good but you were polite," said Peggy.

"You know what? Joanna showed up, just as I was leaving."

"You're kidding. How did she get here so fast?"

"The charges were dropped and she got a good flight."

"That's good—but what will you do now?"

"I'm not sure I need to do anything," Con said.

"Of course you do! She spent a night in jail!" said Peggy, her temper suddenly engaged.

Con was not bothered when Peggy spoke sharply. She knew it was style, Brooklyn style. If Con had ever had that sharpness, the years in Philadelphia had worn it off.

"That's what Joanna says," Con said. "But she was drunk. I think bartenders and cops are pretty careful—they know what's legal."

"We don't know she was drunk, and she had a right to speak even if she was." The waiter was hovering again. Peggy opened her menu, and spoke quietly again, as if she'd made up her mind to postpone this topic. "The lasagna here is better than my mother's," she said. "You were so lost and sweet and young, that week."

"Was I?"

"You seemed thirty years younger than I was."

"What's the lasagna tonight?" said Con. The specials were scribbled on the blackboard.

"Pumpkin, for the season," Peggy said. "That sounds stupid."

"Big slabs of pumpkin, like butternut squash?" said Con. "Are you getting it?"

"No."

Con felt young again, as she had apparently been all those years ago, young and naive and ignorant, too stupid to order the right thing in an Italian restaurant, insufficiently critical of Peggy's dead mother's lasagna. She tried to remember whether Peggy's mother had cooked it for her on purpose because her own mother had died. She thought she and Peggy had met a few times when her mother was alive.

"I didn't think that would have happened—what happened

to Joanna," Peggy said. "I knew things were bad, but I didn't think a girl would be arrested in a bar in this country for saying the war in Iraq is a bad idea."

"I know. Maybe it didn't happen quite like that."

"She wouldn't have lied," said Peggy.

This was true; Joanna didn't lie or even exaggerate. Sometimes she made herself sound worse than she was. But she was confused about this incident. "If they asked her to leave, that's legal," said Con. "First the owner had to ask. Then the cops had to ask. I admit that she says they didn't ask her to leave—that they told her to be quiet."

"Then you have to do something," Peggy said.

"What can I do?"

"You're a lawyer."

The waiter showed up. Con inquired of her taste buds and found she wanted pumpkin lasagna. Peggy had fish. They tore off bits of bread. They ate salad.

"I don't practice in North Carolina," said Con. "That's what Joanna said: 'You're a lawyer.'"

"But you know how these things work. Maybe have a local lawyer write a letter?"

The food arrived. The lasagna was wonderful. There was something she didn't want to think about, something that had come up in this conversation. She liked the music in this restaurant. "Who's that singing?" she said.

"Barbara Cook?"

"Maybe."

"It's Barbara Cook. I know this recording," said Peggy.

"Okay, okay."

"And anyway, nobody else sounds like Barbara Cook."

"*Okay*," said Con.

"At least they turned off the radio and put on a tape," Peggy said, fork in hand. "The news came on before you got here, and each story was worse than the one before. They're activating more reserves and sending them to Iraq. Bush signed the ban on partial-birth abortions. Also, I didn't quite get this, but there's some kind of story that at the last minute, Iraq tried to avoid the war, and our guys just wouldn't budge. They were just determined."

"I can't stand to talk about it," Con said. She tore up a piece of bread and ate it. She ordered a second glass of wine. Then she changed the subject. Peggy liked hearing about her work. She talked about employment discrimination against victims of domestic violence.

It was unusual to feel bad when she was with Peggy, whose sharpness was kind, with the ease afforded by love. They often disagreed, and pretended to insult each other. Con felt prettier near Peggy, who took the trouble to look nice though she was older than Con. When Peggy was around nobody could say older women weren't sexy. "I can't wait to see Marlene," she said. "What does she want to do?"

"You'll never guess. She wants to go to the El Greco show at the Met, and something at the City Opera. *Turandot*. I wonder if I can still get tickets."

"What a day!" said Peggy. "Buy me a ticket. And let's bring Joanna. It will do her good."

"She won't come. She doesn't like Marlene."

They ordered coffee. Con had decaf but Peggy could still drink coffee right before bedtime. "What's new at work?" Con said. They talked about that, and then about Peggy's lover. Con always spoke of him as Paul, but his name was Phil.

"I've been seeing Phil for two years," said Peggy, "and you've said Paul every time you've mentioned him."

"He looks like a Paul."

"You met him once."

Phil's wife was sick; she had aggressive breast cancer. "Oh, poor lady. Does that make him want to break up with you?"

"No, he needs to talk about it."

"Are you hoping she'll die?" said Con, putting cream in her decaf.

"What a thing to say! I care about her!"

"Oh, come on," said Con quickly. "You've been sleeping with her husband for two years!"

"I care about her quite a bit."

"Don't tell yourself what isn't true, Peggy," Con said. "You've been sleeping with married guys so long you've forgotten it's not the basic reality, as if everybody came in threes: a man, his wife, his mistress."

"Isn't that how it is?" said Peggy. She drank coffee black, but she stirred it first to cool it.

"You think Jerry had lovers? Or Fred?"

"What went wrong, if it wasn't that?" Peggy stirred her coffee again, blew, tasted it and put the cup down. Still too hot. "I mean Jerry. Fred probably hadn't gotten around to it yet."

"Jerry's coming tomorrow, I think," Con said. She was certain he hadn't had a lover.

"Oh, right, you said. Staying for weeks and weeks. Well, it's your life."

"A week. It's one of his trips."

"Are you going to bring him to the opera?"

"Oh, no, he'll be busy." Peggy sounded as if she thought it was stupid to let Jerry come, but Con was too tired to argue. She wanted to go home, not just because of Joanna.

The waiter asked if they wanted anything more, and Peggy said, *"Il conto, per favore."* They split the check, but as Con was shrugging into her jacket, Peggy said, "Wait a minute. There was a reason I was thinking about the week your mother died. Do you remember asking me about a man named Lou Braunstein?"

"Asking you? No, I never heard of him." She stood. "I'm exhausted."

"Toward the end of that week—the week your mother died—something upset you. Well, your mother died, of course that was terrible. But then something else upset you, and it had something to do with a man named Lou Braunstein. You wouldn't tell me what it was, but you wanted to know if I knew anything about him, and I didn't. But I wrote down the name. A few weeks ago I was cleaning out a drawer and there's a piece of paper that says, 'Lou Braunstein—find out and tell Con.' And I remembered you asking me. We were outside, somewhere."

Con didn't want to think about whatever did or did not upset her fourteen years earlier. "I'm sure it doesn't matter," she said.

"No doubt. But for whatever it's worth, I Googled him. He was a gangster from Brooklyn in the forties. He went to prison a couple of times."

"I can't imagine why I would have known the name," Con said.

"We'll never know," said Peggy, as she kissed Con gently.

Their apartments were in different directions. Con spotted a taxi and waved it down. She was uncomfortable all the way. The too-smooth upholstery seemed likely to spill her at every turn.

Joanna was watching a reality show in the tiny room Con called her living room, knitting her greenish twine. On the program, a young woman was lost and exhausted. A smug young man said she was the last person to arrive, and she cried.

"This makes me feel like a shit," said Con, looking at the young woman's face.

"You're supposed to laugh," said Joanna. "You're only supposed to feel guilty about what's on public television. Guilt makes you give them more money. With commercial television, you feel superior, so you buy things for yourself."

"Well, you must be feeling better!" said Con.

"No, I'm not," said Joanna.

"Sorry." She thought for a while. "I didn't make you break up with him."

"I know that."

"Do you want to talk about it or would you rather I kept quiet?"

"Probably he's a bastard. But I'm sorry I ended it. So I feel as if he ended it, which doesn't even give me the satisfaction of ending it."

"Are you going to be friends? When you get back there?"

"We'll see. We'll see if I get back there," said Joanna. "Maybe I'll find a teaching job. I'm sick of working with fiber anyway. I should do something different. I'll get white lung disease if I keep this up."

Con had wondered about breathing the stuff. Little threads

were everywhere. "By the way, would you vacuum around them?" she remembered to say. "Marlene is coming, as you know—and do you know Dad is coming for a week? It's one of his trips."

"A week?" said Joanna. "Why did you let him do that?" She had turned off the television and dropped the knitted mess on the floor. Now she stood, fingertips in the small front pockets of her jeans, looking down at her mother, who was again perched on the arm of the big chair, in her jacket. Two of Joanna's green creatures loomed nearby, like attentive but helpless listeners.

"God knows."

But Joanna had turned to leave the room; soon Con heard the rise and fall of her voice as she talked on her cell phone.

First thing Thursday morning, still in her bathrobe, Con went online and found the City Opera Web site. Tickets for *Turandot* on Saturday night were still available. She retrieved her credit card from her purse and was just about to buy three—surely Joanna would not want to go to the opera with three old ladies—when she heard her daughter shuffle down the hall to the bathroom. When Joanna came out, it turned out she did want to see *Turandot*. "I've heard it's decadent," she said. "The music is supposed to be great but the story is sick."

The four of them couldn't sit together, but Con bought two pairs of tickets, not far apart. Of course she'd sit with Marlene. She hadn't been to an opera in years. She checked the *Times* Web site, which featured the various items of bad news Peggy had delivered the night before.

"You deserve a night out after the week you've had," she said over her shoulder to Joanna, but her daughter was no longer lingering in the doorway. She'd gone back to sleep, and Con didn't see her again before she left for work. It looked like rain and she took an umbrella.

"Here I come," said an e-mail from Jerry, which she read when she got to the office. She e-mailed Peggy about the tickets. "Joanna's coming," she added. She e-mailed Marlene, who responded with her itinerary. She'd arrive at LaGuardia at 5:33 the next day, Friday, and stay for two nights. It would be good. They'd talk. Con could still say anything to Marlene. Friends envied her for Marlene. Marlene had never been predictable, and was not hard of hearing though she was old. She had remained grouchy but cheerful, while Con couldn't remember when she herself had last felt cheerful. "Turandot," Marlene wrote, "is about a Chinese princess who kills her would-be lovers!"

Thursday was the first day in a long time when Con felt clear about what she was doing, and as if she and her colleagues weren't working against one another. She received no more personal e-mails, and worked hard all day. At six thirty a familiar but unfamiliar shadow—not a visual shadow, a sense of the shape of a body, a laden body—became present behind her, and she turned, thinking it was one of the lawyers with whom she'd consulted intermittently all day. But it was Jerry, resting by dropping big nylon bags and stretching his long arms up and forward and out. Con stood. Jerry's arms were stretched wide. His way of being pleased with himself was to look down the length of his nose, or seem to; Con knew you couldn't look at your nose without being cross-eyed and Jerry did not look cross-eyed when he looked over his long nose and pursed his lips with pleasure, not exactly at seeing her, of course; at being seen. He was a little boy who knows everyone loves him, and divorce had not changed his mind. Exuberance makes any cluttered office look more purposeful and any floor less dusty, so Con, in her abruptly more attractive workplace, touched his outstretched arm though she didn't hug him. He leaned toward her and she stretched to kiss his cheek. "What are you doing here?" she said.

"Your colleague pointed the way," said Jerry. "I came by train." It had seemed simpler to meet her there than in Brooklyn. It didn't seem simple to Con, but never mind. She kept him waiting while she answered a few e-mails and came to a stopping place. She turned off her computer. "You come when you like, you come to my office. Anybody would think we were married." With some surprise, she heard affection in her voice.

"We sort of are," he said.

She put her arms into her coat. "We haven't been married for a long time, Jerry." Now she sounded appropriately severe.

"So what? Let's go out for dinner." He had behaved almost this way when she was married to Fred. He'd behaved like her brother.

"Joanna's at my apartment," she said.

"Oh, is that where she is?"

"She wants me to pursue this," Con said, "but I don't want to. Going to court over a young artist who got drunk in a bar."

"It doesn't sound to me as if she was drunk."

They took a taxi to Brooklyn because of Jerry's bags, which seemed immoderately large and full. He'd have to sleep on the sofa. The shape of the apartment was amorphous enough that she sometimes dreamed of rooms she'd overlooked, but there weren't any. She'd manage, but it would be crowded.

As they stood at the curb with his luggage while a cab slowed for them, he said, "Some of what's in here is yours. A package came for you."

"But I haven't lived there for so long." The bags went into the trunk of the cab and they got inside. "When did it come?"

"A week ago, maybe two. I didn't open it."

"I didn't order anything—and I certainly wouldn't have given *that* address," she said, wondering if she *had* somehow given that address.

"No, it's a priority mail bag addressed in handwriting."

"A present from somebody I haven't thought of in fifteen years?"

"I guess so."

Joanna and Jerry had both walked in on her unexpectedly. They'd done this before, she thought. It suggested power. Joanna took after her father—or imitated her father—in ways Con couldn't quite keep up with. Con herself always let everybody know exactly when she'd turn up, and phoned if she was late.

In the cab they talked first about the potential sale of the house in Philadelphia, then about Jerry's reason for coming. "It's a huge Brooklyn secret that everybody could know about—but nobody does!" he said. "Except me." He laughed and squeezed her shoulder, as if she too knew the secret.

"What was that name you mentioned? Marcus something?"

"Marcus Ogilvy. Wonderful character. Early-twentieth-century transportation genius. Crazy genius. I'll tell you." But instead of telling her, he grew silent for a moment, then said, "But shouldn't we do something about what happened to Joanna? Getting arrested for speaking her mind? And maybe for looking ethnic?" They had arrived, and Jerry paid. They eased his bags across the sidewalk and through the slightly crumbly but ornate doorway into her building. "We can't just let it go," he went on.

"What do you want me to do?"

"I didn't say I wanted *you* to do something," he said, holding the door for her. "I want *us* to do something."

"What us?"

"We're still an us. We'll always be an us. Also, I'm moving to New York. The house should sell quickly, and I'm moving here."

"That's nice," said Con.

"You don't sound pleased."

"I'm pleased," she said.

They got out of the elevator. "Joanna told me she hasn't had more than two beers at a time in the last three years."

"Hush," she said. "She's probably here." He set his bags near her desk, where Joanna had set hers the night before. But she motioned him to bring them into the living room, down the hall. As he put them down, Joanna came ambling out of her room, talking on her cell phone, raising a finger to show she'd be off in a minute. She gave a little ironic wave at her father. She was beautiful. Con knew that already, but sometimes when she saw Joanna for the first time after a few hours or days, she was struck as if newly by her daughter's sturdy, glowing body and face. Maybe the cops had been harsher because she was a beautiful woman of uncertain race. No wonder she'd become a sculptor; she must have been inspired by her own body. Her limbs were thick, tan, and rounded, her breasts firm and well-defined. Her head had volume. Joanna hung up and Con crossed the room and reached to take her daughter's wonderful head in her hands. But in another moment they were arguing. Joanna quickly determined that her father too believed they should pursue her case, and her rage at the police and the people in the bar rose and escalated until she was screaming at her mother. "They carried me off to jail. They locked me up. What does it take to make you care? What does it take?"

"Did they treat you badly?" said Jerry.

"No," said Joanna, quieting a little. She'd been in tears. "I will stipulate that they were polite, once I got there. I was given weak coffee. I was called Miss."

"But it was terrible anyway," Con said. "You know I care. I just don't—" She had e-mailed several people about Joanna's case already, but she'd equivocated, saying, "Given Guantánamo Bay this is trivial, but . . ." Maybe she'd dissuaded while persuading.

"Let's get something to eat," said Jerry.

They walked—almost a family—and it was cold. Joanna in a puffy parka was warmer and bigger and walked faster than her parents, and Con felt like a small scurrying animal, the urban kind with matted fur, hustling to keep up in a light wool fall jacket that wasn't warm enough. She hadn't yet worn her winter coat this season. Jerry was never cold, and he strode long-leggedly along the street as if he'd lived here all his life, his open raincoat swinging and puffing behind him. Jerry always wanted Chinese food if possible, and he started negotiating the order before they got there. He liked to share, and scrupulously consulted his fellow diners, but had strong ideas and usually prevailed. Joanna let go her grievances to think about shrimp or scallops. They hadn't decided when they got there, so they ordered winter melon soup while they studied the menu.

"Barnaby agrees with me," Joanna said then.

"Who's Barnaby?" said her father.

"You know," Joanna said.

"Oh, right, your sculptor."

Barnaby seemed to be back in favor. Con wanted wine but didn't want to order a glass lest Joanna feel encouraged to do the same, not that she'd drink too much while eating a quick Chinese dinner with her parents. Then Joanna ordered a glass of wine and Con did too. Jerry shook his head. He rarely drank; maybe he so enjoyed being exactly as he was that he didn't want even the mild alteration in mood and thinking brought on by a glass of Chardonnay.

"What does he agree with you about?" he asked Joanna.

"Did you go to his studio today?" said Con.

"I talked to him. He was horrified. I mean, we all know there's intense pro-war feeling, but who would have thought I'd spend the night in jail? That's what Barnaby said."

"What does an apprentice do?" asked Jerry.

"I'm not an apprentice. I wish I were. Then he'd have to teach me until I know everything he knows. It's a three-month internship."

"So you prepare material?" Jerry persisted.

Joanna sighed. "I haul things around. Sometimes I just clean. Sometimes it's wonderful and he shows me how to do things, holds my hand when I use the tool. Sometimes I go out for a sausage and pepper sandwich and bring it back to him. Then I pick up the pepper strips that fall on the floor."

The waiter came and they ordered a couple of main dishes. They'd decided on shrimp.

Joanna continued talking as the waiter moved away. "Barney's eye is wonderful. Sometimes he won't talk—but *sometimes* he thinks aloud, and my head tingles," she said. "A lot of it is knowing where to stand. Once I stand where he was standing, I see it just the way he did. I say 'How do you know where to stand?' and he says, 'I look at the window and then back to the piece.'"

"So it has to do with light?" Con said.

"I don't know," said Joanna. "You do it a lot and then you see. I notice how he moves, how slowly or quickly he moves. I can tell when he's thinking and when he makes up his mind."

"He lets you see that!" said Con.

"It's more intimate than sex," Joanna said, looking up at her with a flash of frank pleasure in being understood.

"So I guess I'll have you around the apartment for a while?" Con said. "I gather you're not going back to North Carolina in a hurry." She was glad.

"I shouldn't have said what I did to Tim," Joanna said. "I think I'd better stay away from him and from that bar. At least until I grow my hair down to my knees or shave it off. And have a nose job." She paused as the food was brought and took rice, then reached for the shrimp dish. "But no, I'll find someplace else if I stay in New York. Barnaby might have some room."

"Isn't he married?" said Con.

"People sometimes have an extra room." She waved down the waiter and asked for another glass of wine.

"That's not what I meant," said Con. This piece of the conversation was over, said Joanna's chopstick, describing a boundary in the air.

"When I bring everything from Philly," said Jerry, "there won't be much room."

"What?" said Joanna.

"*What* are you talking about?" said Con. "Room in the city of New York?"

Jerry looked startled, maybe embarrassed. "In whatever apartment I can get," he said. "I assume I can't afford a big one. So I may not have room for Joanna to stay with me. But if it's possible—come live with me!"

"I'm not sure you can afford *any* apartment in New York," said Joanna, "but don't worry, I'm not going to live with you."

"I've had enough of your opinionated remarks," Jerry said cheerfully. "I put the house on the market. The real estate agent thinks it will bring in quite a bit. I may be able to afford a palace."

Con thought Joanna was rude but probably right. "It gets harder every week," she said.

Jerry changed the subject. "So, is he leaving his wife for you?" he said to Joanna.

"I don't think that's an appropriate question," said Joanna. "He isn't always at home. He's got a couple of rooms in the back of the studio. His house is in the suburbs somewhere. I didn't mean I'm going *there*."

"That sounds awful," said Con, but Jerry was saying, "See? Barnaby has room. I'll move in with Barnaby!"

Con pressed "play" on her mother's answering machine and heard her own voice. She sounded confused, childish, and pathetically ignorant of what was coming. "I don't know how to stop the machine," she had said. Marlene had said, "I have to tell you something." When her voice said "she died," Con was physically shocked again, as if she hadn't known. She heard her own stunned, angry, helpless cries. In the background, Marlene was saying—tentatively at first, then more firmly—"It's for the best. She was going to have a terrible time. It's for the best. But think how it was for me, Connie. I woke up to it."

Finally, Con's muffled voice asked, "Are you sure?"

"Yes," said Marlene.

"Did you call 911? Are you really sure?"

"I called my doctor. He certified that she's dead. Don't worry, Connie, I knew enough not to call you first, if she could have been saved. But it's good that she wasn't. When people are brought back from something like that, they're never the same, and she was already—"

Now Con's voice was firmer. "Please tell me what happened."

"Oh. I guess I didn't. I woke up," said Marlene. "You know how I am. I wake up fast and I want to get going. She was on the foldaway bed in the living room. I got a neighbor to open it for me the day she came. I can't do it myself—I'm afraid of straining my back. We kept it open, so she could lie down. So I went right past her and into the kitchen. I started coffee and got out things for breakfast. She never got up first so I didn't think anything."

"Okay, then what?" said Con's voice. Again she sounded like a child.

"Then something made me go check on her," said Marlene. "I'll never know why. I touched her forehead and I knew."

"She didn't look different? You didn't know until you touched her?"

"She looked the same. The doctor said she had a heart attack in her sleep. You know her blood pressure wasn't good. A stroke would have been worse. Sometimes people can't talk. Or they're paralyzed. Or the confusion—it would have gotten worse and worse. But it's awful." Marlene paused. "I loved her."

That was when she began talking about the funeral home and the burial. Then she said, "I can't believe it's all over. Just last night—she was maybe a little better. We watched television. She wanted to watch *Dynasty* and *All in the Family*. Before that, after dinner, there was an interview with Yasir Arafat. I was surprised she remembered who he was." Soon after that, they'd hung up. Now Con listened to the recorded conversation once more, and didn't erase it. She took a shower. In the shower she decided that maybe Marlene was right. Her mother was old. She was losing her mind. It was better to have it over with all at once. When she got out of the shower, she leaned naked on a towel—her mother's towel—and wept with her face to the towel. How could this pink towel, frayed on both sides, have survived, while Gert—who no doubt had dragged it to the Laundromat in her shopping cart only a week ago—was dead? Con stood clutching the towel. Then she understood that the towel would have to be laundered again, and she was the one who would have to launder it, that the towel now belonged to her, or to her and Barbara—that she was responsible for everything in the apartment. For a second she felt a certain elation, as if there might be treasure. Then came dread of the work, the time it would take. Then she found herself planning to explain to her mother that there was no way she could do it quickly, that she'd have to keep the apartment for a few months and come for weekends when she could, to sort and clean, that her mother would just have to understand that. But her mother was dead. Con had to tell Barbara that their mother was dead. She called, but got no answer and didn't leave a message. She didn't want to deal with any more answering machines. It was intolerable not even to know until after the sixth ring whether she would have to deliver this news immediately or not. Again she was trapped in her mother's house, but in a different way.

She should call Jerry and Joanna. She postponed that.

By now it was noon on the first day Con had no mother. She had had nothing to eat. Deliberately, with an emphasis she recognized as Gert's—an effort to stay clear—she made herself a cup of coffee and some toast. She ate a little, and then called the motel. Joanna answered. She'd have to do to Joanna what Marlene had done to her. "Joanna, honey, I have to tell you bad news," she said.

"Something happened to Grandma?" said Joanna.

"How did you know?"

"I figured," said Joanna. "Is she dead?"

"Yes. She had a heart attack at Marlene's house." There was a long silence.

"Are you all right?" said Con.

"Did Marlene call you?"

Con told her the story. "Where's Dad?"

"He's coming," said Joanna. "We went out for breakfast. I went ahead to the room. I hate it here. What he's doing has nothing to do with history, it's just being in a motel. Do we have to go to Rochester for the funeral?"

Con didn't know what to do about a funeral. Her mother had not been religious. "No. We'll do something in Brooklyn," she said, improvising. Barbara would come. She would know what to do.

"I'll tell Dad," Joanna said. "That way you don't have to tell him."

It was the first moment of kindness since Marlene's announcement, and it made Con cry. She cried for a while and thought she heard Joanna crying too. Then she said good-bye and hung up and tried Barbara again. "I was going to call you," said her sister.

"I have to tell you something," said Con. After this call she could go to bed again.

After Barbara cried, the sisters told each other a few of the familiar truths about the deaths of mothers. Barbara said she'd come, and they'd figure out something to do. A Jewish funeral would be nice. "Or maybe a Jewish memorial service?" she said. "Have her cremated."

"I should have her cremated?"

"Yes, if she's cremated we can't have a real Jewish funeral, so that will take care of that. We'll make up something sort of Jewish, instead of having to do the real thing."

"I should call the funeral home and tell them to cremate her?"

"Can't you do that?" said Barbara.

"I don't know the name of it."

"Marlene knows."

"I don't want to call her," said Con, and she thought about the money Marlene had taken from her mother during the war.

Barbara said, "Should I call her?"

"From London? I'll call her."

Which meant there was more to do. She called Marlene, said she was having her mother cremated, and called the funeral home. Marlene approved of cremation, but the man at the funeral home was difficult, first about cremation and then about money. It was awkward, he said, because there was no contract. Mrs. Tepper had not made her wishes known. If she had come in and talked to them, they could have worked it all out. It would not have been necessary to pay all at once.

"She didn't plan to die in Rochester," said Con. She was sure her mother had not made an arrangement with a funeral home in Brooklyn either. "Do *you* have an arrangement with a funeral home? I don't."

"As a matter of fact I do, with this one, but it's simpler because I work here," said the man. "I do understand. Now—" Con would have to get a death certificate. She would have to . . . Suddenly she was responsible for money again, and still didn't have a credit card, and still wasn't home. At that point she began to sob and apparently that was what was required. The man said he'd get the death certificate himself and cremate Mrs. Tepper and wait for his money.

At last Con went to bed in her clothes, and lay under the covers, looking up at different light—afternoon light—as it came through the window, partly obstructed by a building. After a while, she might get up and have soup. Her mother had laid in so much canned soup that Con suddenly realized soup was her legacy. She could stay here, rising only to eat canned soup, for weeks and months. Or maybe she shouldn't touch it until her mother's will was probated, and this idea struck her as so funny she laughed, which enabled her to cry a little more.

It was Friday, but her mother was not coming on Saturday. What would she do with the chicken? And what would she do with the cat? Did she have to live here?

The phone rang again and it didn't occur to Con to let it ring. She picked up the receiver. "This is Mabel," said the voice on the line. "Is this Constance or her mother?"

"This is Constance. My mother—well, this is Constance."

There was a pause. "What is it?" said Con.

"You told me to call you today."

Con tried to remember and then she did. To keep the house from being closed down, she'd have to file an appeal by Monday.

"Is there something I should do with that paper?" said Mabel. "Should I call somebody?"

"I should do it," Con said. She was interested to see that the part of herself that could have this conversation was still present. If Joanna had died, she found herself thinking, she couldn't have spoken like this.

Again Mabel was silent. Con didn't know how she could file this appeal from Brooklyn. She didn't want to involve Sarah, who already thought she was incompetent. Then she found herself explaining to Mabel how very small the chance was that an appeal could work, and she understood that she didn't want to involve Sarah because she didn't agree with Sarah. Mabel was all right, but she wouldn't know how to make this house and these women seem more presentable.

"But we're doing so well," Mabel said. Her voice was hushed, and Con could tell that this was the first moment that she believed the house might actually be shut down.

"Even now, it's hard," Con said. "It will get harder."

"You mean I should give up?" said Mabel. "I thought you'd talk me out of giving up."

"Do you want to give up?" Con said, conscious that she was doing something wrong, but unable to stop.

"Sort of," said Mabel. "My boyfriend thinks I should give up. He always thought this was a little crazy. He wants us to move to California and do something different."

"Do you want to think about it?" Con said. She knew she'd persuaded Mabel—or she'd let Mabel see what was realistic. Maybe it wasn't so wrong. "We can negotiate and get you a few weeks, I'm sure," Con said, and she thought to herself that a few weeks would not help the women who lived in the house. They would not make it. Some of them wouldn't make it even with the house, but without it, they'd all be back on the streets, or back in jail, quite soon. She knew this. But maybe there was nothing she could do about it. She'd ask Sarah to take over and negotiate a little time for the house to be closed and the women to look for other places to live. Maybe Sarah could get a few months, not just a few weeks. That would keep Sarah busy and it might even make her happy. Con considered how easy it would be to let that deadline go. In a week or so, she'd tell Sarah about her mother, and could imply that she didn't know about the deadline until it was too late. That was almost true. She and Mabel talked for a while longer, but Con sensed that a decision had been made. After a while she realized she had not heard anything Mabel had said for a while. But she felt better. Maybe she'd quit this job and never try anything hard again. When she was tired of lying in her mother's bed, she'd get a stupid and simple job, working with objects that would stay where she put them. They hung up and Con slept.

When she awoke it was dark. She couldn't remember what day or time it was, but she was hungry. Should she finally cook the meat sauce? She didn't want canned soup after all. As she lay where she was, she saw her life stretched before her. You eat a specific number of meals, and then you eat your last meal, and then you die. After supper, she'd be that much closer to death; you always moved closer, never further away. She didn't want to think that this darkness would give way to light, because another piece of her life would be gone—this life that didn't feel particularly terrific right now but was better than death. At times all her life, Con had known how it felt to be her mother, known from inside, because their bones had the same shape. Now she almost knew what it was to die.

Con wished she knew what Gert had eaten for supper the

night before, but didn't think she'd ask Marlene. Had there been dessert? Probably not; Marlene was thin, weight-conscious. If Gert had a visitor for a week, she'd put in a supply of desserts, but Marlene didn't think that way. They'd watched, of all things, an interview with Yasir Arafat, and Con tried to decide what her mother might have thought about that. She pictured her looking at the TV, silent, trying to remember who he was.

Con's mother had brushed her teeth, put on her nightgown. Gert's innocence, as she did these things, assuming she'd do them again, was heartbreaking. Often, Gert had thought others were foolish, and Con hated to think of her mother made a fool by death, going about her business as if it weren't waiting for her, just as Con had foolishly gone abut her business, that first night, as if the back door weren't unlocked.

If Gert had lived, she might have become too confused to derive satisfaction from life, but that time had not come, and Marlene was wrong if she thought it had. Of course, Marlene had not claimed that Gert had died at the best possible moment, only that this was better than years of suffering. And maybe that was so.

Again, Con couldn't seem to get herself out of bed. It got later and later and she grew more and more hungry. Finally, she got as far as the table and sat there for a while, but it was stupidly dark. She stood and put on lights. Then she went into the kitchen and cooked meat sauce. She filled a pot with water and cooked spaghetti. While it cooked she poured some sherry. All week, she'd been careful not to drink too much of it. Her mother, who hardly drank at all, wouldn't have begrudged Con the sherry, but she might have thought Con was an alcoholic if the level of the bottle had gone down noticeably. Con was pretty sure her mother would never drink alone, and had kept the sherry for company. Now there was no reason not to drink it up. Con drank and ate.

There was also no reason to be here. Or she now owned Sandy the cat and must stay forever. Again, she had forgotten to feed him. He emerged from hiding when she opened a can of food. After he ate, she held him for a while.

She hadn't been outside all day and now it was evening. She didn't know what had happened in the world. She turned on the news. There were photographs of demonstrations in China. Thousands of people marched, and thousands more filled the main square in Beijing. The next story, once again, was about the oil spill in Alaska. Investigators were still trying to figure out why the *Exxon Valdez* ran aground. Con imagined discussing this news with her mother. How frustrated Con would have been, explaining over and over what the *Exxon Valdez* was and why it mattered, what was happening in China. Her mother, she decided, would have understood the news from China. She'd have liked this news—the faraway place, the excited, hopeful crowds.

Chapter 4

◇◇◇◇◇◇◇◇◇◇◇◇◇◇◇

Waiting for the check and fortune cookies with her daughter and former husband, Con studied Jerry. His light brown skin looked young, and his eyes had the same ironic alertness that had attracted her the first time she saw him, the same delight in the great adventure of being Jerry Elias that had charmed and infuriated her, by turns, when they were married. Jerry thought almost everything was just slightly funny, and rejoiced in doing so. The check arrived and he reached for it. Jerry liked nice things, and she saw that he had a new leather wallet.

"Did someone buy you that?" she said. She hadn't heard about a girlfriend for years.

"The last time I went to see him," Joanna said, "his wallet was worn out. I saw this in a store and I sent it."

Con was jealous when Jerry and Joanna spent time together. The wallet was sleek and smooth, minimal. Con would have chosen something chunky and folksy, and Jerry wouldn't have liked it as much.

Orange sections had come with the cookies and Joanna ate them. Only Con took her cookie. She read the fortune aloud—"You will receive a surprise"—and looked at her ex-husband and daughter. "Sorry," said Joanna. "I bought only one wallet."

The walk home was quiet. Jerry carried the bag of leftovers. Fed, they were warmer and Joanna was kinder. After a block or two she dropped behind and soon they heard the rise and fall of her voice—intimate and exasperated—on her cell phone.

"How does she afford that thing?" Con said.

"I help," Jerry said. "I'm doing all right. People expect to pay a consultant pretty well."

Their daughter caught up. "Could I have the leftovers?" she said.

"You're hungry?" said Jerry.

"No—Barney hasn't eaten." She took the bag from her father and waved down a taxi a few minutes later. "I'll stay over," she said, and raised a friendly hand to her parents as she got in.

"At least she's not in jail," Con said after a silence, as they walked.

"And they dropped the charges," Jerry said. "Still . . ." It was late; the streets had a late feel, with a few dogs out for a bedtime walk. Their owners waited impatiently, then stooped with a plastic bag or glanced around and kept walking. Jerry seemed to study a big shapeless black-and-white dog as it loped behind its owner, stopping to sniff. "Who do you think we should talk to?" he said.

"I wish she hadn't been drunk," Con said again.

"Con, I don't think she was drunk. You can relax on that topic."

"She was in a bar. She was drinking. She has a history of drinking."

"She says she wasn't drunk."

Con sighed. The dog and owner had gone around a corner. "Why am I the one who has to deal with this? Joanna's an adult."

"Aren't you pleased that she's turned to you?" Jerry said. "And you're a lawyer. But it's a damn good case, and it would bring attention to the problem. Maybe wake up a few people who can't seem to realize how different things are."

"Are things that different?" said Con.

"Since Bush came in?"

"There have always been bad guys. During the Vietnam War I couldn't stand to read the paper."

They were silent for the last half block, their footsteps sounding on the sidewalk. Footsteps sounded different in winter. Then Jerry said, "It's different. Blacks have an early-warning system."

"And you think Jews don't?" said Con. Whenever they remembered they were a black and a Jew (sometimes they remembered they were two Jews) they'd either quarrel amiably or become silent together; one way or another, they were getting along. At such moments it seemed they had not been changed by divorce. Con's two-year marriage to Fred seemed dreamlike. She remembered only details: they'd had an apartment with red linoleum on the kitchen counters. Fred, a bald man, had sung as he walked about the house. He sang well, but his songs were unconvincingly cheerful. He'd left her, but he'd said, "I'm doing this so you don't have to work up to it," and she had known—after a few days—that she'd been working up to it. Con had been his first wife. "What did he know?" she and Peggy had said.

In Con's apartment, they crowded into her little living room because Jerry wanted to look at the news. The Pentagon had announced that a covert force was hunting Saddam Hussein. Bush had requested that Iran, Syria, Egypt, and Saudi Arabia make an effort to establish democratic institutions. "Do you mind if I turn this off?" Con said. She was half-sitting on the arm of the big gray chair. "I can't stand it."

"I'm tired," Jerry said, and his left arm stretched in her direction even as his right was fumbling for the remote. "Con," he said. She moved close to him and tucked her head against his chest, so she felt his body's sounds through her scalp. Then she put her arms around him for a moment because that still felt natural. She stepped back and pointed out the sofa where he'd sleep. When he'd visited before, he'd stayed in the room Joanna was using. Planning where she'd put Marlene—in that same room; Joanna would sleep on an inflatable mattress in Con's study—she went to the linen closet in the hall and returned with sheets and towels, which she handed to Jerry. Then she said good night, stopped in her study to check her e-mail, and went into her bedroom.

At ten o'clock at night on the day Con's mother died, the doorbell rang. Wondering ruefully if the burglar had come back at last, Con put the chain on the door before she opened it. There was Peggy, in a bathrobe.

"I'm not going to make a habit of this," she said. "I mean, I know you're leaving in a day or two, but I won't call you at home with my pathetic little life. Though I hope we'll be friends."

"Yes," said Con. She opened the door.

"My boyfriend's mad at me," Peggy said. "I need a sensible woman to tell me whether I should apologize or be mad back. But if I'm intruding, tell me."

"My mother died," said Con.

"*What?*" said Peggy. "She had a heart attack?"

"I guess so."

Peggy stepped forward and put her arms in their quilted sleeves around Con, who had not been touched since she'd had the news. She sobbed in Peggy's arms and felt faint. "I have to sit down," she said. "I didn't know I was going to do that."

"Tell me," said Peggy.

Half an hour later they returned to the topic of the angry boyfriend. Con said he had no right to be mad. She pretended she was more sure than she felt. She wanted to keep Peggy. They finished the sherry and parted with hugs at midnight. She was not asleep when the phone rang. It was Jerry. "I didn't know what to say," he said. She hadn't minded his silence. She was shocked that she hadn't minded. Hours had passed since Joanna had told him about Gert. They'd gone out exploring and returned. "Do you want me to come?" he said.

"No," she said. "Let's talk tomorrow. I'm so tired."

Jerry was standing in the hallway when Con, still dressed, came out of the bathroom, and as she turned toward her bedroom he came toward her. He'd put on the long T-shirt he slept in. Again he took her in his arms, and she remembered his odd remark about his possessions taking up room. He smelled like her youth. She started to step back when she felt his penis stir, but he took her hand. "Con—do you think?"

It had been so long (five or six years; she'd cheated once with Jerry in the waning months of Fred) that he was someone new—but not new. She knew the ways in which he was a jerk, but just then she didn't care. And she knew the ways in which he wasn't a jerk. She leaned into his embrace, and they went together into her bedroom. She hadn't slept with anyone in a long time, and she was postmenopausal; she rummaged in a drawer for lubricant.

Sex with Jerry was athletic, funny, companionable; it was not especially personal, so it wasn't sentimental—and therefore it wasn't sad. She sometimes forgot that sex with another person was more satisfying than masturbation, which provided Con with frequent, sharply pleasurable interludes, but did not lift her spirits. Sex with someone else made her charitable. Jerry's egotism was not annoying after sex—it was sweet, like a child's. He stayed inside her for a long time. Then he withdrew, sleepily kissed her under one eye, and slept. He took up room in her bed. She tried to establish a hollow for her bottom, shoving slowly against his back. He didn't move. At last she stood up, took her robe, and wandered down the hall to her little living room. They had never turned off the lights, and the sheets she'd given Jerry were still folded on the sofa. She sat for a while. Jerry's bags—a gray nylon duffel bag and a soft-sided black suitcase—were in the middle of the rug. He'd unzipped the black one, apparently just for his T-shirt and toothbrush. Con got up just enough to pull the duffel bag closer, so she could rest her legs on it. A hassock would be a nice thing to have.

Then she remembered that Jerry had mentioned a package addressed to her. He wouldn't mind if she opened the bags. He had no secrets. She reached down, unzipped the gray duffel bag, and reached inside. Amid socks and shaving equipment was a wrinkled Priority Mail bag. She pulled it out. It was stuffed full. When her hands took in its weight and shape, she recognized it without being able to say what it was. It was soft, but not like a pillow. As Jerry had said, it was addressed to her at the Philadelphia house in handwriting, with no return address. She ripped open the flap, her hands trembling, and drew out a black nylon purse, shaped like a briefcase but smaller, with "Le Sac" embroidered on its trim. A piece of white paper came out as well. "Found this—hope it reaches you. Pete."

Con's hands trembled. She held the bag. The person who had mailed it—Pete, whoever Pete might be—had wiped dust off it. It was streaked, but not grimy. She continued to sit, holding the bag but not opening it, for a long time. When she went to the bathroom she carried the bag—lightly, as if it might be dangerous to touch—and placed it on the edge of the bathtub while she sat on the toilet, then brought it back to the table. Then she filled the kettle and stood warming her hands near it until it boiled, then made herself a cup of Lemon Zinger with sugar in it. She still couldn't bring herself to touch her old purse.

The apartment was cold at night. Con wanted her pajamas under her robe, and finally left the bag so as to walk carefully into the bedroom and get them without waking Jerry. She decided that if he woke up, she wouldn't tell him what she'd received. But he didn't. In the kitchen, the bag was still on the table. She was relieved, as if leaving the room had been taking a risk. She took off her bathrobe quickly—eyeing the bag—put on the pajamas, put the robe on again over them, and tied the belt tightly. Then she drank some tea. Then, at last, she opened the bag.

As I've said, this is not a story about memory, and in November, 2003, Con hadn't been thinking about the week in 1989 that I've chronicled. If anything this is a story about forgetting. Con had forgotten that week as much as it is possible to do so. I don't blame her. Fourteen and a half years had passed. If we're accustomed to reading novels, we're used to stories told by someone who remembers, much later, the order of events, who said what, and how each person moved and gestured. Of course we all have detailed, possibly accurate memories of striking scenes from the past—but not of what happened an hour later, or the next morning. In real life, aside from vivid flashes, we usually can't remember the exact words of a conversation we had minutes ago. We remember, a week or a year later, that someone's story made us uncomfortable, but not necessarily why, or what the story was about. So, Con had forgotten a great deal, but any of us might have done the same. Maybe not quite the same; Con had tried to forget.

During the week in 2003, the earlier week had come to her mind only once, when Peggy talked about how they'd met. And even then, Con got it wrong. Marlene's coming visit might have reminded her of that week, but Marlene had visited several times since Con had moved to New York, and Con had had a lifetime of contacts and associations with Marlene. In the first week of November, 2003, Con was not thinking about her mother's death or, indeed (except when Peggy talked about her), her mother. She carefully and habitually did not think about her mother.

But some things are unforgettable, and she knew, of course, when she had lost the bag: the night she arrived in her mother's apartment, at the beginning of the week in which her mother died. Something in the bag was hard, with corners. She pulled out the hard object first, and it was a wooden box on top of which was a copper plate engraved with a map of France. A girl in wooden shoes stood at the side, pointing at the map. Con gasped, because she had known it all her life. It had belonged to her mother. It had her mother's jewelry in it. It was locked. When she was young, her mother used to let her take the key, open it, play with the contents, and lock it up again.

Now she put it aside and drew the remaining contents of the bag out, one thing at a time, handling the objects carefully as though they might crumble on contact with the air. On the table, she lined up objects that looked familiar but were also new. In the bag were a red nylon wallet with bent edges. Inside were no bills but some change. There was a small orange plastic hairbrush with reddish hair on it, brighter than her present hair, and a five-by-eight-inch notebook with a green cover and spiral binding. The notebook had been old when she lost it, and the point of the spiral binding had worked loose. When she picked it up, the tip grazed the side of her hand in a way that felt familiar. There was a copy of the Sunday *New York Times Magazine* of April 16, 1989, opened to the crossword puzzle, which was partly completed. A pale blue plastic tube that contained two tampons, something she no longer needed. Keys on a big ring with a big brass ornamental key on it. An unreserved Amtrak ticket to Philadelphia and a Northeast Corridor schedule that had expired in October, 1989. A checkbook in which the checks said "Constance Tepper and Jerome Elias."

In the wallet's zipper pocket were two quarters and a handful of pennies. The plastic slides had in them a Visa card, an ATM card, a driver's license with a startled young face and her address in Philadelphia, a photograph of Joanna looking plump and impatient, a photograph of Barbara waving from the steps of a red London bus—and then she remembered taking it, and how the bus took off with Barbara and without her, and how she'd chased it, laughing. A photograph of Jerry, looking like a boy.

A red address book. For months, back then, she hadn't had people's addresses or phone numbers. After her mother died she had spent a few days each week in the apartment, trying to deal with everything. Barbara had been little help, but she had put together a memorial service and had somehow found relatives to attend it. They'd had a fight about something of her mother's, which Barbara, in the end, had taken. Con had wept as if it were her mother that Barbara wanted and had managed to secure, but now she couldn't remember what the object had been, or whether she'd taken it when Barbara died, whether she'd even thought of it.

A bottle of aspirin, 325 milligrams each. Now her headaches often didn't subside even if she took extra-strength aspirin. A lipstick. She looked at the keys again. One was the key to her mother's apartment, one to their car. Now she didn't have a car, and Jerry had a different one. She didn't recognize some of the keys, though they all looked familiar, looked as if her fingers might have identified each one in the dark.

Jerry stood in the doorway. "What are you doing?"

"You forgot to give me my package."

"What was it?"

She stared at him. He was naked, his forearms long and tapered, like a young man's, his legs thicker—middle-aged—but held lightly, as if he might spring away. He'd grown hairier—on his arms, his shoulders—as he grew older. His belly was still almost flat. He worked out at a gym. His hands had always looked too wide for the rest of him, and they still did; he had the hands of a wide, squat, muscle-bound man, but he was a long, narrow man. He had a way of turning his palms so he looked as if he wore something on his hands; they were small mitts. His hair was graying but still mostly dark; it had the texture of a black man's hair.

"It's my purse," she said.

"What purse?"

"It was stolen. Years and years ago. The week my mother died. From her apartment."

"Are you *kidding* me?" said Jerry. "Is the money in it?"

"Just some coins," she said, "but lots of other things." Then she said, "Aren't you cold?"

"Not particularly."

She found herself standing, anyway, as if to warm him with her body. She took him in her arms and wept a little.

"What is it?"

"I don't know. It's beautiful, but sad, somehow. Look." She showed him the keys, the wallet.

"Come to bed," he said.

"I don't know what to do about Joanna."

"It's the middle of the night. Don't you have to go to work in the morning?"

So she followed him back to bed and pulled herself next to him, leaving what she'd found on the table. She wouldn't let him sleep in her bed when anyone else was in the apartment. She slept, then awoke once more and went to look at the bag. She couldn't thank Pete, who'd found it and mailed it, who'd spent several dollars on postage, mailing what he'd found to someone who might be dead or might never receive it. She couldn't let him know it had reached her. She was sure Pete wasn't the burglar. Someone who didn't bother to take the coins from the wallet would not bother to return the bag, even if he'd had a change of heart.

She looked at the old crossword puzzle. She'd filled in half the blanks. She remembered that she used to work crossword puzzles, but she didn't remember doing one before her bag was stolen. It was called "Name Game." For one across the clue was "salami purveyor" and she'd written "deli" in ink. Five across was "provoked." She had not written anything there. She didn't let herself find a pen and finish it. Jerry was right. It was the middle of the night. But before she returned to bed, she turned some of the pages, starting at the back of the magazine. The recipes were for shrimp and vegetables with champagne, salmon fillets braised in red wine, asparagus and mushrooms with fresh coriander. Fancy food. Con strained to remember reading the food page—probably on the train from Philadelphia. She couldn't. In the Style section an article said, "Now, at the end of the 1980s it is the height of high style to wear almost everything a man does, in versions scaled to a woman's physique." The sentence seemed innocent—old-fashioned and simple-minded. She couldn't imagine a time—only fourteen and a half years earlier—when this sentence might have seemed like something to write and read. She left the magazine and returned to bed. She didn't know she slept, but she must have, because what awoke her next was not a nightmare—it had no story—but perhaps the residue of a nightmare. Con felt herself falling, falling into emptiness that was featureless and unending. In a moment, if she didn't stop herself, she would be no one, not there, not anywhere. Nothing held her, nothing kept her from falling into featureless space or timeless time except the thought of Joanna, and she screamed and in her mind reached to hold onto someone. She reached for Jerry and held his arm, and when she sensed that she'd touched someone, she clung harder.

"Con, wake up, it's all right."

She had thought she was awake. She *was* awake, but it didn't help, because she still felt that letting go of this human arm might release her to fall over an edge, into a cessation of everything. She held Jerry's arm and he turned and surrounded her with his body, and soothed her like a baby. Any decent human being would have been enough to keep her from falling, but what if nobody had been in her bed? Usually, nobody was. Usually she was alone in the apartment. She sobbed with her whole body.

In the morning she slept through the alarm clock. "Con?" Jerry said, finally. He was standing in the doorway.

"I'm staying home," she said and slept again. When she awoke, sunshine told her that hours had passed. She heard the shower. She went into the kitchen. Jerry had moved the objects from the bag closer together, so as to make room for a cereal bowl and a coffee mug (which sat near them, with a little milk in the bottom of the bowl, and some coffee in the mug), but he had kept Con's things in the same relation to one another: the bottom left corner of the green notebook, with the twisted spiral of metal, rested just below and to the right of the wallet, and so on. The wooden box was off to the side. She tried to open it again. She'd have to pick the lock. It was a simple lock and probably she could open the box without trouble, but she wanted to wait and be careful, so as not to mar the wood.

She phoned the office and said she was sick. It was almost true. Her head felt wrong. She would not finish the task she'd set this week; it would have to wait. She poured herself a cup of coffee, took the notebook, and went back to bed. When Jerry emerged from the bathroom, wrapped in a towel—he still hadn't unpacked, and indeed there was no place to store his clothes—she said, "I'm looking at something" and waved him away. He padded into the living room and didn't come back.

The first page of the notebook was dated March 3, 1987. She'd been carrying it around for two years when it was stolen. Now she didn't carry notebooks like that.

"Jo to doctor 4/6 4:00" was written on the first page. Under it she'd skipped a few spaces and had written "Office meeting Wed. 3" Then came a list of jobs she'd planned to do, maybe over a weekend: laundry, buy shoes Jo, call mother.

She turned the pages. Nothing was funny. She'd been an earnest, hardworking mother. After a bit came notes from the visit to the doctor. Joanna's height was five feet, four inches: she'd already been taller than her mother. Under that was "Plaintiff's lawyer—Bernstein" and a phone number. She'd been so sure, at the time, that she'd know which plaintiff was meant that she had not written it down. And then she suddenly remembered Bernstein. She'd liked him. They'd settled that case.

Con read reminders of errands, notes about work. Sometimes she had copied a few sentences from a newspaper article or a book. Sometimes she argued with herself on paper. "If due process violation, then—" she'd written. Then nothing, but two pages along came the working out of the argument. "It's a due process violation," she'd written. "Plaintiff should have offered notice and a hearing. As in Hendrix. But Hendrix had to do with firing. But still."

Next came a few pages of what looked like a letter, but then she realized it was a journal. She had rarely kept journals or diaries, only when she was upset. "Another day, no phone call," the diary began. Maybe Jerry had been on a trip. But he never called from his trips.

She'd gone on, "She wouldn't give up on me, never has in all these years, yet always the sense that it's because she knows I'll never do such-and-such, never say such-and-such. But I don't know what such-and-such is, so I might have finally said or done it. Last time—more disdain? When M. bragged about the ribbon?"

Could she have meant Marlene? Or was M "mother" and "she" was Marlene? Surely Con had never felt that embarrassing sort of need for Marlene.

There were more names and phone numbers, plans for work, shopping lists, lists of people to phone: her mother; Barbara. A flurry of facts, names, and numbers, in the last used pages. Addresses. Directions. This must have had to do with the case she'd been working on when the bag was stolen, the last case she'd worked on for that job. Everything had ended at once: her marriage, her job, her life as a daughter. This notebook.

The next-to-the-last entry said "Mountain View Motel" with a phone number. The last was a note to herself in blue ink, followed by another one, in black. The first said, "Mabel Turner and her gang not terrific clients. Possible to dump them? Find different but comparable client? Ethical to dump them?" Then came a space. The second note was in larger handwriting, as if Con had been excited. "NO," she'd written. "NO. Nobody's consistently terrific. Nobody's terrific. The point is how we describe them. Orange stripe on white can be honestly described as white stripe on orange." She stared at the sentence. It seemed like something she had always known—something everybody had always known—but also something she still didn't know: that there was more than one truth, more than one way of telling the truth.

Her mother had had a striped tablecloth, and that was what

Barbara had taken. Losing her mother had made loss the theme of Con's days; losing Barbara was only part of the life of loss. She looked back over fifteen years and saw nothing but loss, nothing but sorrow. As with the stripe on the tablecloth, this was one way to see it. She took a shower and washed her thinning, graying hair, feeling kind toward it for once.

When Con awoke in her mother's bed on Saturday morning, she thought the problem was that she'd lost the cat. Then she remembered. She'd forgotten to offer the cat to Peggy the night before. But why would Peggy want him? For a long time Con couldn't bring herself to get out of bed. For once, the phone did not ring. She made up her mind to go running. Then she'd figure out how to go home. She still didn't have keys to her house, and Jerry and Joanna were still away from home. Now it seemed cumbersome to imagine the burglar going to Philadelphia and finding his way to University City so as to hurt Joanna. Now she knew he just wouldn't have the energy, as she herself, the day after her mother died, did not have the energy to get out of bed.

She wanted things. She'd known the dark red glass ashtray all her life. Now she knew that Marlene had taken it from a hotel—cheating on one alarming lover with another—and given it to her mother. Barbara must not have it; Con must have it. What if Marlene had lied, and her mother came home from Rochester to find Con packing her belongings or giving things away? Maybe her mother was fine and Marlene was demented.

Con put on her sweatpants and running shoes and took her mother's new key, which she first stuck into her sock—where its sharp edges nicked her skin—and then into the pocket of her T-shirt. She remembered the man at the funeral home, someone besides Marlene who believed that Gert was dead. She made her way down to the street. The fresh new morning was kind; she stretched against an iron railing and took off slowly. A man passing said, "Way to go, girl." But she was soon breathless. She gave up and walked. Now she wanted to be back in the apartment, where she could cry.

On her way to the shower, she considered her mother's enormous collection of towels. Her mother had acquired objects with abandon; apparently she thought she'd never die. Instead of taking a shower, Con moved piles of towels to the sofa, then began taking clothes from the closet and laying them on the bed. She found dresses her mother had made years ago. How could Con dispose of them? She had never properly appreciated her mother.

When she was finally bathed and dressed, she called Marlene. "It's hard," Con said, when Marlene said hello in her ordinary voice.

"Oh, Connie, my old friend," said Marlene, and at that Con began to cry loudly and openly. She had no tissue, and walked with the phone—it was the kitchen phone—as far as she could, looking for one.

"It's for the best," Marlene said again.

"No, it isn't!" Marlene never talked like that. She never made the remarks people habitually make to keep from noticing how bad they feel.

"She was terrified," said Marlene. "She'd say something that didn't make sense, and then she'd point out what she'd said."

"There are medicines."

"Which *might* slow it down."

"It still isn't better that she's dead." Con remembered something her mother used to do. When a decision had been reached, she'd pat the furniture—a table, the top of a bookcase. A little tap, as if to say, "So."

"Nobody can pick the best moment to die," said Marlene. "The moment when you start enjoying life only forty-nine percent of the time."

"I don't think I enjoy life forty-nine percent of the time," said Con, "and I'm not ready to die."

"Her last act was traveling, visiting a friend," said Marlene. "Would you want her last act to be having her diaper changed?"

"Was it a good visit?" said Con. "Was any of it good?"

"Connie, don't idealize your mother. I loved her, you loved her, but at best she was a little boring, and now that her mind was going—well, forgive me, honey, but it was excruciating. You'd have felt the same way."

This could be true. Maybe she was as bad as Marlene. Con couldn't bear this conversation, so she thought about the percentage of time she was happy. She decided it wasn't a matter of percentages. Working, she was often unhappy, but the happiness of accomplishment was intense. She said, "I know you're right, but I can't feel it."

"It would have been selfish to keep her alive—if we could have," said Marlene.

"No," said Con. "If I could have decided, I'd have kept her alive for her own sake, not mine."

"I've always loved the way you think," said Marlene. Then, "Have you found her will?"

"I haven't thought much about it," said Con. "I have to figure out what to do with this apartment. I have to get home. My job—"

"Well, I have a copy," said Marlene. "I'm her executor."

"What?" said Con. She should have thought about her mother's will a long time ago. "How did *that* happen?"

"She asked me to help," Marlene said. "A couple of years ago—I was visiting, and she brought it up. She had a will, but it was way out of date. There are things you have to do—otherwise, the taxes—well, you know. So I took her to an old lawyer friend in New York. Don't worry, you and Barbara get all her money. What there is."

"But I didn't even know!"

"She didn't want to bother you. You were busy."

Con was too dispirited to protest—and what good would that do now? At least she didn't have to deal with it. Off the phone, she determined that she should stop looking at old clothes and pay more attention to financial records and documents, but she didn't. As the hours passed she was surrounded by larger and larger piles of her mother's possessions. Barbara was coming—she didn't know when. She had to hide anything she wanted from Barbara. She put the red glass ashtray into her suitcase. It was huge. She loved knowing Marlene had stolen it. Sometimes crime is interesting, not so terrible. Nothing she wanted was mixed in with her mother's dresses. Her mother had a desk in the bedroom. Con should look at the contents of the desk. She should find her mother's will.

The desk did not contain the will, but it contained canceled checks going back many years. Con found a used envelope, full of birthday and Mother's Day cards from Barbara and herself, and a few handmade cards from Joanna. She threw out all but the handmade ones, and put the canceled checks into the envelope with them. Then she found a pen and wrote "CANCELED CHECKS." She left the envelope on the dresser so as to pack it later.

She continued taking things apart, and found something else of interest. Her mother had written letters on unlined pads of paper in pastel colors. Several pads were in the second drawer. It seemed Gert wrote drafts of her letters and kept them—at least in recent years. Con found none from the war years. Maybe she hadn't written drafts in those more spontaneous days, when even Gert had been young and knew what she thought. Con took the pads, and with only a moment's hesitation sat on the sofa to read them, pulling her legs up under her.

Gert wrote conventional letters to a few relatives, who'd have to be notified now. Con looked around for her notebook so as to make a list, forgetting for a moment that it was gone. She postponed this task. Gert had placidly delivered her own meager news and news of Con and Barbara, always given a positive tilt. Sentences reappeared year after year: "Barbara enjoys living in England."

The only letters worth reading were those to Marlene, but reading them wasn't pleasant. The blandness disappeared, and

Gert complained about Con and Barbara. Now she wrote drafts not to polish polite sentences but to calm herself down. In one letter the sentence "Connie despises me" had been crossed out. Then she'd written, "I keep thinking that Connie despises me" and she'd crossed that out too. The sentence that remained was "I know Connie doesn't despise me but sometimes she talks as if she does. She must be having trouble with Jerry. He isn't an easy man to live with." Con didn't bring Joanna often enough, though "Joanna is crazy about her grandmother, I'm happy to say." Gert's complaints about Barbara were more familiar, because Gert had complained about Barbara to Con more than once (and, presumably, about Con to Barbara). But she'd let herself be more honest in her letters to Marlene, and her disapproval of Barbara was unqualified. Marlene had apparently argued with Gert about her daughters. "Maybe you are right about Connie," Gert wrote once, without further explanation. Parts of the letters were less interesting, and at times Con found something unintelligible—answers to questions Marlene had presumably asked. Several times Gert wrote, "It hasn't come yet" and once she said, "Could you explain better about that money? I don't understand." Could she have meant the tax money that would be saved if Marlene had the will redone? That was possible.

If Marlene had written about her, Con wasn't sure she wanted to find those letters, but she put the drafts in her lap aside, and began searching again. She wished she had thought to talk to her mother about her will, about taxes and the estate. Or that her mother had asked her. It made her squirm that Marlene had done it when she had not. Marlene had always advised Gert about money: it would have seemed natural to Gert to put her in charge of the will.

Each time Con had looked through her mother's possessions, she'd skipped the second drawer in one of the dressers against the wall. It was stuck. Turning from her mother's stationery pads, she pulled out the drawer under it, and was able to reach in and remove something that had worked its way partway over the back of the drawer. It was a single letter in a thick envelope addressed to her mother: old, creased, and stained. She recognized the return address, on Albemarle Road. Her mother used to speak of a time "when Marlene lived on Albemarle Road."

Other than this envelope, the drawer contained only baby clothes her mother had made, knitted hats and sweaters. She took the letter and returned to the sofa, where her mother's drafts were still spread out. The letter was typed. Of course she read it immediately. By now there was no stopping.

Albemarle Road
Brooklyn
March 3, 1949

Dear Gert,

You are probably wondering why I'm writing you a letter when I could pick up the phone. Or you are wondering why I am writing you a letter when you may have thought I would never have anything to do with you again. Or Abe has not told you a thing and you are won-

dering what I am talking about. Or maybe you are wondering how the corner of the ashtray broke. I am talking
about the ashtray Lou and I took from the Plaza during
the war. I promised I'd give it to you, and then I did give
it to you, although by then it didn't matter so much who
saw it, with everything that happened.

Now, who knows, with what your husband has
done, a whole lot more may be about to happen. Maybe
he didn't tell you what he's done. I better start at the
beginning. This was last Saturday when you were in
New Jersey for your uncle's funeral. I was sorry to hear
about that. I know you hadn't seen him or your aunt in
a long time but it's hard to lose anybody, and you don't
have many left in that generation. Anyway, Lou and I
had a fight. Sometimes I wonder why I married him,
we got along so well before, but now it's just accusations
and worrying and wanting to know if I love him. And
somehow he got it into his head I was fooling around
with Abe—which for heaven's sake I hope you know is
not true. Frankly he's not even my type. What with one
thing and another, it ends up with Lou dragging me into
the car and we go over to your place. He swears he's
not going to say anything, he just wants to see how Abe
looks at me when the door opens. Well, you know how
Abe looked at me—he looked how Abe looks. He always
has the same look, as if he's counting inside and he's not
allowed to talk until he gets to five. So he stands there
looking at us, holding the door.

Pardon me if I'm not being so complimentary about

your husband. And pardon me for this long letter. I can see it's going to be a long letter. So after a while he says "Gert's not here," and I say, "Could we come in, Abe? How are the girls?" Of course the girls are asleep, and he comes to his senses and lets us in and he even offers us tea, but Lou says, "I don't suppose you have any whiskey?" so he brings out a bottle and we have a little drink. The radio is on and I think this will be all right, we'll just listen to the music and have a drink and go home.

Lou sits there fiddling with the big red ashtray, turning it and playing with it, even though it's full of butts. You know how he can't ever keep his hands still. And wouldn't you know, after a while he gets to talking, and I guess he'd had a few earlier because the drink made a difference and he takes another one, and the next thing you know he's saying things about Abe and me. I thought I'd die. Whereupon it comes out, and I hope you had no idea about this, that your husband knows all about the little investment Lou talked you into, that we said was going to be a secret. I don't know how he knew and I hope you didn't tell him, but after pretending to be friendly it turned out Abe wasn't so friendly, he had something to say to Lou, and the upshot of it is, Abe accuses Lou of stealing your money—his money—and Lou throws the ashtray. He can get like that. Of course he didn't throw it at Abe, he threw it at the wall, but Abe got upset, and he ran to see if the girls were all right, for what reason I don't know. A corner of the ashtray broke off and I picked it up. It was sharp and I threw it in the garbage. But it broke off cleanly and the rest of it wasn't sharp so I put it back where you keep it on the corner table. The butts were all over the floor and I cleaned them up, with Lou saying, "What are you doing that for? Let him clean it up." We got out of there quickly but this is not all.

Gert, why did you tell him about that investment? It was your money from what your father left. Maybe you didn't tell him. I suppose there are a lot of ways he could tell, if he's looking at everything. But here's what he did. Or, I think he must have done it. At least, somebody went to the cops, and now they're looking at a lot of things Lou does. You know Lou's business, it's complicated and I don't ask questions, and I know as well as you do that it's not all on the up-and-up but he does no real harm to anybody and that's just the way he is. He's always been that way, as we both know. So now he may have to go back to prison and heaven knows what.

You see why I didn't just pick up the phone. This is a lot to explain, especially if Abe didn't tell you. And if he did, you may be very angry. Or Abe may be angry with you about the money, or maybe he hasn't said. Anyway, he knows. So I thought it was best just to write instead of calling when for all I know he's home, or the girls ask questions.

Gert, there is something else I want to say and maybe I'm just not the kind of person to say this out loud and maybe that is another reason why I am writing you a letter, which I hope you will read and destroy immediately. It's been good with Lou but, Gert, if I have to choose, I am not letting go of what I have with you and

I hope you feel the same. I mean, I do not expect you to choose between Abe and me. Abe is a much better husband than Lou Braunstein and I know that. But if Abe isn't going to let you see me or call me, I just want you to know I'm not going anywhere and when you can get in touch I will be thinking about you already.

Hug the little girls for me and take care of yourself. I won't call but you call me when you can. Even if Lou goes away for a long time, I may blame Abe but I know why he did that and I don't blame you.

With my love,
Marlene

When Con finished reading the letter, she walked back and forth across the room, again and again, rapidly. She didn't want to know all this, or to think through what it meant. To distract herself at last, she picked up Gert's drafts once more and looked at the most recent. "I need to visit you," Gert had written to Marlene. Her prose had become simple, her handwriting shaky. "I will tell Connie she has to stay in the apartment to take care of the cat, but it is because I think her husband hits her. It is all I can think to do to get her away from him."

It was Saturday: Peggy would be home. Con put down the letter, left the apartment, walked quickly down one flight, and rang Peggy's doorbell. "I'm crazy," Con said. "Could I come in?"

"Of course," said Peggy, and drew her inside. She turned off the television set. Her apartment was shaped like Gert's but was furnished in a more old-fashioned, elaborate way, possibly by the aunt whom Peggy had replaced there. It smelled of cigarettes, but surely they too weren't left over from the aunt. Con had not seen Peggy smoke.

"I found some letters," said Con.

"You're reading your mother's letters?"

"Yes. Is that wrong?"

"I suppose so."

"So I deserve whatever I find out?"

"Maybe," said Peggy. "You need to get out of here. Let's go for a walk." Peggy needed groceries, and Con accompanied her. The fresh air felt good on her face. "When are you going home?" Peggy asked, in the store.

"I don't know. There's so much to do."

"You can't do it all at once. You'll come back."

Con felt like a child, following her friend as Peggy made adult decisions about vegetables and cheese. "You must think I'm an impossible person," she said, standing behind Peggy at the cash register.

"Your mother didn't interest me," said Peggy. "Sorry." She examined her change and put it into her wallet. "But I like you," she said as she picked up the bag. "I can't like you less for reading her letters. Can I tell you what's going on with me? Maybe it would distract you. Or are you too sad?"

"Did you ever hear of somebody named Lou Braunstein?" Con said.

"Lou Braunstein? I don't think so. Who is he?" They were leaving the store.

"Someone my mother knew."

"Is it important to know who he was?"

"It's all upsetting," said Con.

"I'll try and find out," Peggy said. She took the receipt from her bag of groceries and scribbled on it.

"Now tell me about you," Con said. Peggy was a little self-centered, but she seemed to know it, which made it all right. She listened as they set out for home. Con found she thought of it as home. She should move back to Brooklyn. Little is more absorbing than affairs with married men, and it seemed Peggy would always provide her with distraction of this sort. A Brooklyn resource. They had tea when they got back to Peggy's apartment. Her kitchen was a mess. Then Con went back upstairs. As she climbed the stairs, she realized someone was sitting on the floor outside Gert's apartment. She didn't let herself be afraid. The person was leaning against Gert's closed apartment door, and was Joanna.

Con dropped to her knees and seized her curly-haired big girl and rocked back and forth, clutching her and crying. She had not yet recovered from the burglary, and from thinking Joanna was hurt or missing. Her feelings had been interrupted by anger at Jerry, then by Gert's death. The thought made her angry with Gert. Jerry had never hit her. Jerry would never conceivably hit her. It was a ridiculous paranoid fantasy. It was demented. Well, Gert had been demented.

Joanna stiffened in her arms—"Oh, for God's sake, Mom"— and then gave way, and Con felt her firm body grow thicker and more flexible as it settled into her arms. "I miss Grandma so much," Joanna said. "Nobody loved her as much as I did. That woman killed her. She killed Grandma."

"Marlene?" said Con, standing up and brushing herself off. She unlocked the door. "She didn't kill her."

"You're already getting rid of stuff?" Joanna said. "We didn't even have the funeral."

Piles were everywhere. "We'll deal with that later," Con said.

"We should call a rabbi," said her child. "Grandma was Jewish."

"I don't know any rabbis. *She* didn't know any rabbis."

"The Yellow Pages," said Joanna. She carried the backpack she used for school, stuffed with clothes. She set it down. The cat approached, and Joanna sat down on the floor to stroke and hug him.

"You're been out of school all week," said Con.

"The week went by fast."

"Not for me."

Maybe Con could just stay here with Joanna. It would be a way of leaving Jerry. She'd get a job in New York, and Joanna would go to a Brooklyn high school. The thought of a job made her remember she had never called Sarah, and now it was Saturday. She had to feed Joanna. They'd spend the night here and go home to Philadelphia in the morning. She'd had contradictory thoughts one after the other, as if one led to the other: stay here, return home.

"Did you come on the bus?" she said.

"Yes. Dad's meeting us at home. I wanted him to come with me but he said there was someone he still needed to talk to."

"Some retired soldier from the Revolutionary War?"

"Something like that." Joanna laughed. "I knew you needed me." Then she cried again. "There was no reason for Grandma to die."

"She was old. She had a heart attack."

"That woman killed her."

"Marlene is complicated," said Con, "but not like that."

"She doesn't love us. She likes hearing about us so she can laugh at us," said Joanna.

"When did you even meet her?" said Con. They were still in the living room, Joanna on the floor, though the cat had walked off.

"A long time ago, but I was a smart little kid. She looked at me thinking 'What can I laugh at?' I could hear it. I was ten or eleven. I was fat, and she thought she'd never be fat. Never never never."

"You weren't fat," said Con. She was cold. She went into the bedroom for a sweater and Joanna followed her, then began looking at what Con had spread around the room. "What have you been *doing*?" said Joanna. She picked up a photograph.

Gert's drafts of letters were on the sofa but Con didn't know where she'd put Marlene's letters from the war. She began tidying ineffectively, then said, "Let's make supper."

She wasn't angry with Joanna anymore for joining Jerry. She was angry with Jerry, but it seemed inventive and surprising of Joanna to have gone to him, then to her. "What did you learn?" Con asked, but Joanna just shrugged.

"It's dirty in here," she said. "So dusty. Isn't it giving you a headache?"

Con opened a window and the noise of the street came in. "I did need you," she said. She led the way to the kitchen and put together supper. There was more meat sauce, and she cooked macaroni.

"Daddy told me you want to leave him," said Joanna, as they sat at the table. The striped tablecloth had become dirtier all week and it was quite dirty now, but it was still pretty, with the brilliant stripe.

"He promised not to tell you."

"He said you might tell me, but he says you don't mean it."

Con felt the weight of actions she'd need to perform. She would have to persuade Sarah to forget the house for former prisoners. She would have to find a rabbi in the Yellow Pages. She would have to get rid of nearly every object in this apartment. Barbara would want three ceremonial relics of their mother's existence, and she would want ten. Plus the letters. And Joanna would take half a dozen, and Marlene could be given the painting of the sand dunes and a few other things. Her mother's odd, inexpensive necklaces and pins were gone. Con remembered a few things from the wooden box: a copper pin her mother had loved, a string of small red stones.

Leaving Jerry, right now, seemed not an expression of what she felt, believed, or wanted, but an unending series of additional tasks: sorting, packing, moving, setting up a household. Jerry would be slightly amused as Con tried to accomplish leaving him. His amusement was different from Marlene's. Joanna was partly right about Marlene, but Joanna was jealous because Con had always liked Marlene too much, and so she couldn't see her. Marlene had pulled Con slightly off center. A child would know that. Marlene had made Con feel adult and significant when she was ten or fourteen. It was not good that Con still looked to her for that reassurance, but it was so.

"Have you been living on spaghetti?" said Joanna. She stood up, her food half eaten, to search in the refrigerator.

"I should have made a vegetable," said Con, surprised she hadn't.

"Is there ice cream? said Joanna. She checked the freezer. "Grandma had Häagen-Dazs!" she said.

"No, I bought it," said Con. "She had ice milk."

"Well, it's healthier," said Joanna, defending her grandmother's choice, whatever it had been.

Jerry knocked on Con's bedroom door as she was getting dressed. "What?" she called grouchily.

"Never mind."

She was not sorry she'd slept with him, but now she wanted him to become, once more, the slightly formal guest. Jerry had not done badly, all these years, impersonating that guest, though he'd looked slightly bewildered and self-consciously adventurous, like somebody playing charades. Several times he'd had dinner with her and Fred. He'd looked amused on those occasions too, as if *she* had been playing a part, and he didn't think she was good at it.

When she came into the living room, dressed in jeans, she marveled at the sunlight, which was usually wasted on an empty room while she sat in her office with its dirty window. Jerry was sitting in shadow with a laptop on his knees.

"Sorry," he said, not looking up. He was closing a file. "I had a thought, and I was impatient to tell you."

"What's the thought?"

"You could come with me."

"Come with you where?" she said.

"It's just Brooklyn."

"Oh. Marcus Ogilvy? Was that it?"

"Yes."

"What did he do?" she said. "Who was he? Where are you going?"

She sat down. She wanted him to leave, so she could keep on looking at her old and newly recovered objects, or figure out how to open the box. But she remembered her wild jealousy of Jerry on his trips, her wish to go searching with him in some unlikely place for the remnant of a fact nobody cared to know but Jerry and Con. "Tell me," she said, but she was wary.

"What do you know," said Jerry, "about the history of the subway system?"

Con didn't know anything, and for the next half hour, Jerry told her stories. She didn't know—this, he made clear, was *not* the particular secret he was investigating—the famous secret about the lavish two-station subway, in which a car was propelled by a big fan. It was built by a nineteenth-century entrepreneur before the subway system existed. The businessman had pretended he was building a pneumatic tube just for mail, not passengers, so the Tweed gang wouldn't stop him. Con didn't know about the man who finally put down the money to build the first real subway, the IRT: the incomparably rich August Belmont. He was the son of August Schönberg, a Jew who became an Episcopalian and translated his last name, "beautiful mountain," from German to French. The son also built the Belmont race track and bred Man o' War. She didn't know several other famous subway stories. And Con didn't know about the bit of New York history that had caught Jerry's attention this time—Marcus Ogilvy's mad scheme of the 1920s, the Brooklyn Circle. "That's what we're going to find," said Jerry. "It was never finished, but parts of it were built. The books say there's nothing left, but my guess is there are perfectly obvious fragments. You Brooklynites are so used to crazy, incomprehensible structures, you probably walk past these things every day, and nobody notices."

She admitted it to herself: she was interested. Marcus Ogilvy was another Jew who was not quite a Jew, and obviously that was part of the appeal for Jerry. Marcus Ogilvy even had one black grandparent on his father's side. His mother was a German Jew and Ogilvy had studied architecture in Europe as a young man, late in the nineteenth century, then returned to his native New York and made a small fortune developing new neighborhoods in Brooklyn and Queens. He was in his thirties when most of the subway was built, in the first decade of the twentieth century, but he was never enthusiastic about underground transportation. Before the subway had been built, elevated trains, including the famously defunct Third Avenue El, crossed parts of the city. They were noisy and regarded as dirty, and up-to-date thinking at the start of the new century was all in favor of the subway, which was considered a startling improvement when it was built.

"Ogilvy loved el trains," Jerry said, gesturing so expansively that Con felt as if she'd been reduced to someone at the back of a lecture hall. He went on to explain how Marcus Ogilvy had built a mansion on Arlington Avenue in East New York from which he could hear the reliable rumble of the Jamaica El as he fell asleep at night, and he'd enjoyed standing on the platform of the Cleveland Street Station, gazing at the city around him, taking in the relatively fresh outdoor air and the relatively clear light, up closer to heaven, instead of descending to a tunnel he always feared would collapse, or at least would harbor rats and snakes.

Ogilvy was especially troubled about one characteristic of the subway system as it extended to Brooklyn. The lines stretched from Manhattan like tentacles of a sea creature, but (as Con had known all her life, from the story of how Gert and Marlene became friends) nothing connected them except in a very few places. From some locations in Brooklyn, it was necessary—it is still necessary—to travel into Manhattan and back in order to reach someplace else in Brooklyn. Or it is necessary to take slow and ponderous buses. Ogilvy had proposed to change all that with an elevated line that would not be ugly. Jerry opened a map. Across Brooklyn, he'd drawn a curved line in pencil. The Brooklyn Circle was to have been an elevated arc linking the Parkside Avenue Station of what is now the Q train, to the Winthrop Avenue Station on what's now called the 2–5, then to the Crown Heights–Utica Avenue Station on the 3 and the 4, and finally to the station now called Broadway Junction, on the J (the elevated line that Ogilvy listened to from his bed), where the J meets the A and C subway lines—just being built when Ogilvy made his plans—and the elevated line now called the L, which goes to Canarsie.

Ogilvy's favorite word was "elegance" and in his designs and the impassioned articles he wrote about them, he actually referred to some features of the European Gothic cathedrals he'd admired as a young man, like pointed arches in the supporting pillars, to let more light into the street, and groined vaults underneath the tracks. He wanted people's eyes to be drawn upward, their moods lightened. He wanted pedestrians to feel as if they were walking under a delicately designed street arcade, not a looming and potentially dangerous dark shape. The pillars were to be white. At that time all the subways were privately owned—the city didn't own them until 1940. Ogilvy secured the necessary permissions, found backers, and began building supports and tracks.

"Bits of the line are still there," said Jerry. He stood up and walked to the window, as if it might be possible to glimpse these shapes even from here. "I *think* they're still there."

"What happened to it?"

"Oh, what do you think? 1929 happened. He lost everything. His backers were shaky in the first place—sane people had doubts about elevateds. The worst accident in the history of the subways was on an elevated line. And of course they're noisy."

"Did he kill himself?"

"No, he just gave up. He went to live with his daughter in Geneseo, New York. I was there last month, but there's no trace of the house."

"You went looking for Marcus Ogilvy's daughter's house?"

"That's what I do." His back was to her, and the sunlight framed his bony shape, his boyish curly head.

Con knew better than to ask anybody *why*. Nothing has a why. Why did she want to go with Jerry to look for Marcus Ogilvy's unfinished elevated railway instead of spending a pleasant sick day at home getting ready for Marlene—who would arrive in only a few hours? She didn't know why, but she wanted to do it. Before they left, she tried again to open the wooden jewelry box. She'd need to use something like a paper clip or a bobby pin, and she didn't know exactly what. Jerry was impatient to get started.

The weather had turned even colder. Con put on her winter coat, which had to be ripped from a plastic bag, and smelled pleasantly of dry cleaning. Jerry still wore his raincoat. As they left the apartment they bumped into each other, and Con recalled that doorways narrow when new lovers try to go through them together. Not that they were new lovers. They emerged from the building and walked toward the subway. Jerry said they'd take the train to Parkside Avenue. As they went down the steps into the station, Jerry said, "Funny thing—for a while I had a girlfriend around here."

Con pretended more nonchalance than she felt. "Around here?"

"A couple of blocks from here. She used the same station."

"Maybe I know her."

"No," he said. "You don't know her."

Just before Parkside Avenue, the Q train emerges into modified sunlight, not as an elevated train but a simple railway, running in a ditch that's open to the sky. The station is unusual: it has no steps, like a train station in the country. Con had always liked it; sometimes, as a girl, she went to her mother's office after school. But she was sad, coming out now. "My mother worked near here," she said. "P.S. 92."

She didn't know, come to think of it, how many women had been in Jerry's life since the divorce. She was in touch with him often enough that names or incidents might have come up, but apparently he concealed names and incidents. If there was one there could have been ten. There was no reason for that to be bad, but it was bad. Maybe it simply meant they weren't as good friends as she'd thought. She might have run into him in a local restaurant with another woman. She might have made a new friend who referred to "My boyfriend, Jerry," and it would be her Jerry. Her former Jerry.

Which would not have mattered. "So you're not seeing this woman anymore?" she said.

"Who?"

"My neighbor."

"Well, she's not your *neighbor*." He paused, looking toward Prospect Park and then toward Parkside Avenue, getting his bearings. "No, I'm not. We go this way."

Solid, square apartment houses looked well cared for. There was no sign of a failed elevated train line, and Jerry said most of this construction was more recent than the Brooklyn Circle; developers would have obliterated everything. Con had lost some of her initial eagerness. She tried to care. Jerry became not tense but a little quiet by the time they reached the school. Before then, he'd been talkative and buoyant. This must be the way he always was at the start of a trip: sure of himself, with the confidence of a detective in a story, a detective who never gets shot and always solves the murder by the end of the book. But Jerry could be arrogant; it was one of his failings. She hadn't thought of his failings since before they'd gone to bed together. He wanted to play by himself: he didn't know how to be with someone else. Now he was showing off, she felt, casually mentioning women to upset her, casually pretending to know what he was doing. They would find nothing. Con should have gone to work, and as she walked she thought of the notebook entry she'd found the night before, in which she'd written down that quick thought about truths. She knew it was relevant to her search for the perfect client, the perfect abused woman suffering employment discrimination. The thought made a difference: having a thought like that seemed to justify a holiday, and Con felt, suddenly, as if she'd been locked indoors for days—for years—but now was out in the cold sunshine, the brief sunlight of November. She wouldn't tell Jerry she'd suddenly understood what was wrong with her as a lawyer, that she was here to celebrate, here in her clean winter coat. He didn't tell her things, and she wouldn't tell him either, but she was tempted.

P.S. 92 was a massive, plain structure with a small paved yard. It tolerated no nonsense, its unequivocal architecture seemed to say; any scraps of lost train lines would have been swept away. But Jerry drew her closer to the fence behind it. "That's the sort of place we'll find something," he said. Between the school and other buildings was an amorphous lot with a low structure. Con saw an old iron pillar, but surely not the right sort. They turned on Nostrand Avenue, where there were stores, and began zigzagging—one block north, one block east—peering through gaps between buildings. Con had decided Jerry was deluded and she was not interested, but she was interested in spite of herself.

"So are you glad you dumped Fred?" he asked as they walked.

"Well, that was a while ago," she said. "I don't think about it much. After the fact, it became a foregone conclusion."

"I knew all along it wouldn't work out," said Jerry. "You should have ended it sooner. You should be different as a lawyer, too. Less timid."

Now she was angry. He could be superior about bits of history if he knew something she didn't know, but not, please, about her own life and her own judgment. "What, you're some sort of oracle?" she said, and her voice was sharper than she'd expected. "Why don't you tell me right now—is there anything you are quite sure you *don't* know?"

"Oh, sure," said Jerry mildly. The more she revealed what she felt, the blander and more reasonable he would become. Now he explained, as if their entire conversation had been impersonal, that the Brooklyn Circle line had passed not along the street but through the blocks, behind the houses. "It wasn't going to be as tall as some of the elevateds," he said. "About level with the second-floor windows."

Con didn't answer. Again, she spotted a steel upright object, this time with a crosspiece. She waited to see whether he'd speak, but he didn't.

But half a block later Jerry suddenly grew extremely quiet: his long limbs slowed and it was as if he were completely alone. Then he put an arm on her shoulder. At least he hadn't forgotten she was there. He pointed. It was a stretch of three pillars with fretwork and arches intact between them, in the middle of a block off Winthrop Street, in a parking lot. She knew in an instant that what she was seeing was like nothing she'd ever seen before. The pillars did not resemble fragments of other elevated train structures. They were gray metal, and the pointed arches between them were sharply cut. They looked light. They didn't seem high or heavy enough, she said out loud, but Jerry said, yes, they would have supported the tracks and the trains; the design was what made it possible, as in the cathedrals of Europe.

He'd brought her along, after all. She had almost decided to let go of her anger, to delight in him the way she would in a child who'd produced such a discovery: to let herself see it without living in their past, hers and Jerry's. She wanted to touch these pillars but they couldn't get close enough. Jerry had a small camera, but they were too far to take a picture that would mean much. From his pocket he produced a stack of three-by-five index cards. He scribbled with a ballpoint pen, leaning on his knee and then, after a grunt asking permission, on her shoulder.

They continued walking, now passing attached houses with aluminum siding. On New York Avenue, there was something between two buildings, but so fragmented Jerry said he couldn't be sure. Then, near Wingate Park, off Brooklyn Avenue, was a good-sized section. A wall had been built but Con was pretty sure she could see tracks. Jerry took photographs this time, and filled more cards with scribbles. Con lent him her leather purse to lean on, then regretted it because he wrote more. She was cold.

The houses became smaller and more suburban-looking, and the streets were quieter. All the avenues were named after New York cities. They'd seen few people as they walked, but a man on a stoop now called "How y'doing?" Everyone they saw was black. Now there was plenty of room behind houses for dilapidated bits of an old elevated railway, and twice they spotted single pillars, then another set of three. Now Con could recognize them easily, with their distinctive pointed arches. Near Utica Avenue they found a complete set of track work on six or eight pillars. A light, sturdy structure, it was just visible behind some houses. Jerry stopped a man in the street. "Can you tell me what that is?"

The man looked. "Part of the Long Island Rail Road they no longer use," he said authoritatively.

"Oh, thanks," Jerry said.

"People look at it out their windows," said Con. "They have to wonder how it got there. Maybe some of them know."

"No," said Jerry, a little impatiently. "They don't know. They think it's part of the Long Island Rail Road, if they think at all. New York is full of mysteries. Do you know about the High Line, in Manhattan?"

Con didn't. "An old railroad. People see it all the time and aren't curious, but that's not surprising. If you were curious about everything you'd have a heart attack every day."

"You just like feeling superior," said Con.

"No!" Jerry actually sounded hurt, and she put her hand on his arm.

"Just teasing," she said.

At Utica Avenue—a busy street full of stores—Con almost forgot about the Brooklyn Circle. She lived not far away, but had never been here. In a Korean grocery they bought apples and pretzels and bottles of water. Con had hoped for lunch.

They crossed Eastern Parkway. Now the neighborhoods became shabbier, and Con and Jerry seemed more conspicuous. "Are you a teacher?" a little girl asked Con. Near Pacific Street—almost at the end of their walk—was another set of tracks. It was wedged between small apartment buildings, as if removing it had been too much trouble, or maybe it even helped support the buildings. The tracks crossed a narrow vacant lot strewn with garbage and glass. Jerry walked confidently into the lot to get a better look at the tracks, just twenty feet from the street, but Con remained on the sidewalk. "We're almost at the end," he called. "I'd given up on finding something like this." The tracks were somewhat different from the others, with double pillars linked by small platforms.

Con was tired and cold, and pretzels and apples had not satisfied her. She stayed where she was, and at last Jerry returned. They began to walk slowly past the structure. "You're not as interested as I thought you'd be," he said.

She didn't try to be fair. "You're a solipsist," she said finally. "You don't quite know anybody else is real."

He stopped where he was and looked at her. His buoyancy was gone, and suddenly he looked older, somehow both more Jewish and more African American. His face was less handsome, but maybe better, and Con was sorry she'd spoken. "What do you mean?" he said.

"I shouldn't have said that." They'd stopped, and she was cold already, but it seemed necessary to wait right where they were, at a street corner a few yards beyond the structure. "It's beautiful," she said quietly. "I should have said it's beautiful."

"But you don't really care?"

"You want me to care."

"I want everything about you, Connie," Jerry said. "Yes, I want you to care!" Now he sounded angry. "I want you to care about Marcus Ogilvy trying to build a train line. I want you to care about Joanna being arrested for saying what she thinks! I want you to care about me trying to figure things out—but you—you don't look. You don't see what there is to see."

"Of course I do," Con said with some irritation. "That's not the least bit fair." They were arguing like married people. She needed a consultation with Peggy to decide whether he was right or not—whether he was unreasonable to make her want to admire broken-down train tracks in cold weather without lunch, or whether she was unreasonable not to see the romance of it.

Of course, in part, she understood. "I do see that what you've found is wonderful," she said. She thought again of Peggy, of what Peggy had told her about the question she'd asked long ago. "Does the name Lou Braunstein mean anything to you?" she said then.

Jerry turned just then, as if to go back the way they'd come. "Lou Braunstein? Sure. Forties crook. A wonderful guy. Behind some of the biggest scams in those years. He went to prison for some kind of complicated tax and investment thing, but even before that—during the war—he was one of the big guys. Why? He might have had something to do with the money for this project—why Ogilvy ran into so much trouble. Of course, Braunstein was a kid at that point—he was just the errand boy, if his group was in it all. Ogilvy got lured into a bad investment scheme, but the D.A. never quite succeeded in pinning it on anybody organized; some guy with a green eyeshade went to prison, but he was just following orders."

"No kidding," said Con.

"Why are you interested in him?"

Con tried to think why she was interested in him. Why she'd been interested, fourteen years earlier, in Lou Braunstein. Why she'd asked Peggy who he was. It was so hard to remember that week—the week she'd lost her bag; the week her mother died. She had flashes in her memory, moments. Sitting up in bed talking to Jerry, sitting up in bed talking to Marlene, coming up the stairs and finding Joanna leaning against the door. "He had something to do with Marlene," she said.

"Really? Lou Braunstein?"

"I think he was Marlene's husband," Con said. "Is that possible?"

"Well, I suppose anything's possible," Jerry said, "but it doesn't seem likely. Don't you think you've confused him with some other guy with a Jewish name?"

"I suppose so," said Con, but now they were walking back to the short, graceful section of Marcus Ogilvy's tracks. Sunlight coming through the fretwork made patterns on the ground. They stopped and looked.

"We could climb that," said Jerry.

"Are you crazy?" But she wasn't angry anymore.

"Why not?"

Con's black woolen coat was so clean. And it came down to her knees. If she'd expected to do any climbing, she'd have dressed differently. "It's illegal," she said.

"I don't see any signs."

"Of *course* it's illegal."

He began slapping his thigh lightly, rhythmically, like someone getting ready to move vigorously. They stood under the tracks, and afternoon sunlight touched their faces and clothes. Jerry gazed up. He pulled out his note cards and scribbled, then moved to another part of the lot and scribbled some more. It was a section of track about fifty feet long, and everything that had supported it—that still supported it. Jerry photographed it from every possible point. His pleasure was palpable. In truth, the pillars didn't look hard to climb, with cutouts in the gray metal just right for a hand or a foot. Still, she was relieved when he seemed to have forgotten the idea.

But then he said, "Okay, let's go up," as if they'd already agreed. She was curious too. She could have her coat cleaned again. They started up. Jerry went first. Con had no trouble. Nobody was in the street, and they seemed unobserved. What they were doing didn't feel unsafe. It felt like playing on an innovative playground. In summer, the neighborhood kids were probably all over this structure. Looking up, Con could see cleaner spots, places in the elaborate fretwork below the tracks where children had held on as they climbed. She confidently put her hands where they wanted to go. Her purse bounced on her back.

At the top they heaved themselves over a metal fence and onto a track bed. The tracks were still there, ending at the back of what looked like a warehouse. They were not dirty. They would not be hard to walk on, but maybe she wouldn't try that. On either side, faceless apartment windows seemed to ignore everything. Maybe the residents weren't home, or maybe they didn't look out these windows.

Jerry gingerly stepped along the tracks. Con crouched, holding the barrier she'd just climbed over, watching her ex-husband and new lover, watching his graceful legs. Maybe she would keep him as her lover.

"Come on," called Jerry. He was leaning on his knee, writing. Next he stretched in several directions to take photographs.

"I'm fine here," said Con.

Then Jerry took a misstep between the tracks, and yelped, coming down hard on an ankle. He'd had a weak ankle for years, she recalled. And there was a knock on the window behind Con. Still holding on, she turned. A man stood at the window, an elderly man in a white shirt. He was waving his hand as if to shoo her away, frowning. She smiled reassuringly and turned back to Jerry. "Are you all right?" she called.

"I don't know yet." He was grimacing, stooping. He slowly stood up and put weight on his foot. "Not all right. But maybe it'll stop hurting in a minute." Carefully he raised his foot and shook it. There was little danger of his falling between the tracks to the lot below—there were plenty of crossbars and underpinnings. But he might have got a foot caught in one of Marcus Ogilvy's graceful openings and cutouts, the ones that had allowed the light to touch them when they stood below.

"Can you come back here?" she said. She didn't know how they'd get down. She looked behind her. The man was still watching, a flash of sun on the window glass hiding his mouth but his forehead and eyes visible. He looked puzzled. She wasn't sure he could see Jerry, who was beyond her, along the track.

She gestured. She smiled again. The man looked. His skin was bright brown, the color of dark cherrywood, his forehead big and shiny.

He knocked again, and when she turned he frowned and shooed her once more. She shrugged, and started—as well as she could—toward Jerry. The wind up here was strong, and she had a sudden fear of falling through the spaces between the tracks after all. Now that she was closer, she could see that the spaces were larger than she had believed. She would die. She would die trying to make her way toward Jerry, and she remembered holding him in the night, and the feeling that she was at the edge of something, or fast disappearing into something, that without his touch and the thought of Joanna she'd be obliterated, gone. He should never have ventured out on the tracks. He should never have wanted to come up here. It was sooty. Her coat—still with the conscientious smell of recent dry-cleaning—was already dirty. If only she'd worn her short jacket. The coat flapped and caught at her legs. She might trip on it and plunge through the spaces between the tracks. She took a step. Now there was no place to put her hand, so she leaned over carefully and got down on her hands and knees, but her coat was seriously in the way, and her bag—a flat, attractive, moderately expensive leather bag—thumped at her side. She considered letting it go, dropping it through the space in the tracks and forgetting it. Were things that bad? Could she let her purse—and what was in it—go? For she knew that even in this quiet neighborhood, someone might well come along and take it before she got down.

The thought of the other bag made her more willing to drop

this one. If it was *that* sort of universe she lived in, where what is lost may be returned—well! But she didn't. She backed up and left the bag on the ledge where she'd been clinging, just below the window of the cherrywood man. He seemed to be gone. She considered taking off her coat but was afraid to move that drastically, afraid that its breadth might make a sail in the wind and pull her down. She opened the coat, got back down on her knees, and with one hand yanked the skirt of the coat up in back, folded over on itself, so it was out of the way. She began crawling toward Jerry, stopping twice to refold the skirt of the coat.

Jerry was leaning over, clutching his ankle with his free hand. Con didn't know what she could do for him, but she continued toward him. At last he reached forward and touched her shoulder.

"Be careful. We'll both fall," she said.

"We won't fall. There isn't room to fall," said Jerry. "Kids come up here all the time. If they fell down and died, you'd have read about it in the paper."

"Not in New York," said Con. She meant New York was so big, nobody would hear about it. She was sure parts of Brooklyn weren't even on the map. "Can you walk?"

"If I could lean on you, maybe," Jerry said.

Con didn't see how this could be done. She tried to stand and found she could. "I don't want you to lean on me," she said.

"Just a touch on your shoulder," said Jerry.

Con heard the sound of a window opening. "I've called the cops," called the man with the broad forehead, leaning out.

"We're going to be arrested," said Con.

"But the cops will get us down first," Jerry said.

"But I don't want to be arrested," Con said. It was too absurd—mother, father, and daughter running afoul of the law the same week. She'd die of humiliation. She'd be disbarred. Jerry looked cleaner than she felt, almost dapper, his white shirt still looking crisp through his open raincoat. He smiled at her. "It's going to be okay," he said. "Then we'll get married again."

"I don't think so," said Con. She turned and got down on her hands and knees again. She began crawling back. Below her she could see the pattern of the tracks in shadows on the lot below, but it looked far away, so she looked ahead instead of down. The tracks might be poorly fastened. The fastenings would have loosened over the years, and wouldn't have been kept in repair. Con and Jerry's combined weight might send the whole section, with them on top, crashing down.

"The cops are on their way over," the man called.

Con reached the window and looked up at the man, like an actress playing a dog or cat. She had an impulse to say "Woof." Then, as the man watched, she moved her hands up the short walls at the side of the tracks, so as to get upright again. Jerry was crawling behind her. He hadn't needed to hold on after all. "My husband is crazy," she heard herself say. "I'm sorry. He's a historian."

"You're not allowed to be out there," the man said.

She said, "Of course not. It's not safe. He's nuts, and now he's hurt. Can we come through your apartment to get down? He can't get down the way we came up."

"I don't know if I can let you do that," the man said. "I don't know anything about you."

"I live on Sterling Place," said Con. She almost said that Jerry lived in Philadelphia, but remembered she had called him her husband. "We live on Sterling Place. Prospect Heights?"

The man considered. "My brother lives near there," he said, as if that proved something. "Wait." He closed the window.

"I don't know if I can make it down," Jerry said. "This ankle is killing me."

"He'll be back," said Con. The man returned and opened the window again. Con retrieved her bag and brushed off her coat as best she could, then made her way over the sill. "I'm sorry to be so dirty," she said. When she got inside, the man was standing to the side—not blocking her path but leaning against his stove—holding a knife pointed at her. She turned, raising her hand, to tell Jerry to stay outside. Maybe he could scream. Maybe the cops had really been called, and would arrest but also protect them.

"I'm sorry, ma'am," said the man. "I have to be sure. You can't be too careful."

Con stood still, studying him, then understood. "You think we're going to hurt you?" she said.

"I let you into my home," said the man.

This was true. "It's all right," she said to Jerry, who climbed onto the sill and sat there for a moment. He couldn't put weight on the injured ankle and had to try several times before, with a cry, he ended up on his hands and knees on the man's kitchen floor. Now Con supported him as he stood and leaned against her. With the cherrywood man remaining where he was—apparently protecting his stove—they moved side by side, leaning together, across the kitchen, through a sparsely furnished, extremely clean living room, and out into the corridor. There was no elevator, and it took them a few moments to figure out how to get down the stairs. Finally, Jerry hopped, and Con waited below to steady him if he started to tumble. At last they reached the downstairs lobby, crossed it, and, leaning together, made their way outside, stared at by two middle-school kids and a woman with a stroller. There was no sign of any cops. "Where's the subway?" said Jerry. "We'll never get a cab around here."

Con wanted to try, but first insisted they walk a block away from Marcus Ogilvy's abandoned, cathedral-like structure, soaring in an abbreviated way between apartment houses. She didn't want to see any cops, just in case. And then they kept going. She kept an eye open for a cab but never saw one. It took most of a cold hour to reach the subway station and then they couldn't quite find it. The Long Island Rail Road, running down Atlantic Avenue, was between them and the station. At last a young woman came along, and in answer to Con's question said, "Oh, the mystery way" and pointed out an underpass that would take them through the railway station and upstairs on the other side of it. They had to climb down many stairs, then up many more. But beyond the railroad, in the fading afternoon light, was the Broadway Junction Station, the proposed terminus of the Brooklyn Circle. The el could be reached with an escalator.

If Marcus Ogilvy had had his wish, they could have traveled back to Con's apartment much more quickly. Maybe there was something else they could have done, even as things were, but she was too tired to figure it out. They went all the way into Manhattan and back. Jerry's ankle started to swell. Con remembered that she'd had almost no sleep the night before, and almost no lunch. She fell asleep leaning against the window of one of the trains, and when they got off the last train, Jerry with his bad ankle supported her. It was dark out. As they made their way slowly up the street and along the last block to Con's apartment house, she remembered Marlene, arriving at 5:33 at LaGuardia. It was ten after five. She was starving. She was dirty. Marlene had no cell phone. Still in the street, Con dialed Joanna's cell phone with her own. "I don't even know what I want you to do," she began.

"Think what it is," Joanna said. "I'll do it."

"Where are you?"

"I'm at Barney's."

"You've been there all day?"

"No—I was home for an hour or so," said Joanna.

"Your dad has a sprained ankle," Con began. Should she explain her day to Joanna now, or later, or never? "We're just getting home, and Marlene's arriving in twenty minutes." Joanna said she'd call the airline and have Marlene paged. "She can take a taxi," she said. "She doesn't need you to meet her. I'll ask them to tell her to take a taxi."

"Can she really do that?"

"Of course. Which airline?"

Con would even have a little time. She could change her clothes. She could eat something. She could get Jerry off her shoulder and put him to bed somewhere. They made their way, he hopping, up the three steps to her front door, then up the difficult marble step into the lobby, then into the elevator and down the corridor into the apartment. She noticed something odd as she passed the open kitchen doorway, but deposited Jerry on a chair in her study before she went back to see. Her mother's wooden box was not where it had been; it was on the counter instead of the table. And it was open. Next to it was a bent paper clip. Joanna had opened it. Con glanced at the tangle of necklaces and random objects, then gathered up the jewelry box and her old black nylon purse, brought them into her bedroom, and stuffed them into her bottom drawer. Then she stripped off her clothes, put on a bathrobe, returned to the kitchen, and ate six crackers. Then she went into the bathroom and filled the tub with hot water.

Even though her mother had died while Con was staying in her apartment, it didn't mean she'd be trapped there forever. Joanna had the key to their house, but it was too late to go there now, on Saturday evening. If Con had been alone, she thought she might have just taken up her mother's life where Gert had left it, used up the soup and bought more. Joanna wouldn't let her do that. Con made up a bed for her daughter on the sofa, where she herself used to sleep, though she was tempted to offer Joanna the bed, which seemed to close around Con each time she got into it. The loss of her purse was just the first sign of Gert's death, a symptom.

After she put sheets on the sofa, she got into her pajamas and returned to the living room to turn out lights. Joanna was in bed, maybe asleep.

Just then the phone rang. Con reached for the nearest phone—the one in the kitchen. She was sure it would be Jerry, but the caller was Sarah.

"You're in the office?" Con said, trying to keep her voice low. "It's Saturday night. It's midnight."

"No, I'm not in the office," Sarah said. "Constance, why haven't you called me?"

"I know," said Con. "I've been crazy. My mother died."

"Your mother died? I thought she was visiting her sister."

"Her friend. She died there." There was a long pause, and she could hear the drag of breath on a cigarette. Sarah smoked only when she was upset.

"Then didn't you have all the *more* reason to call me?" Sarah said. "I'm sorry. I'm sorry about your mother. But Constance. I stopped by the office to pick something up today, and while I was there, Mabel Turner came in. I know she lost the hearing, and I know the appeal probably won't win, but we have to file it. We have to keep that house going. It's a principle we need to establish, aside from everything else. When did your mother die?"

Con wondered if Sarah believed that her mother was dead. "During the night. Thursday night. Her friend called me yesterday morning. Then Mabel called me. She's giving up the house. It was never working, Sarah. The whole idea—well, it was an idea. Just an idea. Not practical."

Con wished she had taken this call in the bedroom. Now Joanna was sitting up on the sofa, looking at her.

"This house has worked for two years," Sarah said. "It's one of the best there are, and it's legal under the disability laws. If we lose the appeal, we might be able to go to federal court. Look, I know Mabel called you. And we're supposed to protect the house, whether it's perfect or not. We have until Monday to file an appeal, and I'm filing it. I'm taking you off this case."

"I think Mabel never intended to stay," Con said.

"Mabel intended to stay, and Mabel is staying. And if she didn't, someone else would run the house. But it doesn't sound as if you gave her much encouragement."

"I'd just found out about my mother."

"I'm sorry, Con. I really am sorry. I lost my mother, and I know how it feels. But all you had to do was call me. All you had to do was tell *her* to call me."

"I'm sorry," said Con.

"I'm sorry too," Sarah said. "Constance, I don't see how you and I can keep working together. You simply gave up. You encouraged the client to give up. I don't think there's any excuse for that, and I'm sorry to say this at such at time. Well, let's talk next week. Let's both calm down and talk next week. Take it easy." Sarah hung up.

"Who was that?" said Joanna, as Con put down the phone.

"I don't want to think about it," Con said, and went to bed. How quickly could she forget everything about this week—this entire week?

As soon as she'd washed the grime of the Brooklyn Circle off her body, Con called the airport to track down Marlene. The plane had landed; the message had been given to Ms. Silverman. Con poured some scotch, then ordered sushi to be delivered, considering that Marlene would like the idea of something exotic, whether she liked the way it tasted or not.

Glass in hand, Con went into the living room, where Jerry lay on the sofa with an ice pack. As he turned his head and she began to speak her hands seemed to become lighter, harder to control, so she had to put her drink down on a bookcase. She wanted to touch him, but didn't. Her hands—not the rest of her—wanted to touch him. Her hands had acquired a layer of softer but more highly charged air than that in the rest of the atmosphere; they had their own opinion. She pressed them to her sides. "You need more ice?" she said. "Or scotch?"

"A glass of water would be good. Thanks. The ice is still okay." As Con went for the water, her hands still felt lighter and larger than usual, pleasanter than the gray cold hands she'd carried for years. Jerry's eyes, when she handed him the water, gleamed as if he knew. It was infuriating, really. She hadn't forgotten his faults. He looked back at the television screen. Six Americans had died that day in a helicopter crash in Iraq. Soon it would be four hundred Americans dead, many more Iraqis. Con returned to the kitchen and drank, looking at her hands. Then she looked around for something to do. There had to be dozens of tasks, but she couldn't think of any. She went down to the street and looked up and down for taxis.

Joanna came home. To Con's relief, she didn't ask just how her father had injured his ankle. Her shedding green sculptures were still everywhere, and nobody had vacuumed around them. Con's eye fell on one in her study: grayish and large, it was made of ungainly—but pleasing—twisted braids. It established itself. Maybe she'd buy it when Joanna finally left. What would Joanna charge her mother? "How's Barney?" she said. "Acting fresh?"

"Same as ever." Joanna sat down at Con's computer and began typing. "Look, Barney's a sexy guy. He has sex on his mind—sex and art. Sometimes it's hard to know just where one ends and the other begins."

Con lingered in the doorway. "So he wants to make sculptures out of his interns?"

"Something like that," Joanna said. "What can I do? I've never learned so much in my life. The tricks he shows me with metal—I never did anything like this in school. And the guy's sense of shape is incredible."

"You're sleeping in here tonight, remember?" Con said. "On the inflatable mattress."

"Should I get my stuff now," said Joanna, "or can I answer my e-mails?"

"No hurry." The sushi arrived. Con had ordered many maki rolls. Marlene didn't come, and Con called the airport again—hungry, tense, distracted by Jerry's ordinarily unmomentous presence. She was on her way from kitchen to bedroom, when she happened to glance at the apartment door as it opened on its own. Marlene was quite late, but here she was, walking in without ringing and somehow without the look of someone arriving. She carried nothing but a black tote bag with a map of the London underground, which swung from her shoulder. Her glasses were lopsided on her strong face, and the reflection on them from an overhead light fixture made her look like a Cubist painting.

She didn't seem to know where she was, despite the confident step. Con peered into Marlene's face and saw the moment at which Marlene recognized her—saw her intelligent, greedy pleasure. Con stepped forward, shy, and hugged her friend. She reached up to run her hand over Marlene's well-shaped head, as she might with a child, though even in age Marlene looked formidable, with her white hair waving a little around her ears, emphasizing her big, haughty nose. The hair felt not quite clean. Now the tote bag, which looked heavy, slid to the floor, and Marlene grasped Con's shoulders. "My daughter!" she said, in a familiar, slightly mocking falsetto; the tone mocked the supposed daughter and somehow confessed sincerity at the same time, because it was self-mocking as well. The eyes were dark and annoyed. She straightened her glasses. "The cabbie has my bag," she said. Now her voice was deep. "He took all my money, the bastard, after driving me all over the city."

"You've been driving around all this time?" said Con.

"Oh, I waited for a while at the airport. I thought maybe you'd show up after all."

"I'm sorry," said Con. "I'll get your bag."

"Apparently you don't bother to lock your doors, here in the country," Marlene said. Her perfume, which suggested air and wind, had never changed over all these years. "Downstairs," Marlene continued, "as I was about to ring, somebody came along. I guess I don't look like a terrorist."

"Sit down," said Con. Con led Marlene into the kitchen and went downstairs. She retrieved a black wheeled overnight bag from the cab and brought it to the elevator, enjoying the brief, tired, relieved solitude, and even the elevator's familiar creakiness, in which she took the kind of pleasure a real country dweller—who could legitimately keep doors unlocked—might take in the ruts on his untraveled road.

Marlene was not in the kitchen but in the study. There, a half-finished sculpture lay on the floor. Balls of twine surrounded a central solid shape; but Marlene was considering something large and dark red on the table. "Is this an ashtray?" she said, picking it up. She had always been slim, with long, narrow hands. ("I should have been a pianist," she'd said in Con's girlhood; the tone suggested that playing the piano was a slightly hilarious concept. At other times she said, "I should have been a poker player" or "a gun runner" because she could lie without getting caught.) Con had no ashtrays. She'd forgotten that Marlene smoked. Surely she didn't *still* smoke? What did doctors say to women in their eighties who smoked? "No," she said.

"Where did you get that?" said Marlene.

"Do you need to smoke in here?" said Con.

"No. Maybe one. That ashtray was mine."

"It was my mother's," said Con.

"She liked it, so she took it," Marlene said.

"If you have to smoke, I'll give you something," Con said. "I don't use it as an ashtray." As a child, she remembered, she had run her hand around and around it. It would be dirty with ashes, and her mother would tell her to stop. Her mother stopped smoking and it remained an ashtray, and then her mother stopped letting friends smoke in her apartment, and the dish became a candy dish, or just a pretty object. "Do you like sushi?" she said.

"Raw fish?"

"That's part of it."

"Is that what we're having? As a matter of fact, I had a snack at the airport."

Con got her into the kitchen, which was too small for so many people. She set the table. "Jerry's here," she said.

"Your first husband?"

"That's right."

"What's he doing here?" Marlene tapped on the table. Obviously she wanted to smoke.

"He comes to New York on business these days," said Con. "He stays here sometimes." She didn't want to talk about the afternoon, about Marcus Ogilvy's secret that was not a secret— but was, since nobody knew about it but Con and Jerry. She had been too lenient with Jerry.

"Just don't let him get too close," said Marlene presciently, as Jerry hobbled into the kitchen, apologizing for not coming to say hello right away, shaking hands, glad to see Marlene, whom he'd known only slightly when he and Con had been married. Con called Joanna. "I've got Joanna, too," she said.

"I thought we might be alone," said Marlene.

By the time they ate, it was nearly ten, and Con was glad; there need not be an evening. Marlene ate maki rolls matter-of-factly with her long fingers, not bothering with chopsticks, soy sauce, or wasabi. The four of them ate everything Con had ordered. As soon as the food was gone, Marlene produced a cigarette from her pocket and lit it. Joanna left the room, and Con went to make up a bed for Jerry on the sofa. If they'd been alone, she'd have invited him back to her bed. She noted that Joanna had brought an armload of bedding into the study.

Marlene was not in the kitchen when Con returned there. The cigarette had been stubbed out on her plate. Con cleared the table, then went to the closet in the hall for more sheets and blankets. Someone was in the bathroom—Marlene, she assumed—so Con opened the door to the extra room, now vacated by Joanna. Naked, Marlene was just lying down on the bare mattress. Her slimness made her look young when she was dressed, but without her clothes she was an old woman, with slack, sagging breasts, and loose flesh at her belly. Like a victim of some disaster, she drew herself into the fetal position. "Oh— I'm sorry!" Con said.

"Did you bring me a pillow?" said Marlene. She didn't lift her head, but the tone made her question seem not helpless but amused, as if Con was too young and foolish to have thought of a pillow.

"Don't you have a nightgown?" said Con. Marlene's bag was still in the study, and Con brought it in, opened it, and found a pair of dark blue satin pajamas. "I have to put a sheet on," she said. "Should I help you?"

She was exhausted too. She disliked coaxing Marlene's arm into her pajama top, then supporting her as she pulled the other sleeve into position. She got Marlene to stand, helped her into the pants, and made up the bed. Then she awkwardly kissed Marlene's faintly lined cheek and left her standing next to the bed.

Con's toes hurt where she'd bruised them on the train tracks. She had an anxious moment as she got ready for bed: Jerry might find another woman, one who'd last longer than the un-named woman from her neighborhood. Well, none had lasted so far. And if he did, maybe he'd cheat on her with Con.

She'd kept her own bed for herself. That night she awoke only once, and felt sleepers on all sides of her. How good to have Joanna temporarily near her, neither in jail nor in Barn-aby Willis's ambiguous studio, and not in Tim's North Carolina apartment either. As Con fell asleep again, her mother's ghost—dark gray, not white, looking as her mother looked in photographs from the forties: stocky, alert, kind, with a black coil of hair at her neck—moved toward her as if down a dark street. Con could recognize her perfectly though her mother's shape was dark and the street was dark. "It's Mommy," she said to Barbara, who was there too. "I see Mommy."

"So do I," said Barbara, before she returned to being dead.

Chapter 5

$\diamond\diamond\diamond\diamond\diamond\diamond\diamond\diamond\diamond\diamond\diamond$

Before Marlene or anyone else woke up on Saturday morning, Con took a good look at the untidy contents of her mother's wooden box. Gert had used it as a place to stick anything small, and it contained buttons, safety pins, and bobby pins, as well as a tangle of necklaces and other jewelry. It all looked familiar—a string of dark red beads, a square copper pin decorated with a copper twig and leaves. Turning them over, Con's hands were unsteady.

Today she'd have to manage Marlene and Joanna together, but she'd have Peggy for comfort and help. Joanna, just now, seemed calm; apparently she planned to join them for the whole day. Con still couldn't figure out why she had suddenly decided to return to New York when Marlene was mentioned; maybe Joanna's complicated interior had coincidentally shifted just as Con mentioned Marlene.

Con ate some cereal and then Marlene came into the kitchen, dressed in black pants and a sweater. She said, "What's funny is that I don't remember going to bed last night."

"You had a long day," Con said. Marlene liked grapefruit juice in the morning, and Con had bought some.

"Was I appalling?" Marlene asked. Her voice was lower, without its usual ironic lilt. She sat down.

"You were fine."

"I thought we'd talk, finally," Marlene continued, sounding more like herself, "but you were looking after your ex." She sat up straighter, and Con felt the same question from Marlene she'd sensed all her life. Are you with me? Shall we be outrageous together? But her actual question, as well, seemed to linger in the air. Was I appalling?

"We can talk now," said Con. It was eight o'clock. Maybe Joanna and Jerry would sleep late. She poured coffee and made some toast.

"He was certainly making much of that ankle," Marlene said.

"It was a bad sprain."

"Not as bad as he'd like you to *think*, of course."

In the past, Con might have joined in the joke. "It wasn't a *fatal* sprain," she could say. "Jerry would like us to think it was a *fatal* sprain." But Jerry had not made too much of the sprain. She said, "I had a good time with Jerry."

"I hope you didn't go to the El Greco show," Marlene said. "Or if you did, I hope you don't object to going back." She broke her toast into fragments. "Of course, I can go alone."

"We'll go together," Con said. She was tempted now to talk

about the dazzling, vestigial structures of the lost Brooklyn Circle, but Marlene would claim she'd known it all her life, and the secret would be spoiled. It had been a good day despite the sprain, despite the risk and craziness. She remembered being afraid she'd be disbarred.

Marlene and Con, as a pair, were not what they'd been. Pace had been everything; the conversation was just slightly slower. And there was a touch of panic behind Marlene's remarks. Are you *still* with me? she seemed to ask. Even if I'm old? Con had the frightening thought that at last *she* had become the powerful one.

Then Marlene said, "When I was young, in Brooklyn, my boyfriend and I—whatever boyfriend I had—if we had a free day, we'd take the subway to Coney Island and walk on the boardwalk. Even in the winter. Especially in the winter."

"Jerry and I should have done that," said Con, which was almost like admitting they had become lovers.

"I have a *brilliant* idea," said Marlene, and though her tone was ironic, Con knew that she mocked only the word, not the idea. "Let's do that. Let's go to Coney Island!"

Con instantly wanted to go—to be Marlene's confederate in making this slightly outrageous plan—but she didn't say so right away. "It's cold," she said. "And the El Greco show . . ."

"We'll do both. Coney Island in the morning, El Greco in the afternoon. Do you have walking shoes? You're not one of those women who sacrifices comfort to fashion, I know *that* much about you!"

"Of course I have walking shoes. Peggy's coming too, you know."

"Well, I hope Peggy has walking shoes!"

"And Joanna. Everybody has walking shoes."

"Joanna?"

"My daughter."

"Of course," said Marlene. "Quite a party. Is your crippled former husband coming along?"

"No," said Con, smiling, giving in. "He's going to stay right here on the couch and recuperate from his horrendous injury." Walking together on the boardwalk in sun and bright air—Coney Island was an excellent idea.

"When the dogs had sprains," Marlene said, "we immobilized the leg."

"I forgot you worked in an animal hospital."

"For years. Supposedly I was the receptionist, but I could keep the big dogs quiet, so they'd call me back when there was trouble. I don't know what the rest of them were afraid of." She put down her mug of coffee and looked at it steadily, as if it were a troublesome dog.

"Yet I don't think of you as a person who goes for pets," Con said.

"Pets, no. I never wanted a pet."

"But you said you were so good with them."

"A professional relationship," Marlene said. "I'll take a shower now."

But Con heard the shower running. "Joanna's in there," she said, but it must have been Jerry in the shower, because just then Joanna came into the kitchen, scratching under her arms, in sweatpants and a gray T-shirt. Her exuberant black curls were all over the place.

"That doesn't make sense," Joanna said grouchily, glancing at Marlene.

"What's wrong with it?" Marlene sat down again.

"There's only one kind of relationship with an animal. Either they trust you or they don't."

"They trusted me to know what I was doing. I never encouraged them to *like* me. I didn't want them shedding on me and kissing me."

"Is that why you didn't take Grandma's cat?" Joanna said. "I still feel bad about that cat."

Con didn't remember a cat. Then she did. She'd gone to her mother's apartment in the first place to take care of a cat, a fat creature with orange fur that came off in handfuls. "But what happened to it?"

"Well, Marlene wouldn't take it. I asked her after the memorial service. She said, 'Take him to the vet and have him put down.'"

"No!" said Con. Surely they hadn't done that.

"Just because I understood them doesn't mean I sentimentalized them. An electrician doesn't necessarily like electricity."

"Of course he does, if he's a good one," said Joanna, but Marlene was still talking. "Sometimes I had to give them injections. If you're sentimental, you're not going to stick a needle into an animal—but they needed those shots."

The bathroom door squealed on its hinges and Jerry appeared in a bathrobe. The door had been squealing since Con had rehung it. Joanna moved toward the bathroom, then turned. "They taught you to give injections?" she said.

"That's right."

"Marlene would like a shower too," Con said.

"I'll just be a minute," said Joanna. "When are we going to the museum?"

"In the afternoon," said Con, while simultaneously Marlene said, "Coney Island first, in the morning."

"All right," Joanna said.

"It's cold out," said Con, sniffing the air at the bottom of a slightly open window. "You don't have to come."

"Not that cold," Joanna said. "The parachute jump. If they called it outdoor sculpture they could charge people to look at it."

"Haven't they taken that down by now?" said Marlene, but Joanna was gone and Con didn't know.

They were alone again. Con put away the breakfast things, then sat down opposite Marlene yet again and picked up her coffee cup. "Marlene, you can't imagine what happened," she said. She had decided to tell Marlene about the return of the bag, but not about the Brooklyn Circle.

"You know," said Marlene, "you look like your mother. I always said you didn't, but you do."

"Really?" said Con. She didn't know if she wanted to look like her mother.

"Of course, the hair is similar, and the height. I always thought your eyes were different, and your expression," Marlene said. "But I found myself seeing her when I looked at you."

"So—the oddest thing happened," Con said.

"Of course, at the end she looked so confused. My god she could be stupid—stupid and boring." Con drew in breath sharply, but Marlene kept talking. "But up to then. It's a timid look—"

"Timid?"

"Well, alert. As if there's something you might see if you turned your head, but you're not sure you *want* to see it."

Now Marlene smiled slyly at her across the table. She seemed, just now, younger than Con, who was an old, frightened lady, struggling to understand the choice Marlene was asking her to make. The jaunty Marlene whom Con had loved as a girl had made her way gaily and bravely—somehow—through the Depression and World War II, and had never given up that gaiety, though her tone was skeptical and cynical. The stories she told, even of those hard years, were about success and pleasure. When she'd spoken of the Depression to Con, she had mentioned not poverty and joblessness but freedom to try anything. Marlene's elbows in the black sweater braced her upper body on the table. Her flesh was old but her posture was sloppy and youthful, as she leaned forward smiling at Con. "You're a nice girl, Connie, you always were," she said with what sounded like pity. Her voice was low, now, and steady. "Now it's my turn for a shower."

"But you loved my mother," Con said in a low voice.

"That goes without saying," said Marlene.

She stood, and Con rose as well. "Marlene," she said quickly, "what was your husband's name?"

Marlene stopped, looked at her. "Lou," she said.

"Lou what?"

She hesitated. "Brown," she said then. "Lou Brown. You must have known that!" She left the room.

Sunday morning and Con was still in her mother's apartment, but as soon as she got her thoughts and the apartment organized, she and Joanna could leave. Today was the day, Con decided—as she lay in the dusty morning sunshine—that she would learn to control her memories. Sarah had said something Con didn't want to think about, and she wouldn't. Today she would think only practical thoughts. She would get herself and her daughter out of the apartment, to Penn Station, onto the train, and home to Philadelphia. That thought made her remember Jerry, someone else she would keep out of her mind as much as possible.

She hoisted herself from bed more briskly than at any time all week, put on the clothes she'd worn the day before—she'd run out of clean ones—and set the table for herself and Joanna. Soon she was eating while gazing out the window at the elaborately irregular edge of the sky, a sleeping daughter behind her, and thinking what she recognized as her mother's vaguely worried thoughts. Had she inherited the mood, which seemed to grip her face from within? Did moods fly out of a dying person's mouth and attach themselves to survivors?

The phone rang, and it was Barbara. "I'm in New York. I got a cheap flight, but I had to come right away."

"I thought you weren't coming yet." Con had assumed she'd have time to prepare for Barbara.

"I saved a lot of money. Now we have to hold a funeral."

"Joanna's here. She wants a rabbi. Where are you?"

"A motel in Queens. I rented a car."

"Oh, Barb," said Con. They cried.

"Have you found the will?" said Barbara.

"No—but, Barb, did you know Marlene is the executor?"

"Marlene? Why? Why did you let that happen?"

"I didn't know," said Con.

"How could you not know? What's wrong with you?"

"Look, I didn't know. I'll see you soon." Barbara was right, of course, but Con was not going to add something else to feel guilty about. She was pleased she'd see her sister soon, and wanted to stay pleased. "Just don't think," she admonished herself out loud—then glanced at the sofa, but Joanna was still asleep.

For their outing to Coney Island on this November morning, Con wore a heavy sweater under her jacket, though it made her look bulky. Her winter coat was dirty. When she left the apartment—the others had preceded her—Jerry was at the table with coffee. He reached a long thin arm up and tapped her shoulder. "Wasn't that fun?" he said.

Con wondered whether he meant bed or the Brooklyn Circle.

"Even though my ankle hurts," he continued.

"It was stupid to go up there. I'm glad we found the old train line, but I'm not glad we did *that*."

"Isn't that where I proposed to you?" said Jerry.

"Is that what it was? Do you want cereal?"

"I'll find what I need," he said. "Come closer."

"I don't think so," said Con, but then she leaned over and kissed the hair behind his ear.

Peggy knew the subways so well she had told Con just

where her party should stand on the platform, so as to meet her on the train. She'd been surprised but not unwilling to add Coney Island to the outing. Marlene didn't seem to mind the subway steps, though she gripped the handrail tightly. On the swaying train, she and Peggy greeted each other with theatrical glee. Peggy was beautifully dressed in a calf-length tan skirt and a short jacket. She sat down next to Joanna and that left Con with Marlene, who talked about how much she hated the war in Iraq.

The Q train ran above ground much of the way; Marcus Ogilvy would have been pleased. It turned creakily at Brighton Beach and continued parallel to the ocean. At the first glimpse of the sea between buildings, Con cried out. Then she saw the parachute jump, the Ferris wheel, and the roller coaster, larger and stranger than she remembered them, extravagantly tall, or round, or undulant. Con, Marlene, Peggy, and Joanna emerged from the Stillwell Avenue Station just a block from the boardwalk.

As predicted, the day was cold but sunny, and though it was only the beginning of November, the sun had the low sharpness Con associated with winter, when you always knew from which direction the sun was coming at you. She didn't mind the cold, and decided not to worry that anybody else might. They were all more strong-willed and stubborn than she was. They had been free to stay away and had chosen to come.

On the boardwalk, old people who seemed unchanged from those she'd seen years and years ago still sat on the same benches, huddled in coats and sometimes blankets. Marlene belonged to their demographic group but was not like them.

Her black coat was open at the neck, and she'd knotted a white scarf under it loosely, so it left her throat exposed and rose and fell in the wind. She wore no hat. Her face with its prominent nose seemed large and individualized compared to the squashed faces of the people on the benches. Did other old people sink into anonymity? Marlene's eyes were hooded, looking even darker than they had looked the night before, aware and critical. She turned to Con as they walked. "Gert and I picked up sailors here a couple of times," she said. "We went under the boardwalk and kissed them."

"Not my mother!" said Con.

"She was already married," Marlene said. "She took off her ring and put it in her pocket, and once, she thought she'd lost it. We went scrambling around in the sand, but it was right there—she'd forgotten which pocket."

Con could imagine her mother taking off a ring and forgetting which pocket she'd put it in, but not taking off her wedding ring, not kissing a sailor. "You're making that up, surely."

"No, we did it. All kinds of things. Your father was in the army. We didn't do anything wrong—just kissed the poor boys. It's nice to do a little extra kissing when you're married."

"Still . . ." said Con.

"They were going off to be killed, and your mother was a sucker for any homesick boy. Even I. I've never been a mother, but I felt like a mother to those sailors. I wanted to give them my breasts." She paused and seemed to consider a thought, then spoke again, glancing at the ocean. "Of course, if they said something stupid, I told them it was stupid."

They walked side by side down the wide boardwalk with its

smooth, clean planks, laid in diagonal sections. It had been re-stored, spruced up. The sand was mostly clean, speckled with the footprints of gulls. The sea was calm, and light scoured everything; anything might be visible, even young Gert and Marlene: two saucy but essentially sensible women taking off their shoes and holding them carefully as they stepped onto the sand. They squinted in the dim light under the boardwalk at sweet, foolish gentile boys—one blond, one redheaded—in middy blouses. Con tried to believe it. "Was it being adventur-ous that made you friends, you and my mother?" said Con. The idea in her mind was of *moderate* license, *limited* license: Gert and Marlene were prudent in their disarray, their disloyalties and experiments. Maybe if she saw it that way, she could imag-ine her timid mother participating in such activities.

"Adventurousness?" said Marlene. "I never thought Gert had much of that."

"Then what *was* it?" Con said. Joanna, with her dilapidated gray backpack hanging off one shoulder, was now walking on Con's other side. Peggy had dropped behind to stare at the water, looking in her long tan skirt like a nineteenth-century heroine. Con followed her gaze, then searched for ships and found one far away—a low smudge.

Marlene had not spoken. "What was what?" said Joanna.

"I was wondering what made Marlene and Grandma such good friends," Con said. "They were so different."

Joanna made an impatient noise, then seemed to become dis-tracted. Maybe her cell phone had vibrated. The next time Con looked for her, she was leaning against the railing at the edge of the boardwalk, shielding the little phone with her body.

Con was trying to remember something. She had found letters from Marlene in her mother's apartment. Where were they? Had she thrown them away? Would she have done that? She remembered the feel of reading the letters, on brittle onion-skin that rattled when handled. Something in the letters had troubled her, but she couldn't remember what it was. "Marlene, did you really think my mother was stupid and boring?"

"Oh, Connie," Marlene said. She stopped where she was. "She was sometimes stupid, and often boring. She just was. But I loved her so—she rescued me."

"Rescued you from what?"

Marlene was silent. Then she said, "After the war—well, it was a bad time." She paused. "For me. Gert got to New York with you kids. Abe wasn't even out of uniform. She found a tiny little apartment, and when I needed a place to go, she just said, 'Don't be ridiculous.' So I went to her. I slept sitting up in a chair, or I slept during the day, in her bed."

"She was kind." Con didn't think of Marlene as someone for whom things had ever been difficult, someone with no place to sleep, even temporarily.

"Not particularly kind," Marlene said. "She was matter-of-fact. About that, about other things—well, it's a boring story."

"I won't be bored. Tell me," said Con, but Marlene had started walking again, and then turned around to look at something. They had passed Peggy, who had gotten ahead of them as they spoke, but now had stopped to talk to some people on a bench. Apparently she had asked for a light for her cigarette. Con sometimes forgot that Peggy smoked, she saw it so little. But Marlene had seen the gesture, and wanted one of Peggy's cigarettes. "Forgot mine," she said. The three older women now walked together, two of them smoking. Con, on the right, closest to the ocean on the wide boardwalk, turned to look at the others. Peggy was windblown, shrewd, beautiful, her gray curls blown back across her face, baring her forehead. Marlene looked mysterious.

"Are you tired?" Con called.

"I'm just starting out."

"Did my mother really kiss a sailor under the boardwalk?" Con said. She was shy about asking for details about the other time—the time after the war.

"I told you she did."

"I can't picture it."

"Well, she wasn't your mother yet."

And then, at the thought of Gert—young, almost thin, in a striped linen dress and a hat, pacing methodically next to her glamorous girlfriend, her wedding ring in a pocket, as she turned to kiss a stranger and make him feel better about the prospect of dying—Con felt something enter her body, something familiar but new. At long last, grief for her mother shoved against her like a clumsy passerby, and she stopped where she was. For a moment the others didn't notice; then they turned.

"Is the smoke bothering you?" said Peggy. Joanna approached, looking as if she had something to say, but Con didn't want to listen. She wanted to negotiate with the spirit that seemed to have entered her, the gigantic disembodied person informing her limbs and torso, pressing its way into her blood vessels and bones. She didn't want to speak, waiting to receive it. Peggy came to stand near her. She put out her cigarette. Con tried to shake her head, to tell her that wasn't necessary, but even that seemed like unnecessary trouble.

Marlene stood where she was, her dark eyes suspicious, her large, skeptical nose even more adept at sniffing out foolishness than usual. "I've lived too long as a smoker to start questioning it now," she said. "Obviously I know all the arguments."

Con had to answer that. "No," she said. "My mother. I was thinking about my mother."

She said it to Peggy, who said, "Let's walk on the sand," stepping back to help Marlene down the steps from the board-walk to the beach. Joanna followed them. They made their slow way toward the water—the four of them, over the packed, damp sand, pocked with summer's cigarette butts, with broken shells and bits of trash. At the sea's edge, small waves rolled to the shore. Con looked for Joanna, and when she came near, put her hand on Joanna's arm. Joanna patted her shoulder awkwardly. Con wanted to sit on the ground but it was too cold. She sat anyway. Her mother had lived so briefly—longer than the sailor, possibly, but any human life is brief—and had done so little—nobody does much—and now she'd been gone for so many years. Con had never missed her mother. She had not enjoyed her enough to miss her. She had thought of her only now and then, of the look of her mother's face, or the shape of her body as it turned, of its puzzled pause on the way to whatever was supposed to happen next. Con had not missed Gert, but Gert missed Gert, that was the horror. Con could do without Gert, and when Con in her turn died, Joanna could do without Con. But Gert couldn't do without Gert. Con could not do without Con.

A radio, turned loud, played distorted music of a kind Con couldn't name, the wailing kind. "Oh, *stop*," she said, almost to herself.

Marlene turned in the direction of the radio. "Turn that down!" she shouted. "We're having a memorial service. This woman's mother died." It was bizarre. The people—a young couple in jeans—didn't understand or didn't care. The loud, ugly music continued. Con stood. Joanna still looked as if she wanted to say something. "What?" Con said. Joanna spoke a few words, but Con couldn't make them out.

Marlene strode across the sand, clutching her coat as if it might have dragged in the sand. Con saw her talk severely to the young people with the radio, and after a while they moved away down the beach. It was possible to hear Joanna above the sound of the wind and the small waves. "Barnaby Willis," she said.

"What about him?"

"I'll tell you later." Con nodded, and put her arms around Joanna's shoulders as they walked together across the sand. "I'm cold," Joanna said.

"We need a hot lunch," said Con. She pulled herself out of her mood. It was like a room she'd entered.

"I'm not hungry," Joanna said. "I'm cold." She pressed crossed arms into her chest and walked more clumsily and heavily than the sand and wind seemed to make necessary. Con looked for Peggy, who came last, still gazing at the ocean. Marlene led the way. Con fell back. She didn't need to feed Joanna or consider Peggy's mood. Now she did miss her mother. All those years, she had said she didn't miss her mother, but she did. She scarcely remembered a time when her mother, a timid woman, had cared for her or even advised her. Her mother was a friendly but unsurprising companion. But there had been something. They had looked out at life together, the two of them, Gert and Constance, with the same—she didn't know how to put it—the same note playing in their heads, the same color filling in the spaces around people and events. Con even knew how the note sounded, and it was the same as the way the color looked: between pink and orange, clear. Not that her mother would have described life as a color, or color as a sound. A certain practical, essentially accepting glance at what was outside of them united Gertrude and Constance Tepper, and all these years Con had had to look around all by herself, without that accompanying gaze emanating from someone beside her. The loss was no less than the shape of thought, and she was astonished that she hadn't known about it. Now she walked carefully, holding onto her mother's absence. For the rest of her life, she wanted to remember and notice the shape of the empty space beside her.

"We've walked to Brighton Beach," Peggy said now, spreading her arms to gather the four of them together. "Let's go to a Russian restaurant." At some point they had returned to the boardwalk when Con was not noticing.

"Of course," Marlene said as they hesitated—as if continuing a conversation that had not been interrupted— "that wasn't all she did for me."

"Who?" Peggy said.

"My mother," said Con.

"Oh, of course," said Peggy. "No, you were friends for years and years, weren't you? What was that like? Did you babysit?"

"Never babysat," Marlene said. "She was perfectly aware that I'd stab them with diaper pins. I didn't do much for her, truth to tell."

"Of course you did," said Con. "She was afraid of everything, until she'd talked to you. 'The oven's making a noise, I'd better call Marlene.' 'The super yelled at me, quick, call Marlene.'"

"Advice is cheap," said Marlene. Con again sensed Joanna's impatience, at her side. It would be better to change the subject. Joanna now led the way off the boardwalk on the side away from the ocean, and they began walking to Brighton Beach Avenue.

"Well, this neighborhood has certainly changed!" Marlene said, as they passed modern apartment buildings. "It wasn't so cozy and safe, you know, in the old days. Coney Island was famous for crime. You had to watch out for pickpockets—all kinds of things. This feels kind of tame, I have to say." She put a hand on Con's arm as if to slow her. Maybe she was tired after all.

"But what I started to tell you," Marlene said, "Now, promise me you won't be shocked. Maybe your daughter will take an interest if I tell her just one story from those days. Maybe this will prove we weren't so boring and stodgy. I think your daughter thinks nothing exciting happened."

Joanna said nothing, and Marlene kept talking. "Well, in the forties—after the war—I had a boyfriend who was—how shall I put this—maybe a little *too* colorful. Nothing he wasn't involved in, one way or another. Of course I didn't realize this when I started going out with him, and when it became obvious, I foolishly imagined I could reform him. Hah. No luck. Meanwhile, though—well, it was a pretty close shave, and your parents saved my skin. His too—at least for the time being."

"What happened?" said Peggy. "What did he do?"

"It was all my fault," Marlene said. Again, she stopped. "Or, sort of my fault. I said I'd go to Coney Island—the story happened right here—with Abe and Gert and the kids, and I thought I'd get bored, so I told my boyfriend to meet me on the beach, and we'd pretend it was a coincidence. Then I insisted we put the blanket down right where I'd told him we'd be, and sure enough, Gert and I are lying there getting a tan, watching you children play in the sand, and along he comes. So I acted surprised, you know—and the two of us went off together. So far so good.

"Anyway—" she put her other hand on Joanna's shoulder and patted it. Joanna shook her off, but Marlene persisted, and Joanna allowed it. Now they walked again. They had reached Brighton Beach Avenue, the Russian neighborhood under the el train, and Marlene was briefly distracted by the Russian signs advertising all kinds of businesses. Everything was in the shadow of the elevated train—the one they'd come on, the usual grimy el, not Marcus Ogilvy's vision of light and lightness, but more than acceptable if elevated trains please you. Peggy pointed out Russian delis, Russian insurance companies and gift shops, a drug store, a travel agency, a Russian psychic.

"Well," Marlene said, "wouldn't you know, my boyfriend and I are strolling on the boardwalk, just enjoying the sun and the day, and what should happen but he runs into a man who owes him money—and they talk, and he says something, and the other guy says something. And the next thing I know my boy-friend slips away from me, and the *next* thing I know there's a scream, and people running and shouting. Well, the upshot was he'd stabbed the guy. Or somebody stabbed the guy, and later the man identified my boyfriend and me. He'd seen me too, of course. I thought my goose was cooked. But Gert and Abe—you never knew this about your grandparents, my dear," she said, patting Joanna's shoulder again as they made their way up the avenue. "I hope this isn't going to shock you. They told the cops I was on the blanket with them the whole after-noon—they said we both were. We got off. The guy who was stabbed was not a great witness, and the cops didn't think they had enough of a case—they forgot about it. You can't imagine how relieved I was. Well, that's the kind of life we led in those days—but you should have heard Abe. I had to promise over and over I'd never have anything further to do with the guy. That was an easy promise to keep!"

"But you didn't keep it, did you?" Joanna said in a low voice.

"Oh, sure I did," said Marlene. "Look, here's a restaurant." She stopped. "My father would have liked this one." They were led through the warm, dark room to a table, and as soon as they'd settled themselves, Marlene declared that they should order the lunch special, several courses. "This is the way it's done," she said. "We won't need dinner. Later, we'll have coffee and cake."

The place was quiet, with Russian ornaments and cloth hangings they could scarcely see in the dimness, and Con felt inordinately grateful for the warmth, for chairs, for the change of scene, which said one part of the day was over and a different one had begun. It would be a good thing if, here at the restaurant, they talked about nothing but food. When the waiter came, Marlene said firmly, "I want Ukrainian borscht, stuffed veal, and potatoes," and he was charmed. Maybe American old ladies didn't usually order so much food. Peggy asked for soup and chicken, but instructed the man to leave out potatoes or rice. "Carbs?" she said, and he nodded. Con ordered a full meal, carbs and all. Joanna just asked for coffee. "I'll pick something later," she said. But the coffee seemed to cheer her, and she talked about the parachute jump and the Ferris wheel. "How often do you see something that big with a *shape*?" she asked. "With *lines*?"

"But the phone call . . . ?" Con said.

"Did you hear I got arrested?" her daughter said, looking at Peggy, who nodded. Joanna told her the story anyway in a low voice, leaning toward her as if to exclude Marlene, but of course it was just the sort of story Marlene liked. She proposed flying to North Carolina immediately to picket the police station and the bar. Then she praised Joanna for criticizing the war in Iraq. "Weapons of mass destruction!" Marlene said, her voice liquid with sarcasm.

"Was the call about what happened at the bar?" Peggy asked then.

"No— Well, maybe. Maybe he's decided my life is too interesting. He likes women just active enough to haul things around his studio."

"Barney," said Con. "The sculptor Joanna works for."

"I went to art school, you know," said Marlene. "I was an artist."

"I've heard," said Joanna. Her voice was flat. She looked at Marlene as if it hurt her neck to turn her head in that direction. Con realized with a mixture of dread, weariness, and excitement that something was going to happen. It had seemed odd all along that Joanna had joined them. Something made her want to be with them—to return to New York in the first place—and it wasn't pleasure in Marlene's company. But for the moment, Joanna ignored Marlene and explained to Peggy who Barnaby Willis was. "One of his former interns needs a job," she said tensely. "He doesn't need two of us."

"This is terrible," said Con.

"He gets *me* for free—the foundation pays," Joanna said. "And he'd *still* rather have her. I suppose he likes the way she sucks his cock. He told me I could do what I wanted and get the rest of the money for doing nothing—he won't tell."

"Does she suck his cock literally or figuratively?" said Peggy.

"Both, I assume," Joanna said.

"Oh, for heaven's sake," Con said, but Joanna shrugged. "I asked too many questions, even about his work. Maybe he does this when the intern figures out he's not God. I don't care."

"Does that mean you're going back to North Carolina?" Con said. "What will you do?"

"There's not much for me there," said Joanna, "but I'll still be a sculptor. That's what I'll do." She shrugged with one shoulder, as Jerry often did. "And make money somehow." She shook her head as if to shake that topic out of it. "I hate borscht. Do they have any other kind of soup?"

She ordered a large bowl of chicken soup with meat dumplings. The other soups arrived, and soon the main courses. The food was good, but Con was sorry she'd ordered so much. Now she was hot. Marlene chewed steadily beside her. When Con raised her eyes, Peggy smiled. Still, the meal was tense, and the tension came from Joanna. It continued to seem anticipatory, and as they ate, with desultory talk about the food, Con felt like turning to see if Barnaby Willis, dragging one of his outsize steel sculptures, was about to stomp into the Russian restaurant so as to discard her daughter more publicly. Or would Tim do it? "Are men ever worth it?" she said. That seemed like a safe topic. The male waiter was out of earshot.

"They have lovely equipment attached to their fronts," said Peggy.

"Oh, if only that was all there was to them!" said Con. Jerry's lovely equipment had made her happy only two days before.

"Loving women is just as hard," Joanna said. "Loving people who don't love back. It doesn't matter if they're men or not. It doesn't matter about equipment."

She said it firmly enough that nobody could disagree.

Marlene stopped chewing. "Loving women," she said. "Are you referring to homosexual love or friendship?"

"Any kind of love," said Joanna promptly.

"Gert never loved me as much as I loved her," Marlene said casually, while sawing through meat. She had eaten almost all her lunch.

"You're kidding me," said Con. "She adored you. She never felt sure of you—I guess she knew you were smarter."

"That may have been the way it looked to you," said Marlene, "but it wasn't how it was."

"But you were so powerful."

"But she had children."

"But you'd call, and she'd go nuts." Now that Con knew she missed her mother, she remembered perfectly those long-ago moments when Gert turned from her and Barbara to lose herself in friendship.

"No, *you'd* go nuts, and she'd be off the phone. Gert didn't know how lucky she was to have me."

Joanna's spoon clattered to the side of her bowl and everyone looked at her, but she said nothing. Then she said, "Tooth."

"You have a toothache?" Peggy said.

"No, I banged the spoon on my tooth." Then she said with a catch in her voice, "It wasn't *always* money you wanted, was it?" She said it to Marlene. Marlene was still chewing, looking at her plate. Everyone else was done—Con had been looking around for the waiter. She didn't know what Joanna meant, whether it was a strange joke or a real question. Peggy looked confused, but didn't say anything. Con wanted to go to the museum. Now Marlene had definitely stopped eating. Con didn't remember seeing the waiter again, but noticed that the check was on the corner of the table. They split it up—not fairly, but everyone contributed. Con didn't know whether Joanna's remark about money had come before or after the check had been put down. A joke about money might make sense with the check on the table.

They left the restaurant. When Con stepped from the darkly carpeted, darkly upholstered interior onto Brighton Beach Avenue, Marlene and Joanna had preceded her, and they stood waiting, apart, each momentarily abstracted. The

Q train's supports and track bed dimmed the street and sidewalk, and then a train passed above them, and as Con looked it seemed that what deepened and filled the complicated shadows was not its shape but its noise. When it passed, in relative silence Brooklyn's interrupted light again speckled and striped the old woman and the young one. Joanna's face was shadowed; Marlene squinted, as a squib of sunlight found her white hair and hooded eyes, and the sidewalk under her shoes.

Con eating breakfast at her mother's table might have been turning into her dead mother—slouching as her mother did, picking with a fingernail at a three-dimensional stain on the tablecloth—but Joanna was not turning into Con; she was a good reminder of Con's present life as she awoke, sat up, and began talking, shaking her big teenaged head from side to side as if her ears needed air. "Who was that on the phone?"

"Aunt Barbara."

"I thought so. Who was it last night?"

"Someone from my office," Con said. She paused. "Aunt Barbara is at a motel near Kennedy Airport. She's on her way here."

"Okay," said Joanna. She scratched her breasts under her pajama top and went barefoot to the bathroom, then came to the table and sat there, but when Con said, "Toast? Cereal?" she said, "I'm not hungry yet."

Con left her at the table and tried making a list of all they had to do before they could leave. Of course they didn't have to empty the apartment yet, but they certainly had to empty the refrigerator. Yet what were they to do with everything in it? She said, "I've gotten to know one of the neighbors," and left Joanna to ring Peggy's doorbell. She didn't have her phone number.

Con didn't ask—yet—about the cat, but she asked if Peggy would take some food. "You have to be willing to throw away good food," Peggy said. "People die in my family every week. You have to be merciless. I'll come up later."

Upstairs again, Con made up her mind to be merciless. She found a suitcase and began putting into it things of her mother's she wanted. Joanna insisted on adding Gert's knitted afghans and shawls and blankets, and even a bag of half-knitted sweaters for babies who'd grown up while Gert searched for more yarn from the correct dye lot.

"It's the most Grandma thing in the place," said Joanna. "Except for the answering machine."

"The answering machine?"

"I'm taking that. I want her voice."

Con didn't think she wanted to own her mother's hesitant voice, sounding baffled about this disturbing invention as she recited her phone number twice. Today Con felt grimly reconciled to her mother's death. She could do without her mother. Yet when she opened the drawer with the photographs, she dropped to her knees and spread her hands on them as if she touched something alive. Her mother had amassed these objects so deliberately: how was Con to discard them?

"Where's her body?" said Joanna, coming along behind her.

"It's being cremated."

"Did it already happen?"

"I don't know."

"Mom, don't you care?" But then she left the room and Con didn't see her for a while.

Barbara and Peggy met on the staircase. Con came out to greet her sister and there was Peggy as well. It seemed amazing that her sister in London could turn so quickly into her sister here in her arms. Barbara felt soft and indefinite. Her hair was waved and streaked, and she looked more professional than Con did. After she and Barbara embraced, Con tried to introduce both Barbara and Joanna to Peggy, but Barbara was exclaiming over her niece, whom *she* then introduced to Peggy. The moment when the sisters would have looked at each other and allowed themselves full consciousness of what they had lost—whom they had lost—was postponed, and felt staged when it happened. Barbara wanted coffee. She had questions. Con felt accused, once more, when she said that Gert was being cremated.

"It makes her so *gone*," said Barbara.

"But you told me to do it."

"You should have said no," said Barbara.

Con said, "And if we had a body, we'd have to have a burial. And a real funeral."

"Well, what *shall* we do about a funeral?"

"Memorial service."

Barbara exhaled noisily and settled herself. "All right, memorial service. But shall we sit shivah?"

"I've been sitting shivah since I got here," Con said. "I sat shivah before she died."

Barbara ignored that. "I'll stay around for a while," she said. "There are relatives we need to invite. . . . Are they all upset?"

Con had not phoned anyone else. She had intended to make

a list, but had not done it. Barbara now listed their father's two sisters and some cousins of their mother's. She carried her coffee to the sofa and took off her shoes. "Shall we plan it today?" she said. "We can check with people. . . ."

"Today," said Con, "I'm going home."

"Oh," said Barbara. "I thought you were going to stay here."

"Why would I stay here?"

"Well, somebody should, for a while, don't you think?" She put the coffee cup down on the end table to gesture, then swept her hand around the apartment. "The cat . . ." Once again, Con had forgotten the cat, but Joanna knew where he hid, and dragged him out and cuddled him.

"Did you think I was going to live here?" Con said. "What about Joanna? What about school? I've already been stuck here a week."

Peggy made an irritated noise. She was taking things out of the refrigerator, her back to the room.

"I just can't *believe* we don't have a mother!" Barbara said. Then she stood up, picked up the coffee mug, and started to walk toward Con, who stood at odds with herself in the middle of the floor, as so often this week. "Joanna could stay with Jerry," Barbara said then. "Besides, you told me you were leaving him."

Con didn't answer. When Barbara lifted her arm and let it drop—a gesture that said "I give up"—Con remembered how she'd always done that, how Barbara had lifted her arm when she wore a red plaid cotton dress to second or third grade, with a handkerchief pinned to her chest. "Barbara," she said quietly, "I'm glad you came."

"Of course I came," said Barbara, with a broad, shaky smile. She had shiny black eyes that became shinier now. She looked pretty and kind.

"Do you want more coffee?" said Con—as if they had all day, as if it were her house. But the phone rang, and it was Marlene. Con told her about the arrival of Joanna and then Barbara, but Marlene didn't sound interested. "Listen, do you have my address?" she said. "When can you send me the financial records?"

"Financial records?" said Con, and she saw Joanna look up sharply. Maybe it would be wiser not to send Marlene the canceled checks, or not right away. She'd look them over, at least.

"There must be canceled checks and so forth," Marlene was saying.

"I saw canceled checks," Con said. "I'll find them."

"It's not a large apartment," said Marlene. "Just get them to me before you go home."

"I have to go," Con said. "My sister—"

"All right, all right." The phone clattered, and she was listening to nothing. Marlene had hung up.

A taxi all the way to the Metropolitan Museum would have been ridiculously expensive, Marlene said, and she didn't mind changing trains. She seemed tired as she climbed the stairs at 86th Street in Manhattan, but the walk to Fifth Avenue was not long. At the museum, the broad, shallow steps—which had made Con feel royal as a girl—were busy with people going both ways under the banners announcing exhibits. Con didn't know why she was nervous. Marlene wanted to rest before looking at paintings, and they sat on benches in the Great Hall. Then she wanted to go to the ladies' room. Then they sat on a bench again. "Connie," she said then, after silence—they watched crowds pass, and Joanna studied a map of the museum—but then she stopped. Her eyes were darker and deeper than ever. Her face seemed less taut than usual, less disdainful. Con was sure Marlene would say she needed to take a cab back to Brooklyn and forget El Greco and the opera. But instead she said, "You'd know this. When did El Greco live? Before or after Michelangelo?"

Con didn't know. "After," said Joanna, who was shifting restlessly in front of them. "Michelangelo died when El Greco was young."

Marlene said, "I was not a good painter, but I actually *was*"— she paused—"a painter. Paint is wonderful."

"Do you paint, Joanna?" Peggy said. "I know you sculpt."

"I've painted. Lately if you give me a canvas I want to cut a hole in it and stick my arm through."

"Learn to paint," Marlene said. "Ugly big lumps will take you just so far."

"I know how to paint," said Joanna evenly.

"I wasn't bad, before the war," said Marlene. "I never went back to it after the war, and during the war—well, nothing was possible."

"Except kissing sailors," said Con, but nobody was listening.

"Shortages," Marlene continued. "Rationing."

Joanna said, "My grandmother, during the war—"

She stopped, and Marlene was silent for a long minute. She stretched her right arm forward, then her left, as far as possible, shaking out the long fingers of each hand. Then she said, "I temporarily lost touch with Gert, not long after we kissed those sailors. She moved to Florida. I'm sure she sent her address, but I never got it." Since Marlene had spoken of her boyfriend the criminal, Con had been trying to remember her letters to Gert from the war years. She remembered almost nothing—mostly a feeling of discomfort. Now she started, opened her mouth to speak, and closed it again. For a moment she'd wondered if she'd only dreamed or imagined the letters. No. Joanna said nothing, and after a while Marlene said, "Let's go." She stood and stretched again, a limber and lively woman in black, carrying a small black nylon purse that hung from one shoulder. She touched Con's arm, and then let her weight rest on it. They began to walk toward the elevator. Con's body seemed compressed by the weight of Marlene's hand and arm, which stayed where they were. She felt her bones move closer together, and she thought of them as lighter, more fragile objects than she usually did. Her bones were those of a fish.

Gert's voice spoke casually in Con's ear, with its old nasal bluntness. "You're tough."

"Something incredible," Con said—to herself, not to any of her companions.

"What?" Peggy turned and looked over her shoulder. "What's incredible?"

She and Joanna paused and Joanna looked at her skeptically. "How long ago did my mother die?" Con said. They all considered, but Con answered her own question. "She died in April, 1989. Fourteen and a half years." They were passing Greek and Roman antiquities. Joanna dropped behind them. "My purse came back," she said.

"What purse?" Peggy came to stand beside her.

"The week my mother died, my purse was stolen," Con said. "Someone mailed it to Jerry's house, and he brought it from Philly. It's at home. I almost couldn't leave today. I didn't want to leave it."

"That *is* incredible," said Peggy. "I remember when it was stolen."

Glad to have a topic other than her mother and Marlene, Con described the bag and its contents. She told them about the wallet—red nylon, worn at the corners—and the cards inside. She described the small hair brush and the light blue plastic tube with two tampons inside. Peggy and Marlene listened, walking past the ancient, distinguished exhibits in the museum, nodding as if Con's rediscovery had equal meaning. As Con spoke she began to cry, and then she couldn't stop. Her mother watched from somewhere in the air—baffled, irritated, loving. Through tears Con said, "And a little wooden box my mother used for jewelry. It was next to my bag, on her dresser, when I went to sleep that night."

"Is the jewelry all there?" said Peggy.

"Oh, I guess so. It wasn't fancy jewelry." Con stopped to wait as they arrived at the elevator and waited for Joanna. They emerged on the second floor, joining crowds moving toward and away from the El Greco show.

"Can we get some rules clear here?" Joanna said. "Do we

have to stick together? I can't do museums with people who insist on sticking together."

"Then I guess we don't," said Peggy, sounding amused, "but I'd like to stay with your mother, if that's all right."

Con thought she'd better stay with Marlene. Approaching the paintings, she tried to clarify her thoughts. She had two goals for the afternoon, and it occurred to her that they contradicted each other. First, she wanted calm—enough calm to look at pictures, to enjoy her friends and her daughter, to hold on to her thoughts about her mother. She wanted Joanna to keep silent and the anticipatory tension she still felt—which had increased when Marlene said she hadn't been in touch with Gert during the war—to go away. But Con wanted something else as well. Anticipatory tension doesn't readily disappear. She felt almost ready to understand something she'd wanted to understand all her life, and she wanted—she intensely wanted—the risk and excitement of discovery. She wanted to know what it had been like to be Gert and Marlene before Con herself was born, or when she was a child: to penetrate that privacy, to be part of it. It seemed dangerous to want to know—she herself would do nothing to try to find out more than she knew already, not today—but she couldn't stop wanting to know. And though she wanted Joanna to stay silent, she also did not want that. Joanna had something to say, that was clear.

As they paused in front of the first paintings, Con firmly put aside these thoughts in favor of calm, in favor of spending the rest of the day taking in the entertainment that would be provided by El Greco and Puccini, not by anyone she knew. The first paintings seemed irrelevant. Why did people hang paintings and why did others come and stand in front of them? Too many people were standing in front of these. The people pretended to be overwhelmed, or didn't bother to pretend and talked about something else. Con was determined not to pretend, but she couldn't keep herself from adopting the pose of an intelligent woman looking at paintings. Marlene marched from painting to painting and said nothing. Peggy read the descriptive placards. El Greco was a disorderly painter, Con thought. She had eaten too much lunch. Disorderly and religious, and Con didn't trust religion. El Greco was a disorderly painter, she found herself thinking once more, and wondered what she meant by it. Around her people with headsets stared as they listened to the instructive voices inside. What did those people know? Would she be better off if she knew it?

He painted standard religious scenes—with elongated figures, of course. Anyone could see that El Greco made no attempt to make the figures realistic, but someone behind Con said, "So real," as if that were the issue, and Con felt a familiar contempt for everyone in the museum but herself, then argued inwardly with her contempt. She was worse than Marlene. She had forgotten to look at the last two or three paintings. Her mother was dead, Marlene had a bad secret, and Jerry had nearly caused them to be killed falling from ancient elevated train tracks, or attacked by neighborhood vigilantes—and she wanted to be with Jerry again, but surely that too was an emotion not to trust.

A heavy swirl of red made her blink. She had been crying again. All she could see of the painting in front of her was red in the center. Then her vision cleared. Hands snatched at the red robe of Jesus while cruel idiots behind him jeered and stared and loved the excitement of what was about to happen. The painting's violence caused Con to make a sound, an exclamation of surprise. "What?" said Peggy, and looked around.

Con smiled at her in what felt like a sentimental way, as if they were looking at a picture of kittens and a baby, not a man being stripped naked by people about to kill him, a scene that compelled her, whatever her mood, whether the man was divine or not. The arm grabbing the red fabric was about to pull it up, which would be dreadful. Jesus ignored all this; he looked upward, and it was hard not to look up with him. His hand pointed to himself and also up. Spears pointed up. There were clouds. But in front of Jesus a man leaned over, incising a hole into the cross, to make it easier to nail Jesus onto it.

Peggy said, "That's his mother." Three women watched not Jesus or the crowd but the man with the awl. One was Mary, and another put her hand on Mary's upper arm to futilely warn her back, maybe even to push her back. "El Greco had a fight with the people who commissioned the painting," said Peggy. "They didn't like it that he put the three Marys in, or that the crowd is higher than Christ's head on the canvas. He got mad and demanded a lot of money, which I think he didn't get."

"Idiots," said Con.

The painting gave her a sadomasochistic thrill about the enormity of the humiliation that was coming. She had seen paintings and reproductions of paintings by El Greco many times before, but had not felt this uncomfortable stirring, almost as if she were a combination of the people in the painting: the brutes, and the mother who watches a calm workman prepare to torture and murder her son. Con did not identify with Christ; she couldn't imagine that calm. Maybe El Greco couldn't either. Con thought none of the prayerful saints looking skyward—in painting after painting—was convincing. They looked more like people trying to read skywriting.

Then, one painting with an upward swoop was *not* unconvincing. "Look," she said. It was the Virgin of the Immaculate Conception, a woman rising into the sky, surrounded by flying angels, with a city below her. The angels' wings looked capable of keeping them up. The painting made Con giddy. "Here," she said, "I *believe* in the verticality."

"He's vertical all the time," said Peggy. Marlene had moved on.

"But usually I don't believe it."

"I don't see the difference."

"Swoosh!" said Con, to demonstrate, and gestured so violently in the crowded hall that she smacked a stranger in the face, a woman coming up behind her to look at the painting.

"Hey!" said the woman.

"I'm sorry!" said Con. "I didn't hurt you, did I?"

"As a matter of fact, you did," the woman said. She was younger than Con, maybe in her late thirties or forties, wearing panty hose and a suit. She put her hand to her nose. "Blood," she said. She showed Con her hand. Reaching her bloodied hand out, she seemed to resemble one of the saints or martyrs in the paintings, perhaps displaying the stigmata. That thought seemed slightly funny to Con, but the woman was neither amused nor forgiving.

"I'm so sorry!" Con said again. "I didn't realize you were behind me."

"But it's so crowded here, you *should* have realized," said the woman.

"I should have. I'm so sorry," Con said again.

"Jen, let me see," said the man with her. "Do you have a Kleenex? I don't seem to have one. You've got to hold something to your face."

What if the woman was a hemophiliac? If she died, Con had killed her. A crowd was gathering. A man handed the woman a clean white handkerchief. Everyone would blame Con and take care of Jen, this young woman with cool blue eyes now looking at Con over the top of the handkerchief.

"What happened?" Marlene now said.

Peggy explained.

"Well, if this woman is going to push her way to the front—" Marlene said loudly, gesturing in her turn. Con raised a hand to stop her, then lowered it, looking around to see if she'd struck anyone else. "I saw her push," Marlene said. "She pushed past me."

"An accident," said the owner of the handkerchief, who had earned the right to take charge by owning and sacrificing such a useful and clean object. The small crowd, like the crowds around saints and Christ in the paintings—greedy for event—dispersed. Con moved along, looking at paintings without seeing them, fighting tears yet again. She was pleased that Marlene had lied for her.

They stopped at a painting Con knew well, because it belonged to this museum: *A Cardinal.* A man in early old age sat on a wooden chair, grasping one arm. Tensely, did he grasp it tensely? He wore a cardinal's red robes and hat, and the skirts of the robe opened to display a white lace garment underneath. The patterned floor under his chair seemed to tilt slightly, and as Con and her party stood looking at it—at a moment when the crowd happened to be elsewhere—the painting seemed to pitch the man forward, toward them. And so the clutching of the chair seemed necessary to keep the cardinal from sliding off it. What Con had long loved about the painting was a scrap of white paper on the floor in front of him, the aberration in the formal pose.

Joanna appeared beside them. They hadn't seen her since she'd refused their company. "Are you almost done?" she said.

"You don't like it?" said Con.

"Too crowded," said Joanna. "What was all that?" She shrugged in the direction of the gallery they'd come from. "Did you guys get into a fight?"

Con said, "It was nothing." Then she said, "Marlene rescued me from an angry mob."

Joanna didn't answer. She looked at the painting in front of her, the cardinal with the scrap of paper. "I hate this," she said.

"Oh, you do not," said Con.

"How do you know whether I hate it or not?" Joanna squared her solid shoulders to look up and down the painting. "This kind of painting," she said. "People find this in it, they find that in it—this one's supposed to be the Grand Inquisitor, but nobody's sure, and once it is, you can see cruelty, et cetera, et cetera. But he's just using tired Christian iconography, that's all it is."

"So the paper on the floor is a symbol of something?" said Peggy. "That's what *I* like, the scrap of paper on the floor."

"It's where he signed it. I guess he was showing off. He didn't want to put it in the corner. I guess it's a symbol—I don't know of what. He somehow manages to be unbearably pious and unbearably egocentric at the same time."

"But it's *odd*," said Peggy.

"I think the guy does look cruel," Con said. The man wore glasses.

"Cruelty, disorder," said Marlene. "Cruelty and disorder."

"It's a show-off painting," said Joanna. "'Look at me,' he's saying, 'I'm violating perspective! Look at me, I'm so religious!' I bet he was obnoxious. This painting is so *male*. How can you stand it?"

"You're confusing him with Barnaby Willis," Con said.

"Oh, honestly, Mother, I know the difference between El Greco and Barnaby Willis!"

"I'd give anything for a cup of coffee," Marlene said then.

Peggy said, "Does disorder have to do with cruelty? The paper on the floor—you can't put it out of your mind."

"Disorder doesn't necessarily have to do with cruelty," said Con.

"Maybe it does," Peggy said.

"Of course it does," Joanna said. "Let's go. Marlene wants coffee. I want food. What time is it?"

The day was disorderly. Reasonable people would be thinking about an early supper. Con, cranky all afternoon, wanted—surely they all wanted—something sweet, something sweet and a cup of coffee. They made their way slowly out of the museum. As they walked, Con found herself thinking about Jerry. Maybe he'd be her third husband. Third husbands were good, Peggy had always said. Third husbands were lovable because you were afraid they'd die, so their faults were adorable. Con didn't think Jerry had high cholesterol, but she didn't know for sure. Something else could be wrong. . . .

Peggy suggested a little place on a side street near Lincoln Center. At last, they took a taxi. Peggy sat with the driver and Con was squeezed between Joanna and Marlene. Marlene talked steadily about Central Park as they drove through it to the West Side. "The leaves are pretty much gone," she said. "When Lou and I got married, it was October and the leaves were glorious. We spent our wedding night at the Hotel Pierre. I said, 'I'd rather have a short fancy honeymoon than a long, cheap one.' I didn't feel like being alone with him for a week in Florida."

"Marlene," Con said suddenly. "Are you pleased with the way you've lived? How should we live?"

"I never wanted children," said Marlene.

Con was sorry she'd asked. When they stopped, Peggy paid and helped Marlene out of the cab. Con walked with Joanna, and Joanna touched her arm. "You know how to live better than she does," Joanna said, and Con turned her head and kissed her tall daughter's ear. Peggy held the door at the little restaurant, two steps down. A waiter fussily seated them and offered menus. They shrugged off their coats.

Emptying Gert's refrigerator took more time than Con would have imagined. Barbara argued with Peggy about the mustard, which she thought Peggy should take. Peggy was willing to take only a bottle of green olives with pimentos. Almost everything else was wilted or crusted over or oddly colored. Con found a bottle of soy sauce and couldn't imagine Gert cooking with soy sauce. She had probably bought it to use in a recipe—so as to impress a daughter—maybe around 1970. Joanna went into the bedroom, saying she'd put clothes into plastic bags for donation. When Con passed the open bedroom door a while later, Joanna was asleep. Later she thought she heard her crying. She went into the room, partly because it was lunchtime and she'd offered to go and buy sandwiches. Joanna was sitting cross-legged on the floor. A half-filled garbage bag was in front of her, and a pile of dresses to one side. She was reading Marlene's letters.

"Where did you get those?" Con said.

"What is all this shit?" said Joanna.

"Old letters. I want to keep them. Put them away."

"I'm just looking."

Con glanced behind her. "I really want to keep them. I'd rather Barbara didn't know about them."

Joanna looked up. "Oh. Okay. Because they're from Marlene? There are letters from Grandma too. Why didn't she mail them?"

"I think they must be drafts," said Con.

It wouldn't be possible to leave that day. She didn't know why she'd thought she could.

"She seems mad at Marlene in this one," Joanna said. "I read one where she was mad at you, too."

"Marlene was always complicated," Con said, with the feeling that she was talking faster than she should have been. "I love it that Grandma stayed friends with her. Sometimes Marlene must have found Grandma a little dull."

"Grandma isn't boring," said Joanna.

"No, of course not," Con said, noticing but not commenting on the present tense.

Con looked around the room. It was chaotic. Drawers were open everywhere. As she stood, perplexed at what had happened to her mother's bedroom, Joanna gathered the letters and stuffed them into the garbage bag.

"What are you doing? I'm keeping them," said Con.

"Oh, we're keeping everything in here," Joanna said. The bag was big, half full already.

"What else did you put in?"

"Knitting patterns, stuff like that." Joanna had tilted forward on her knees, and was reaching deep into the bag. Her thighs were strong and solid. She seemed a little frightening— so full of purpose. Then she sat back. Her face was flushed, maybe teary.

"You'll miss Grandma," Con said.

"What did Marlene do to her?" said Joanna.

"She didn't do anything. It just happened."

"Marlene's not a good person," Joanna said. Con lowered herself to the floor to take her daughter in her arms, but Joanna wrenched away.

Looking around the restaurant, Marlene smiled at all of them— mischievous, conspiratorial. "My feet hurt," she said. "I'm kicking my shoes off."

"Marlene," Joanna said, shoving her chair back slightly, as if to get a larger and longer view of the old woman, who sat diagonally across from her, looking shrewdly around, sizing up the place. "Marlene," she said, "did you go to prison after the war?"

Con was sitting next to Marlene, and she saw Peggy's eyes, across the table, register alarm, then quickly survey the room, as if looking for a distraction. Joanna put her ratty backpack on the table, and began taking things out: a scarf, a water bottle, a fat sketchbook with pages coming out, a black cotton pouch that looked like something a medieval peasant might have carried to market containing his year's wages, a large box of Tampax.

"I looked up *Turandot*," Peggy said then. "The City Opera uses supertitles, but I thought we still might want to know in advance what it's about. I never saw it."

"It's Puccini's last opera," Con said. She was grateful to Peggy for taking the group's attention from Joanna, who had put back what she'd taken out, but was still rummaging in her backpack. It was impossible to know what the question—which Marlene had ignored—had meant, or whether the rummaging was connected to it.

A waiter appeared and everything stopped while they figured out what to order. Joanna wanted a salad. Marlene asked for tea and strudel. Peggy and Con ordered coffee and chocolate cake. The waiter looked disapproving so Peggy ordered a bottle of wine as well. "That's a good idea," Con said, fearing—as usual—that Joanna would drink too much of it, but Joanna refused a wineglass. They returned to a discussion of the opera, and Peggy explained that it was about a Chinese princess who has her suitors slaughtered if they can't answer three riddles.

"It sounds stupid," Con said.

"Is it gruesome?" said Marlene.

"I think so, for an opera at least," said Peggy.

Marlene said, "If you can't enjoy stupid plots, you can't enjoy opera." The waiter poured Peggy a taste of wine, and as soon as she'd nodded, Marlene held her glass out.

"What's odd," Peggy continued, "is that it's a twentieth-century opera, but the plot is like a parody of nineteenth-century operas. A disappointed suitor is beheaded at the beginning. Offstage, thank God. The hero answers the riddle and she still doesn't want to marry him. I think that's the power of it: this woman would rather kill everybody than marry anybody."

"Love of cruelty," Con said.

"Cruelty, or maybe it's the wish to annihilate. To make things go away," Peggy said. Their food arrived. The slabs of chocolate cake were satisfyingly large. Con began eating hers at the edges, comforted to know there was so much of it.

"The opera is not complimentary toward China," Peggy said. "For a long time it was illegal to perform it there. It's his last work—did I say that? He didn't finish it, but somebody else did—so the very end is not as good."

"We'll make certain not to enjoy it," said Marlene, smiling at Peggy. Marlene had a closed-mouth smile; her teeth never showed.

"Cruelty is exciting," said Joanna.

"I don't think so!" Con said.

"Of course it is," said Peggy. "Cruelty and disorder—but not just any disorder. That's why the scrap on the floor works. It's the control in the rest of the painting. The hands on the arms of the chair. That makes the scrap unbearable. It's violent. Don't you have to struggle not to try to pick it up?"

"If we're going to have a good time," Marlene said, "we'd better just decide we like blood."

Peggy went on, "In the opera, the chorus is the crowd around the palace." She tasted her cake. "Sometimes they scream for blood, sometimes for mercy."

"Does the hero marry her at the end?" asked Con.

"Yes, they somehow figure out that they love each other, though I don't think they've actually met," Peggy said.

"Oh, I'm not going to like it," said Con.

"The music is wonderful," Peggy said.

"I won't read the supertitles."

"No, no," Joanna said. "Don't you get it? The pleasure is in the extremes. Puccini's as smart as you—he knows this is an extreme plot. Trust him. Don't just dismiss it. Don't think it's *silly*."

"Have you ever seen it?" said Con.

"No," said Joanna. She had not begun to eat her salad, and now she put it aside and again began taking things from her backpack. The pack, worn and dirty, took up much of the table, its webbing straps scattered amid the food and glasses. Con pulled the wine bottle out of danger. Peggy had ordered an undelicate Italian red wine. Con took some more.

At last Joanna found an envelope, which apparently was what she wanted, and Con recognized it as one of hers, with her bank's logo in the corner. She'd probably left it opened and empty on the corner of the kitchen table, and Joanna must have picked it up to put something into it. From it she withdrew a yellowed scrap of newspaper. The print looked crowded and smudged.

"What's that?" Con said.

"You went to prison, didn't you, Marlene?" Joanna said in a voice that sounded surprisingly gentle and surprisingly weary, all but middle-aged.

"Prison?" said Marlene. "Well, that's a long not very amusing story."

"You went to prison after the war for selling meat and butter on the black market. You were part of an enormous ring—mostly they didn't prosecute, but the man who ran your ring was high up in the crime world, and they were after him. You both went to prison, along with a couple of other people. My grandmother kept the clipping."

"Where did you get it?" Con said.

"It was in that little wooden box with the girl on top. The girl with the wooden shoes."

"It was locked. I saw that you opened it."

Joanna shrugged. "Just a silly little lock."

"You picked the lock?" said Con.

"Maybe I should go to prison, too," Joanna said.

"It was just a week," Marlene said. "It was not boring. I learned quite a bit about my fellow woman."

"I believe it was three months," Joanna said. "He served two years. Then. And yes, jail is interesting, as I learned myself this week. Look, I don't care if you went to prison. What I care about is—Marlene, you killed my grandmother."

"He was my boyfriend," said Marlene. "He thought it would

benefit everyone if we got hold of that meat and sold it. It *did* benefit everyone."

"You were cheating with him on your real boyfriend, who was married," said Joanna. "My point is, you lie habitually. You told me this afternoon that you weren't in touch with my mother during the war, but I've read your letters to her."

"I'm getting old, I suppose," Marlene said. "I'm becoming forgetful. The other day—"

"You didn't forget that. You extorted money from her. In fact, you took money from my grandmother all her life. I think you claimed you were investing it. She didn't really understand—and no wonder, because I don't think she ever got anything back."

"Wait a minute," said Peggy.

Con looked at Joanna. Joanna must have taken the letters all those years ago, and kept them.

"Your grandmother was generous," Marlene said. "I don't know how well you knew her."

Joanna said, "If she hadn't been killed, I might have known her better."

"Joanna," Peggy said, "is this the best time and place?"

"She died of a heart attack," Marlene said. "She was more generous than you can imagine. She pressed money on me, not for some scheme, but for what I needed. She had so little, with two little girls. And later—well, I was sharp about investments, and she couldn't seem to learn what it was all about."

"I think this is probably enough of this subject," Peggy said quietly.

"Right," said Con. "Let's talk about the princess who kills her suitors. A little sadomasochism."

"Pleasure in inflicting pain. The man in the chair with the scrap of paper . . ." Peggy said.

"That's complete speculation," Joanna said, and it seemed she would be willing to change the subject. Con ate more cake. "Nobody is sure he's the head of the Inquisition. This is a speculation after the fact because something about that scrap of paper makes you imaginative types think of cruelty."

"Cruelty is disorderly," Con said.

"I don't think so," said Joanna. "The Nazis. Cruelty can be extremely systematic."

"September eleventh," said Peggy.

Joanna kept talking. "I don't think you even *call* it cruel unless it's systematic. But speaking of being systematic," she said to Marlene, "there's a letter in which you calmly and lovingly offer to tell my grandfather that my grandmother had already given you far more money than she could afford—for your blackmail scheme—and if that isn't cold-blooded extortion, I don't know what is."

"But I didn't kill her. You wouldn't have known her if I'd killed her," Marlene said. She looked down her long nose at Joanna and her black eyes narrowed with disdain.

Con wanted to be on Marlene's side and the wish shocked her. Joanna was embarrassing. She seemed like a child, talking too loudly for a restaurant, and looking scared, so her body seemed almost clumsy. "You didn't kill her *then*, of course not," Joanna said. "Of course not. What do you think I am, an idiot? You killed her when—when she died. She died because you killed her."

Con said, "Joanna, I don't think—"

"You lie habitually and easily, that's my only point," Joanna said, her voice covering Con's words. "You lied to me this afternoon. You lie simply and readily and automatically, so when you told my mother how my grandmother died, there was no particular reason for it to be true."

"I was devastated," said Marlene, in an unusually deep voice for her—a voice without her customary irony. "I was all but incoherent."

"Actually, you weren't," Joanna said. Con remembered moments, scraps of minutes and seconds from the week and day her mother had died. She remembered putting on underpants and a bra after her mother had died, feeling the unfamiliarity of her motherless body. She remembered telling Barbara on the phone. She remembered looking in the Yellow Pages over and over again—or was that at another time? Had they looked for a rabbi, so as to have a funeral? They had had a memorial service. Jerry had spoken well, though she had already told him she was leaving him. She later rescinded the threat, then made it again, then didn't act for several months. Finally, living alone in her mother's apartment in Brooklyn—interrupted by coffee or wine with Peggy—became the norm rather than the exception. She realized she had already left Jerry, and just had to find a place of her own in Philadelphia, so Joanna, who'd been in Philadelphia all this time, could live with her. Now Con remembered Joanna, a teenager, in Gert's apartment: disappearing for hours at a time, sorting the contents of drawers, lying on her stomach under the table to unplug the answering machine.

"What we said was recorded," Con said to Peggy. "I hate to think. Marlene and I were both incoherent. We must have sounded like madwomen." Joanna had taken the letters, and Con had never seen them again. Worse, she'd never inquired. She'd never thought. Her mother had left a little money—very little. She had been surprised there was so little, but too tired to think, too tired to inquire.

"No," Joanna said. "I still have the tape. You don't sound like madwomen."

"You have it?" said Con. "Why?"

"I saved it because I liked listening to Grandma's voice," Joanna said. "I kept replacing the battery because I was afraid there might be a power failure, the battery would be dead, and the message would be lost. I've bought a lot of batteries for that old machine. It's in North Carolina, in the apartment. But I remember everything. After a while I started listening to your conversation." She turned to Peggy, who was gulping wine and pouring some more, looking as if she wanted to be elsewhere. "I guess my mother was in bed, and she didn't pick up in time, so the machine recorded everything they said."

"That can happen," Peggy said. "But Joanna—the machine recorded your mother getting the news, and you listen to that over and over? Don't you think that's a little heartless?"

"What did I do, scream?" said Con.

"I certainly don't remember!" Marlene said.

"You screamed," said Joanna. "Of course you screamed. But then—Marlene . . ."

Con was frightened and excited, watching her child do this. It is exciting to see a taboo violated; Con had a thrilling sense of freedom. But she didn't want to let this conversation go much further. "Isn't this enough, Joanna?" she said. "Marlene is a complicated lady—we all know that. But that doesn't make her a murderer."

The waiter interrupted. Was everything all right? Did they want anything more? Peggy shook her head. "We're fine." He withdrew. Con had the impulse to call him back, just to prolong the moment, but she didn't.

"No, it's not enough," said Joanna. "Marlene, when you found my grandmother dead, why—" Her voice became high-pitched again. She leaned forward. "Why didn't you call 911?"

"Well, I called my doctor," Marlene said. She looked intensely bored, disgusted with Con's badly brought up daughter.

"Why didn't you call 911?"

Marlene looked sideways at Joanna, and the folds of flesh under her chin quivered. "Oh, I did, of course."

"No, you didn't," Joanna said. "You were right the first time. You called your doctor. These things can be checked."

"Fifteen years later?" Peggy said.

"Maybe. But I checked a long time ago."

"And you never told me?" said Con.

"What was the point?" said Joanna. "Mom, I'm sorry. But all these years. You couldn't hear this. You *wouldn't*." She turned to Marlene. "How do you not call 911 when you find someone apparently dead?"

"Well, there wasn't anything to revive, you see," Marlene said. "I don't want to be graphic, but she wasn't just inert—she was dead. She was cold. There was no life to save."

"Still. If you called your doctor, why didn't the *doctor* tell you to call 911?"

"How should I know?"

"Well, I do," said Joanna. "Because he already knew she'd be dead. He was your boyfriend. He'd given you the drug you used. You knew how to give injections from working in the vet's office."

"Now, wait a minute," Peggy said. "This is serious."

"My boyfriend! He was no boy!" Marlene said.

"Marlene slept with her doctor for years," Joanna said. "Dr. Herbert. Nothing wrong with that. He was married, but I don't care about that either." She looked straight at Marlene. "You had a good reason for wanting her dead," she said. "She was telling secrets, wasn't she? Maybe talking about money, and talking about your husband. You didn't want my mother to know who he was—the famous Lou Braunstein, the boyfriend you promised my grandfather you'd never see again. He was quite a character—he had a hand in so many scams and frauds and financial schemes, I couldn't keep them straight when I started reading about them. Did you help him? I bet you were pretty good at that."

Marlene stood. "Are we going to the theater?" she said.

"Year after year," Joanna said, "checks to Marlene. I kept her checks after she died. A hundred dollars to Marlene Silverman, two hundred to Marlene Silverman, four hundred. Over and over again."

"This is ridiculous," said Marlene. "In any case, your grand-mother's death was merciful. You'd have lasted an hour with her—then you'd have wished for it too. The only way I killed her is if wishes can kill."

Joanna kept talking. "I spoke to her real doctor, in Brooklyn.

He was stunned when he heard she had died. Her heart was fine, for somebody her age. She was a little confused, he said, but she had good years ahead of her. They didn't have a lot of drugs then, but he was thinking about antianxiety meds."

"When did you talk to him?" Con said.

"Years ago."

Marlene signaled the waiter. He didn't seem to see her, but she called, "We need the check here. We need to get going."

The waiter cleared the plates and glasses. Con had not finished her cake. The check came. Peggy picked it up and waved away Con's protests. "Joanna," she said, taking out a credit card, "there's something I want to say." As if there might be a way to change everything, they quieted, watching as she put down her card. The waiter took the check and credit card, and quickly returned them. In a quiet voice Peggy said, "Are we possibly talking about assisted suicide here?"

Everyone watched as Peggy calculated a tip and scrawled her signature.

"Assisted suicide?" said Con.

"Marlene," Peggy said, her voice even quieter than before, "sometimes friends protect someone—I mean, did Gert ask you to do it? I don't think anyone here would consider that a wrong choice on her part—"

Marlene looked ironically at Peggy. "Well, I thought you were sensible," she said. "Here you are, joining in the fun after all."

"It's not fun," said Con.

Marlene was pulling her coat on, and Peggy helped her with it. "Well, if that's not what happened, never mind," she said.

Con rubbed her arms with her hands.

"No, Peggy," Joanna said, her voice light and unsteady. "No, she didn't ask Marlene to kill her. On the tape, Marlene said they'd watched television the night before. So Grandma thought everything was fine. You said you watched an interview with Yasir Arafat, and *Dynasty* and *All in the Family*. I looked up the TV listings. It's true. That was what was on. Nobody watches shows like that the night before they know they're going to die. She *didn't* ask. She didn't know. Aside from the fact that it was inconceivable. I don't think there's anything wrong with assisted suicide—but my grandmother would not do it. She'd be too worried about my mother. No matter how bad off she was, she would have figured she had to stay alive to take care of my mother. Grandma would have thought that in a coma."

Con wanted to speak but her voice didn't seem to work. She had the feeling she couldn't raise her arms. They hung before her, her elbows on the table, and she imagined how shocked everyone would be when she couldn't put on her coat.

Gert's refrigerator, by Saturday night, was empty, and Con wiped it out with a damp rag and replaced her own little store of groceries. Nothing else had been accomplished. Barbara kept saying she was jet-lagged, and interrupted everything, proposing different tasks or making objections. As for Con, she was no less distracted than she'd been all week. They had an argument about the striped tablecloth, which Con had come to love that week, and which Barbara insisted she had bought for her mother and should keep. Con knew she'd put the canceled checks into an old manila envelope, but now she couldn't find it, though she searched and searched. She was afraid she might have thrown it out; she knew she was muddled. Together she and Barbara decided nothing and created additional chaos. After a while Peggy politely retreated to her apartment. Then the sisters sat down and talked, as if they'd been impatient to get out of sight of an exacting supervisor. Joanna, in the bedroom, slept. When she awoke they went looking for a restaurant, and found an open bar where they ate sandwiches. Barbara was too tired to drive back to the motel, and after several minutes of negotiation she slept on the sofa while Joanna and Con shared Gert's bed. Con lay awake, next to her lightly snoring daughter.

In the morning, yet again, Con resolved to get control of her life. She had to get Barbara out of there, and eventually that happened—she went off to visit a friend, postponing the question of the memorial service. She seemed to have forgiven Con for having their mother cremated. The thought of Gert in flames was one of many topics to avoid.

Con had given Barbara a key to the apartment. She promised to return the following weekend, when they would hold a memorial service, which Barbara promised to plan. "I know bits of things to recite," she said. "Even Jewish bits. Joanna will recite something."

As soon as she was gone, Con and Joanna filled the suitcase they'd started the day before, and then another one. Joanna took the answering machine and her enormous garbage bag. Con left the tablecloth.

"The cat," said Joanna.

Once again, Con had forgotten the cat. She went down to Peggy's apartment. Peggy promised to feed him. "Cats manage on their own for quite a while," she said, which was what Con had said vainly to her mother a bit more than a week ago.

With her cash jammed into an old brown leather purse of her mother's that didn't have long enough straps to hang off her shoulder—so it dangled from her wrist—and with her mother's old brown suitcase in one hand, her own in the other, Con ushered Joanna out the door of her mother's apartment at 3:30 p.m. on Monday, April 24, 1989, and they made their way to Penn Station.

Con's arms seemed to work, and she put her hands to her face, which felt cold. Now Peggy stood to put on her coat, and Joanna—head down, scowling, silent at last—shrugged into her jacket. Con fumbled to get her arms into the sleeves of her jacket, standing between the tables. A man was passing and she waited and even nodded at him when he smiled. She buttoned her jacket. She was extremely tired. She needed to go to the bathroom, but that could wait.

"And what became of Grandma's cat?" said Joanna.

Peggy turned around. "Don't you remember? My cousin's neighbor took him."

She led the other three out of the restaurant and they turned in the direction of Lincoln Center, just a few blocks away. The traffic was confusing. They spoke only when it was necessary. As they reached the sidewalk just before Lincoln Center, Con said to Marlene, "Is it true?"

Marlene looked at her, disgusted. "Gert was the only human

being I have ever loved." Even now, Con's first thought was *Not me?*

They reached the doors of the New York State Theater. Con found the e-mail reservation in her bag. It was early, and the lobby was not crowded. It seemed inconceivable to attend the performance of an opera right now, but she didn't know what else to do. The others waited while she went to the box office window to pick up the tickets, and as she joined the line, Con remembered meeting her mother in the lobby of this theater years earlier, to watch the New York City Ballet. They almost never went out together; this time, Gert had bought tickets as a present. When Con entered the lobby, excited—Suzanne Farrell would be dancing—she'd caught sight of Gert, waiting for her. Her mother had no idea how to dress up: there she stood in a familiar blue pantsuit with big pockets; Gert wore no clothes without pockets. She looked worried. Maybe she was afraid they wouldn't be able to find each other. Con remembered the moment Gert caught sight of her, the transformation in her face. It was not just relief, it was joy—extravagant, embarrassing—at the sight of her daughter. Gert too must have been abashed at the strength of her feeling, because she greeted Con fretfully: "Is that jacket warm enough?"

But Con had seen the first expression, and knew the truth. At the time, she probably didn't reply, but more than thirty years later, she did. "No," she said to her long dead mother. "No, Mama, the jacket isn't warm enough." She waited some more, then received the tickets and returned to the others. Slowly, they began to climb the stairs.

The ladies' room outside the auditorium had no line. Peggy

gestured, and they all nodded. There was no line inside either. There were four stalls. Marlene, Peggy, Joanna, and Con went into the stalls.

Con was alone for the first time in many hours. She hung her bag on a hook and, again, put her hands to her face and held them there for a long time, feeling her own features, almost as if she had thought her face might have been replaced with a different face. Then she opened her jacket, unzipped her pants, and pulled them down. She sat. To her left and right was silence, and she knew that all four of them were sitting on toilets, waiting for their bladders to calm down and remember what to do. The pause was long.

For a while Con just sat, grateful for solitude. Then—toilets are conducive to thought—she began to think. People don't have moments of lucid, significant new thought often, but I'm almost at the end of the story, and part of the reason for the story is that Con, at this moment, did. She didn't know yet if she believed Joanna. She didn't know if she'd fallen in love, again, with Jerry. But she knew she missed her mother, that was something. And she knew something else. Truths are often false. Marlene might have loved Gert and killed her anyway. And Con should live differently. She should live with more tolerance for forgivable flaws, and less tolerance for unforgivable ones. She heard the sound of urine splashing into a bowl.

All these years, her daughter had kept silent. As they walked, a few minutes later, toward the auditorium, Con put her hand on Joanna's arm and when all four hesitated at the doorway, she handed Peggy two tickets for seats next to each other. Peggy put her hand under Marlene's arm. They received programs. Con and Joanna were sitting to the left of the aisle and Marlene and Peggy to the right, several rows away.

They shrugged out of their jackets and sat down. "Joanna," said Con.

"Are you mad at me?" said Joanna.

"Why would I be mad at *you*?"

"You'd rather not know. You don't think it's true. You want to go on thinking good thoughts about Marlene."

"How long have you been planning this?"

"Oh, years. But I didn't know for sure that I'd do it. I liked thinking about it—but maybe it was just a fantasy, you know? When you said she was coming, I thought, Maybe it's time. But I still wasn't sure. Even when I found the clipping I wasn't sure I'd say anything. I kept watching myself to see if I'd do it."

"I'm not mad at you. But what do you want?"

"What do I *want*? I want my grandmother."

"You might have had an easier time," Con said.

"Do you think I'm right?"

Con considered. "I think you are."

"If Grandma had lived you'd have stayed with Dad. You needed to break up with Dad because you weren't going to break up with Marlene."

"Well, I don't know about that!" said Con.

"I'm not asking you to call the cops," said Joanna. "I don't look forward to testifying at the murder trial of Marlene Silverman."

"No."

"But there is something I want from you," Joanna continued.

Behind them, two women had come down the aisle and seated themselves, an older woman with white hair and a younger one. "*Have* an obsession!" the older one seemed to remark. "*Carrots!*"

"Carrots?" said the younger one, or that is what Con heard. Maybe the old woman meant "carats." As in diamonds.

"I want you to listen to me," said Joanna. "What happened to me in North Carolina. Do something about it."

Con had just decided to live differently. "I should," she said. "I should quit my job and spend all my time trying to make people see what is happening in this country." She flipped through her program without looking at it. "All I care about," she said—and as she spoke it sounded familiar—"is you and the Bill of Rights."

"This once," said Joanna.

"Okay," Con said. "Okay." She thought for a moment. "I'll look at the police report." Then she reached across the armrest and pressed Joanna to her body, and Joanna pushed her big head with its wonderful curls into her mother's face and neck. They stayed that way until they were embarrassed, until the armrest began to hurt Con's side.

The orchestra walked in, in twos and threes, and began warming up their instruments. They each played a note, another note, a run of notes. Con took out her cell phone. She wanted to call Jerry, but she remembered where she was and turned it off. "Turn off your cell phone," she said to Joanna, and Joanna took her phone from her pocket and stabbed the little oval button with her long lovely finger. The phone played its valedictory tones and subsided. Joanna put it away. The theater darkened, and the opera—which, Con reminded herself, would have a doubtful ending—began.

ACKNOWLEDGMENTS

I'd like to thank The MacDowell Colony and The Corporation of Yaddo for residencies during which some of this book was written. For generous help with this novel, I thank April Bernard, Susan Bingham, Donald Hall, Susan Holahan, Andrew Mattison, Edward Mattison, and Sandi Kahn Shelton. I'm endlessly grateful to my loyal and resourceful agent, Zoë Pagnamenta, and my brilliant editor, Claire Wachtel. Thanks as well to everyone in the Bennington Writing Seminars—colleagues, students, alumni, and our late director, the incomparable Liam Rector—for your companionship in the writing life.

About the author

About the book

Read on

Insights,
Interviews
& More ...

Meet Alice Mattison

Paul Beckman

ALICE MATTISON is the author of five novels, four short story collections, and a volume of poetry. Her work has appeared in numerous publications, including *Best American Short Stories*, *The Pushcart Prize*, *The New Yorker*, *The Threepenny Review*, *Glimmer Train*, and *Ploughshares*. She was raised in Brooklyn and studied at Queens College and Harvard University. She teaches fiction in the Bennington Writing Seminars and lives in New Haven, Connecticut. ❧

A Conversation with Alice Mattison

Sarah Anne Johnson interviewed Alice Mattison for the December 2006 edition of The Writer's Chronicle. *She is the author, most recently, of* The Very Telling: Conversations with American Writers. *Her web address is www.sarahannejohnson.com.*

Sarah Anne Johnson: *When asked about making a career of writing, Katherine Anne Porter said: "I've never made a career of anything, you know, not even of writing. I started out with nothing in the world but a kind of passion, a driving desire. I don't know where it came from and I don't know why—or why I have been so stubborn about it that nothing could deflect me. But this thing between me and my writing is the strongest bond I have ever had." How did your writing career first take shape within you, and what have you done to develop your work and foster that bond between you and your writing?*

Alice Mattison: I always assumed I would write. The discovery for me was that other people don't. Everybody writes and everybody draws pictures and makes music as small children. The serious pianist discovers that the other kids are looking for excuses to give up piano lessons but he is not. As a child, I assumed everybody wrote poems all the time. I remember realizing at about thirteen that writing mattered to me but not to everyone. I went to graduate school in literature, thinking college teaching and literary scholarship would be my career. I stopped writing poetry for several years, then went back to it when my first child was a year old, when I was about thirty. I knew then that I had to do it seriously. There was no question. I've been a writer ever since.

As for fiction, that too came slowly. I began writing stories, and I thought maybe someday I could publish a little. It took me by surprise that I could actually do this and define myself by it. I had always wanted to write, and assumed I would do it one way or another, but I didn't ▶

> 66 As a child, I assumed everybody wrote poems all the time. I remember realizing at about thirteen that writing mattered to me but not to everyone. 99

think of writing fiction full-time, for money. I'm like someone who loves to cook, then discovers she can make a living as a chef or a caterer.

Johnson: *When I interviewed Rick Moody, he said that writing in different forms served as relief so that he returned to his fiction refreshed. You've written short stories, novels, poetry, and essays. How does your work in one form impact or influence your work in other forms?*

Mattison: I wrote only poetry for a long time, and then I began writing fiction—short stories. I didn't know I'd ever write a novel, and I certainly didn't think about writing essays. I spent quite some time trying to write both poetry and fiction, and felt obscurely that the fiction was not any good and would not be any good until I turned my attention to it. But that was frightening. I was afraid the poetry would go away, and I wouldn't have it anymore. In 1983, I made up my mind that I would write nothing but poetry during the cold months of the year and nothing but fiction during the warm months. This system was extremely good for my fiction, and that was when I started writing publishable fiction. But poetry did dry up for me. It went away. I don't regret that. Every once in a while it makes me a little sad, but now I'm a much more relaxed reader of poetry. Being a poet is a very, very hard profession. The rewards are fewer than in fiction. There isn't as much money in it, for one thing. There aren't as many ways to get satisfaction or encouragement from the outside world. A book of fiction may get great reviews though it doesn't sell, or it may sell a lot of copies despite few reviews. All those things can be soothing, but with poetry there are fewer ways of being soothed. It was a relief not to be trying to make it as a poet. I love reading poetry, I require poems to read, and reading it now doesn't feel like a duty at all. It's sheer pleasure. But I did give up writing poetry, and for a time wrote only short stories.

Then, somewhat to my surprise, I wrote a novel. I wanted to write something that I could keep secret, that I wouldn't have to show people. Stories were getting done too fast, and I wanted to be alone with something.

Writing essays came about because I teach in the Bennington MFA program. The director, Liam Rector, believes that every writer should write nonfiction, should write about literature. If we are not going to leave our mark as creative writers, we can still write reviews or literary essays—we can contribute to the world conversation about writing. I think that is a wonderful idea and an important idea. I was sitting in Tishman Auditorium at Bennington, listening to a poet talk about writing nonfiction, when I thought I should do it. I made up my mind that afternoon that I would write some essays, and I have. I like doing it. It doesn't feel as essential to me as writing fiction, but it matters.

Johnson: *What inspired the shift from poetry to fiction?*

Mattison: I think it was developmental. I believe James Merrill said that to be twenty and a poet is to be twenty, but to be forty and a poet is to be a poet. I was getting to be around forty, and I changed, as a child changes her interests when she becomes a teenager. My poems began to get more like stories. They had dialogue and characters. I wanted to get more complicated things into my poems—which is still a concern with fiction. Some people like to write a pure story: a woman walks along a road and sees a car accident and reacts, and that's the whole story. I want to think about why it's of interest that she sees the car accident. What was she doing before she saw the car accident? What else is happening in her life? In Elizabeth Cox's story "The Third of July," in fact, a woman does see a car accident and it's the day she's planning to leave her husband, but after seeing the accident and trying to rescue the passengers, she doesn't leave him. That's what I like in fiction, that intersection of two or three things going on in life at once. That's very difficult to get into poetry. Certainly poetry of any kind and any sort can be written, but if you want to write about just one thing and what it's like looking at it, clearing your mind of everything else, then poetry is really good at that. I was moving away from that.

Johnson: *Your books . . . have been compared to the work of Grace Paley. What do you make of the comparison?*

Mattison: I'm delighted. I adore Grace Paley's work. I've been influenced by her a great deal. She's a wonderful, wonderful writer, and her work helped me begin writing short stories. In the seventies, I read Grace Paley and Tillie Olsen, and realized that the short story didn't have to be cerebral, and wasn't necessarily about situations and characters that had nothing to do with me. I had read Henry James's short stories exhaustively and loved them, but nothing in them suggested that this was something I could do too. Reading Grace Paley and Tillie Olsen made me want to try it. My work does not have the political seriousness of Grace Paley's work. I wish it did.

Johnson: *Who are some of the writers who've continued to influence you over the years, and who are you reading now?*

Mattison: I studied English Renaissance poetry in graduate school, and was especially influenced by seventeenth-century poets like George Herbert and Andrew Marvell. Reading them made me aware of exactness of diction and emotional intensity in writing. William Maxwell is someone who has meant a great deal to me, both his short stories and novels. Lore Segal—I just wrote a piece about her for *Post Road*. She wrote two novels, called *Other People's Houses* and *Her First American*, which had something like the effect on me of Grace Paley's short stories: they made me think I could do it too. My favorite novel of all time is E. M. Forster's *Howards End*. I used to read it once a year.

Right now I'm reading *The Wind-Up Bird Chronicle*, by Haruki Murakami. ▶

A Conversation with Alice Mattison *(continued)*

Johnson: *In looking at your recent novels* The Wedding of the Two-Headed Woman *and* The Book Borrower, *the opening sentences stand out as impossible to resist. Many of the writers I've interviewed have that first sentence before they ever sit down to write, while others discover it through the writing. How does that work for you?*

Mattison: I'm somewhat compulsive about first sentences. I can't move on until I have one, and I often write a first sentence many times before writing anything else. I need to imagine it's perfect. As it turns out, usually it isn't right, and I rework it quite a bit. I think the first sentence of *The Wedding of the Two-Headed Woman*—"Nothing distracts me for long from sex"— came readily. The second sentence took years.

Johnson: *What is your process like for writing and revision when you're working on a novel?*

Mattison: It varies. When I wrote *The Wedding of the Two-Headed Woman*, I didn't allow myself to read it until I'd finished the first draft. Each day, I'd print out everything I wrote that day, and before writing I'd read what I'd written the day before, just to remind myself where I was. Writing that way, I got quite mixed up at times. I would forget the characters' names if they didn't appear for a while. Some characters had several names. When I finished the first draft, it needed a whole lot of work.

Johnson: *What was the benefit of that exercise?*

Mattison: It led to greater freshness. It enabled me to discover what was in my head. But I have to say, some of what was in my head—the spontaneous wonderful stuff that we all talk about—was wrong. I had had a notion of what was going to happen, and as I was writing, the characters did something else. I thought it was one of those famous occasions when the character takes it into his head to do something, and the poor author doesn't know, and the character is right and the author is wrong. But no. The characters were wrong and the author was right, so I had to go back and make them do what I had originally set out to do. What I'd written was lazy.

Wedding is the only book I've written without reading and revising as I went along; with some books it wouldn't be possible to keep going without looking back. If you realize two-thirds of the way through that something's really wrong—that you're writing about two brothers and there really are four brothers—you can't keep going. You have to go back and create those brothers. Otherwise, it's going to be dead. When I wrote *The Book Borrower*, I got stuck in the fourth section and then realized that some of the basic premises were wrong. I had to go back and redo the whole book to bring it up to that point, and move on from there.

I'm working on a new novel now, and after I started the first chapter, I looked at it and it was awful, and I went back and did it again. I must've done it fifteen times before I moved on. I've done each succeeding section fewer times, and now I'm trying to push through to the end of the book without checking back, before I start revising. Sometimes, whether it's possible to keep going depends on something as technical as how early in the book the plot declares itself.

Johnson: *How much control do you have over when the plot reveals itself?*

Mattison: I come up with a rough idea of what's going to happen in the book before it starts. I may not know how something will come out—I may not know if lovers will end up together—but I know something about a novel and the basic movement of the story. Some stories have in them more room for mistakes and errors than others. In others, if you don't fix the mistakes right away, you'll be building on error.

Johnson: *How is it different for short stories? Does something about the compressed form of the story play into the writing?*

Mattison: With a short story you can set out without knowing where it's going because there isn't as much room for getting lost. You couldn't leave New York saying you were going to follow your nose wherever you wanted to go and end up in San Francisco. Sooner or later you have to head west on purpose. But if you're just walking around a neighborhood, you have a lot less to lose if you follow your nose. You can walk wherever you feel like walking and then, somehow, amble over to the grocery store, and at worst, it's only a few blocks out of the way. With a short story, you have much more room for fooling around and discovering as you write what's going to happen.

Johnson: *Your novel* The Book Borrower *has been called a classic of female friendship. The story begins in a park when Toby and Deborah, two young mothers walking their children, start talking and Deborah loans Toby a book,* Trolley Girl. *Their narrative is punctuated with passages from* Trolley Girl. *First, how did you arrive at this structure of alternating narratives for the novel, and what did you want Toby's story to gain?*

Mattison: I couldn't imagine how to do it, once I knew there would be a book within the book. One thought was to have one story run across the top of the page and one run across the bottom. As it worked out, Toby Ruben reads the first part of the inner book through the first section of *The Book Borrower*, and then stops. She comes to something upsetting and doesn't want to read any further. She puts it aside. At the end of the book, she picks it up again, and both Toby Ruben and the reader read the rest of it. It's twenty years later, so ▶

A Conversation with Alice Mattison *(continued)*

obviously the character would have to reread what she'd read before, but I didn't want the reader—who presumably has not waited twenty years to finish my book—to have to reread. I didn't know what excuse to give to let the reader see only the part I hadn't included earlier, and finally decided on the simple device of a bookmark. The character puts a scrap of newspaper in the book when she stops, and therefore I could say that she read up to the bookmark, and then include the rest of it.

Johnson: *What draws you to the complicated terrain of female friendship?*

Mattison: What other topic is there? It's the most consistently interesting topic. I'm interested in love relationships, too, and writing about men and women together and about lovers, but I'm fascinated by friendship and the complexity and difficulties of friendship. I suppose it has something to do with me. I have intense friendships and friends who are extremely important to me. I have one husband, but I have many friends, and all the friendships are extremely interesting and complicated and different from one another. It seems to be a richer topic. Someone who didn't have a lot of friends but had many relationships with lovers might feel differently.

Johnson: *You also had to invent the memoir within the novel,* Trolley Girl, *and have it work with the main narrative. Were you at all concerned about pulling this off, not only structurally but in terms of making the story work?*

Mattison: Here's how I wrote *The Book Borrower*: I was at Yaddo, working on stories for *Men Giving Money, Women Yelling*. My friend Jane Kenyon was sick, and we didn't know what would happen. I began writing a narrative about two women friends—who were not me and Jane—in which something happens to one friend, not like what happened to Jane, who had leukemia. It ended with the friend injured, and you didn't know if she was going to live or not, just as I didn't know if Jane was going to live or not. I thought it might be a novella— I didn't know what it was. In the middle of the narrative, in walked an old lady who seemed interesting. I went home and put it aside and didn't do anything with it for a year and a half.

By then, Jane had died. I had finished *Men Giving Money, Women Yelling*, and was ready to write another book. When I pulled that thing out, I didn't know if it would be any good at all. I read it, and it began to seem like the middle of something. It became the third section of *The Book Borrower*. Then my task was to learn how they got into this situation, and who was the old woman, and why was she in the book? I knew the friend's husband would have an obsession. The defining moment for the book was the moment of understanding what that obsession would be. Totally out of the blue, I thought, trolleys. What kind of trouble could there have been with trolleys?

I looked at the *New York Times* index in the library. It lists topics by date. You can look up any topic that was written about in any year. So I looked up trolleys at the beginning of the twentieth century—when the old woman would have been young—and it said "see Streetcars," and I started reading around. Of course, the trouble turned out to be strikes. I read about the strikes that happened, and invented my own strike in my own little town, and it went from there. That's how that book happened.

Johnson: *Daisy Andalusia, from* The Wedding of the Two-Headed Woman, *is a character from the short story "The Hitchhiker" in* Men Giving Money, Women Yelling. *What inspired you to write about her again?*

Mattison: She came into "The Hitchhiker" as the friend of the main character. I really liked the sound of her voice, so I wrote a story in that book from her point of view called "Selfishness." Then I kept thinking about writing about her again, mostly, once more, because I liked the sound of her voice. Daisy had more to say to me, and finally I did write the novel. She's an interesting character because she lies and does bad things. I'm quite fascinated by her.

Johnson: *As the title suggests, Daisy is at odds with herself. She is married, but not faithful. She works organizing other people's clutter, but cannot organize her own thoughts about her life. Can you talk about the conception of this novel? How did the two-headed woman become the central metaphor for Daisy's story?*

Mattison: This was Ricco Siasoco's fault. Ricco was my thesis student in the Bennington MFA program, and he was writing his lecture on fabulist fiction. I thought fabulist fiction was silly, and I wasn't interested in it, but I dutifully plowed through some books so that I could understand what Ricco was up to. It infected my head, and this was what emerged. I had seen a headline— "Two-Headed Woman Weds Two Men: Doc Says She's Twins"—years and years earlier. It came into my mind and I knew that it was something I wanted to work with. But it was Ricco's fault.

Johnson: *Daisy is obsessed with secrets; hence, her impulse to explore other people's clutter. This also explains her fluctuating between her husband, who doesn't reveal himself, and her lover, who shares his secrets. What interests you in general about secrets, and more particularly, about positioning Daisy between these two extremes?*

Mattison: Someone told me that *In Case We're Separated* is full of secrets. I like the idea of secrets, of hidden layers that the outside world doesn't know about. The difference between Pekko and Gordon is not so much how they reveal themselves. Gordon has no imagination, which makes him completely amoral. He can't picture what he doesn't see, so he can't imagine the experience of ▶

A Conversation with Alice Mattison *(continued)*

anyone else. Pekko, although he's a nut, cares about other people. In his peculiar way, he tries to do good. Daisy is tempted by Gordon's detachment because she's not really connected to people. She's tempted and lured by his ability to disconnect from other people, but she ends up with Pekko. Daisy's struggle is not really about secrecy and openness, but about making a connection to other people or remaining solitary. For her, the task of becoming part of a two-headed woman—of joining her body to somebody else—is very difficult, but she does do it, when she and her friend play the part of a two-headed woman in a play. Gordon, who's contemptuous of the play, has no interest in making strong connections to other people.

Johnson: *In* The Wedding of the Two-Headed Woman, *the narrator refers to the story she is writing and to the juicy material that is to come as a result of some event that has just happened. All of this, of course, is to create curiosity and to keep readers engaged. How did you arrive at Daisy's particular style of storytelling?*

Mattison: Once when I was at Yaddo, I met a wonderful man who has since died, the novelist Norman Kotker. He used to say that what's interesting is not so much who is telling a story, but why she is telling it and when she is telling it. I'd never written a whole book in first person before. As I worked, it occurred to me that we all acknowledge a convention that first-person narrators can tell us what happened, down to whole conversations and details of how things looked, in a way that would not be possible in real life. You couldn't write a memoir as detailed as most first-person novels. I wanted to play with the convention, to make Daisy aware of what she was doing. I remembered what Norman had said, and decided that Daisy would be writing the book, not speaking it, and she'd be writing it a year or so after the events because in her mind she kept explaining the story to imaginary listeners. Also, I wanted Daisy to write the story without full moral awareness of what she does, but I wanted her increased understanding to be in the book, too. Finally, I had her brother read the manuscript and comment on it. Daisy hears her brother's comments and changes her mind about her behavior, but it's after she's written the bulk of the manuscript.

Johnson: *In the author's note at the end of* In Case We're Separated, *you explain how the book's thirteen pieces imitate the poetic form known as the sestina, employing repeated ideas or objects in the way a sestina repeats certain words in a dictated pattern. At what point in writing these connected stories did you realize that you wanted the sestina to provide structure for the book?*

Mattison: That was the first idea.

Johnson: *Which stories did you write first, and at which point did you write* "Brooklyn Sestina?"

Mattison: I wrote them in the order they are in the book. I had to. I decided I was going to write a bunch of stories that would be true to my own experience as a kid growing up in Brooklyn, grandchild of immigrants, in a large extended family. Though the characters are imaginary, it would be closer to autobiographical fiction than anything I'd ever done before, so I wanted to add something that would distance it. I also wanted something true to the rest of my experience, which was that I went to Queens College and was suddenly reading seventeenth-century poetry. I thought I'd insert something literary into this story of ordinary people, as literature was inserted into my own ordinary life. I decided to do this by making the collection of stories something comparable to a sestina. A sestina uses six repeated words over and over, and I decided to use six things, six topics. I picked them first. When I wrote the first story, I didn't decide in advance in what order I would use the six topics, but once I had finished that story, if I was going to follow the sestina form, the order of the six topics was predetermined. The second story had to be the second story.

Johnson: *It doesn't feel contrived, and as a reader, I had no sense of the scaffolding.*

Mattison: I didn't tell anybody. I got a contract for this book and *The Wedding of the Two-Headed Woman*. I had written half of this book, and I sent the six stories to my editor and explained the few things I knew would take place in the unwritten stories. I knew I would write about Lilly as an adult, for instance. But I didn't tell her about the sestina thing. I didn't think she'd like that one bit. I didn't tell any of my writing friends either. They'd seen two or three stories at a time, but nobody had guessed. I kept waiting to see if someone would say, "Why are there so many glasses of water in these stories?" When the first story got into *Best American Short Stories*, they asked for a little paragraph about how I came to write the story, and I wrote about the sestina structure. Nobody cared. Nobody was interested until the book came out. Then reviews talked about it. I'm pleased. I find myself an advocate of the sestina.

Johnson: *One of the things you talked about in workshop at the Bennington Writing Seminars was the importance of showing your characters' flaws. You reveal your characters' virtues as well as their flaws, often in the same sentence. Are you conscious of exploring both sides of a character as you put him or her down on paper?*

Mattison: I'm interested in people's flaws and in the contradictions in characters. I like to write against type. I like to discover parts of my characters that aren't predictable given the rest of them. I am conscious of it as I write.

Johnson: *You use several techniques for introducing a character and creating an immediate impression with a brushstroke. For example, "Her father's large,* ▶

well-shaped ears stuck out from his bald head, and his chin was pointed, giving him a resemblance to an alert Greek vase." What draws you to this physical introduction and how do you nail those telling, evocative details?

Mattison: The reader needs something to picture, something that's mentioned more than once. That seems to be the last skill that good student writers learn. I want to see characters move, see what they look like. When I read, if there's a long, exhaustive description, I won't remember it, but if the description says that this person has some characteristic gesture or oddity, I will remember that. It makes it easier for me to keep this character straight. I want to do for the reader what I want done for me.

Johnson: *You also render character with a telling character detail, such as: "he wasn't so in love with me that he couldn't see my faults, about which he was frank." This describes Pekko in* The Wedding of the Two-Headed Woman, *but could also describe Edwin in* In Case We're Separated. *Your sensitivity to character enables you to pull readers right into the dynamics as they play out on the page. How difficult is it to capture this core characteristic?*

Mattison: It's hard. You have to bang your head on the desk or go into a trance for a long time until you know. You have to make yourself be intuitive. You have to try to see the character as clearly as you can until you know why he's different from other human beings.

Johnson: *What do you do when you're not sure or stuck about getting someone on the page in a satisfying way?*

Mattison: I suffer! I keep trying to back away and listen, to hear the character talking.

Johnson: *"Brooklyn Sestina" has a poignant ending in which Ruth tries to understand Lillian's unhappiness, but her own happiness gets in the way. "She stood in her open coat with its empty pockets until she was cold, and then climbed the stairs to Lillian, who was alone in their room, her math book open, her sleeves pulled down over her wrists." Readers are left with the shattering image of Lillian's depression. What do you look for in an ending to a story?*

Mattison: What I'm most interested in when I'm writing it is what *happens* at the ending. The ending of that story in the larger sense is that Ruth sees her sister injuring herself and she has a fight with the guy from the temple and she finds herself saying she's not Jewish. She sees that life is going to be more complicated than she's allowed it to be. She can't go on being a Girl Scout leader. If she's going to make any sense of her sister, she's going to have to change. Her happiness is wonderful—I love it that she's happy, and that she loves literature in this childlike way—but it won't do. The real ending of the story is when Ruth sees that. The other question is, how do you get to stop? You're writing the end of something and you know what occurs at the end, but how do you actually come to the last sentence so that you can put a period at the end of it and go have a cup of coffee? That's different, finding the gesture or the moment that's going to get you out of the story and free you from it. It's hard. I have to do it over and over again.

Johnson: *The interesting aspect of the interconnected stories told from various points of view is that we get to see the story and characters from different angles, but we also get to see how lives unfold over time, how people fail and succeed and hang in there or fall off the edge. What draws you to writing interconnected stories as a form?*

Mattison: Interconnected stories are irresistible. Everybody who tries them ends up doing them. Nobody says, "This isn't any fun." They're more fun than anything. It's not as hard as writing a novel. It's much easier to make up a story over time, and you don't have to sew up all the little holes in quite the same way. You get to make wonderful discoveries, too. The first time I wrote interconnected stories, I didn't know I was going to do it. Then I became interested in having the stories tell me what I didn't know about the characters. I would think, "These people know the answer to that question and I'm going to write until I find out what it is." With *In Case We're Separated*, I had the idea from the first of writing interconnected stories, I suppose because it had been fun the first time.

Johnson: *What are some of the problems you see in the work of new writers?*

Mattison: They use "like" for "as." That error seems almost universal among younger writers. Other than that, I'd hate to generalize.

Johnson: *What advice do you have for new writers working on their first stories, novels, poems, or creative nonfiction?*

Mattison: It's essential to read older literature. Don't read just for practical reasons, but read all kinds of books. The book that teaches you the most may have been written centuries ago or be in a genre other than the one you write in. Whatever you write, read poetry. Also, read the little magazines, university presses, and small presses, and learn how publishing actually happens and where interesting writing is published—presses like Curbstone, magazines like the *Threepenny Review*. Don't limit your reading to books published by big publishing houses in New York.

The second task is to accept the pace of your own development and your own career. I sometimes meet people who are terminally discouraged. I once ▶

knew someone who went to school with David Leavitt, who published his first book when he was very young. She had known him, she was the same age, and she couldn't get over the fact that her own development was much slower. Unlike mathematics or ballet, which you can't do at all unless you start young, writing is forgiving. Some people miraculously have something worth saying when they're twenty-three, but most of us don't. If we do at forty or fifty, that's great. Nobody cares how long it took to write a book we enjoy reading.

And for a new writer, it matters who you know, and I don't mean important people. Most writers need to be part of a community of writers, a group of friends who exchange manuscripts and offer help, and a larger community of people who care about making good writing happen. So it's important to find those friends, to find other people whose work you respect and whom you like. Becoming a writer is so difficult that anyone needs a great deal of support and encouragement and consolation. The way to become a writer is to have writing friends, not to enter the profession as a competitor but as someone participating in a group enterprise, the effort of all of us to write what's worth reading. ∾

Reprinted with permission of Sarah Anne Johnson.

Writing *Nothing Is Quite Forgotten in Brooklyn*

MY FIRST INKLING of this novel came when I found myself imagining four women walking into four adjoining stalls in a women's room in the New York State Theater at Lincoln Center. I understood that it was a relief to walk into the stalls separately and close the doors—a relief for each of them to be alone for a few moments. Something terrible had happened, or they'd heard bad news, or—I didn't know what.

Whatever had happened, they weren't dead or in the hospital or in jail; they were on their way to a performance. Yet I was sure that the event that had just taken place had changed their lives. I began thinking about who they might be, how they were connected, and what could have shaken them so.

Some but not all of the four were from the same family, I thought, and as I continued to imagine them, I decided that two were a mother—a Jewish woman eventually named Constance Tepper—and her grown daughter, Joanna Elias. I wanted to know what had just happened to them and Con's friend Peggy Santoro and the mysterious old woman (an aunt? a friend? I wasn't sure for a long time) who eventually became Con's mother's friend, Marlene Silverman.

I wanted to know what had just happened, but even more, I wanted to know what had happened before that: what had begun the series of events that led to that moment in the women's room? Some novels begin when a writer imagines an opening event and writes a story about what happened after it; this one was thought up backward, as I put together a story that might explain the stunned silence with which those four women closed themselves into stalls, where nobody, for a few minutes, could see their faces.

I keep notebooks with ideas, and when I look over the small, dark-green notebook I began ▶

> **❝** I wanted to know what had just happened, but even more, I wanted to know what had happened before that: what had begun the series of events that led to that moment in the women's room? **❞**

using in the spring of 2003, I find notes here and there about the book I referred to as "The Four Women" mingled with ideas for another book and various random thoughts. At the time—spring and summer of 2003 and into 2004—I was revising a collection of connected stories, *In Case We're Separated*, so I wasn't in a hurry to decide what I'd write next, or how the new book would go. I had time to let the ideas sort themselves out.

Gradually, notes about "The Four Women" become more frequent in the notebook, as I began to know in a vague way what would matter in the book I'd write. In real life the war in Iraq had started, and I knew that would figure in the novel, that the war would have some important, bad effect on my characters.

When I began making up the story that would eventually become *Nothing Is Quite Forgotten in Brooklyn*, it didn't have that title because I didn't know it would turn on objects lost but not quite lost, events forgotten but not quite forgotten, facts concealed but not quite concealed. I thought the book might take place over the course of a single day, at the end of which the women would have whatever experience it was before going to hear an opera. But I soon realized that it couldn't take place in only a day—too much had to happen—and for a while I thought I'd write about a week in these women's lives, a week at the start of the Iraq war. Then it became clear that, as so often happens in anyone's life, a story playing out over a week in 2003 wouldn't have started then either. It turned out that the story that ended the day of the opera had begun fourteen and a half years earlier, on an April morning in 1989 when Con was alone in her mother's apartment, and that parts of the book would reach back into a past much more distant than that, as Con would try to make sense of the friendship between her mother and Marlene, going back over decades. I also knew that Con's marriage would be troubled, but it wasn't until I had worked on the book for a few months that I decided she'd divorce her husband, Jerry Elias.

Jerry is one of those curious, adventurous people who may be a delight to people who don't have to deal with them day by day and minute by minute, but are more difficult for those who have to live with them. I knew that Jerry, a businessman from Philadelphia, part black and part Jewish, would come to Brooklyn with the goal of investigating some kind of historical event that took place there, and at first I thought he'd try to take all the New York subway lines, one after another. Public transportation fascinates me. But then I thought of having him explore a lost, never-completed elevated train line, the Brooklyn Circle, which gives my characters a tangible way to recover a part of the past.

Con also puts her hands on a tangible scrap of the past when she finds and reads Marlene's letters to her mother, Gert, from the years when the Second World War was changing their lives. Maybe we all long to glimpse our parents and their friends before we were born, or before we were old enough to understand what they were up to. Gert and Marlene were up to quite a bit, it turns out. Con discovers that her mother was more complicated, more interesting, than she knew. As for Marlene, I suppose Con always knew she was complicated—even alarming. But Marlene is also irresistibly attractive to Con. Parts of this book were easier to write than others, and Marlene's letters came readily. This book is about many characters and many events, but finally—as far as I'm concerned—it is about Marlene Silverman. ◠◡

Have You Read?
More by Alice Mattison

IN CASE WE'RE SEPARATED

Spanning the length and breadth of the twentieth century, Alice Mattison's masterful *In Case We're Separated* looks at a family of Jewish immigrants in the 1920s and 1930s and follows the urban, emotionally turbulent lives of their children, grandchildren, and great-grandchildren against a backdrop of political assassination, the Vietnam War, and the AIDS epidemic. Beginning with the title story, which introduces Bobbie Kaplowitz—a single mother in 1954 Brooklyn whose lover is married and whose understanding of life is changed by a broken kitchen appliance—Mattison displays her unparalleled gift for storytelling and for creating rich, multidimensional characters, a gift that has led the *Los Angeles Times* to praise her as "a writer's writer."

"Radiant. . . . A book filled with felicitous writing and ferocious insight."
> —Sue Halpern, *New York Times Book Review*

THE WEDDING OF THE TWO-HEADED WOMAN

For years, following an early first marriage, Daisy Andalusia remained single and enjoyed the company of men on her own terms, making the most of her independent life. Now in her fifties, she has remarried and settled into a quieter life in New Haven, Connecticut. She's committed to a job she loves: organizing the clutter of other people's lives. Her business soon leads her to a Yale project studying murders in small cities. While her husband, an inner-city landlord, objects to her new interest, Daisy finds herself being drawn more and more into the project and closer to its director, Gordon Skeetling.

When Daisy discovers an old tabloid article with the headline "Two-Headed Woman Weds Two Men: Doc Says She's Twins," she offers it as the subject for her theater group's improvisational play. Over eight transformative months, this headline will take on an increasing significance as Daisy questions whether she can truly be a part of anything—a two-headed woman, a friendship, a marriage—while discovering more about herself than she wants to know.

"Bracingly serious but without pretension, Mattison's voice is like that of no one else writing today: the demands she makes of her readers are difficult but exhilarating."
—*Kirkus Reviews* (starred review)

HILDA AND PEARL

To Frances, an only child living in McCarthy-era Brooklyn, her mother, Hilda, and her aunt Pearl seem as if they have always been friends. Frances does not question the love between the two women until her father's job as a teacher is threatened by anti-Communism, just as Frances begins to learn about her family's past. Why does Hilda refer to her "first pregnancy," as if Frances wasn't her only child? Whose baby shoes are hidden in Hilda's dresser drawer? Why is there tension when Pearl and her husband come to visit?

The story of a young girl in the fifties and her elders' coming-of-age in the unquiet thirties, this book resonates deeply, revealing in beautiful, clear language the complexities of friendship and loss.

"Accomplished poet, novelist, and short-story writer Mattison adds to her laurels with this quietly suspenseful, psychologically penetrating novel, which is both a perceptive study of adolescence and a dramatic exploration of family relationships."   —*Publishers Weekly*

Have You Read? *(continued)*

THE BOOK BORROWER

On the first page of *The Book Borrower*, Toby Ruben and Deborah Laidlaw meet in 1975 in a playground, where the two women are looking after their babies. Deborah lends Toby a book, *Trolley Girl*—a memoir about a long-ago trolley strike and three Jewish sisters, one, a fiery revolutionary—that will disappear and reappear throughout the twenty-two years these women are friends.

Through two decades, Deborah and Toby raise their children, embark on teaching careers, and argue about politics, education, and their own lives. One day during a hike, they have an argument that cannot be resolved—and the two women take different, permanent paths—but it is ultimately the borrowed book that will bring them back together. With sensitivity and grace, Alice Mattison shows how books can rescue us from our deepest sorrows; how the events of the outside world play into our private lives; and how the bonds between women are enduring, mysterious, and laced with surprise.

"Extraordinary." —*Washington Post Book World*

"An ambitious and original novel."
—*Wall Street Journal*

Don't miss the next book by your favorite author. Sign up now for AuthorTracker by visiting www.AuthorTracker.com.